Coldheart

Justin Robinson

League of Magi
BOOK ONE

CAPTAIN
SUPERMARKET
PRESS

Captain Supermarket Press
info@captainsupermarket.com

First Printing, 2013
ISBN 978-0-9892781-0-2
eISBN 978-0-9892781-1-9

Cover painting by Tae Young Choi
Cover design by Lauri Veverka

Book layout and composition by Lauri Veverka
Typeface: Adobe Garamond Pro

www.captainsupermarket.com

To thirteen-year-old me.
You thought the idea up.
Sorry it took so long.

Contents

Coldheart

- 1 -

SAN FRANCISCO WAS AS COLD as it had been in a hundred years. That's what all the newscasts said. We were breaking records for January, ones that had been set a century ago, in the days before the last blizzard the city had ever seen. Now it was happening again. The creeping tendrils of fog slithering in from the Pacific reached inland, enveloping the city in an icy haze. People, cars, buildings, all emerged from the mist like dreams and disappeared just as quickly. And for someone like me, it was tough to know if it had happened at all.

The phone in my apartment rang on Friday night well after dark, the city smothered under billowing white arms. I had finished another meal of ramen washed down with gritty tap water right as the alarm on my watch beeped. I picked the phone up, numb from a day of meaningless work, the drugs making me as murky as the city outside, and walked from the tiny combination living room and kitchen into my cracked and dirty bathroom.

"Hello?"

The voice on the other end was hollowed out. "Chris? It's Sarah."

Sarah Black. No, Sarah Strauss now. Went back to her old name.

"You sound… are you okay?" I opened the medicine cabinet and took out my pills.

The phone seemed to go dead. I felt Sarah on the other end of the line, but she wasn't speaking. Maybe the words weren't there.

"No. No, I... I saw something." Her throat clicked as she swallowed. "Something terrible."

My tiny apartment constricted around me. "Are you in danger?"

"No. No, I don't think so."

"What happened?"

"There was a murder."

"Murder? Where? Sarah... are you okay? I'll be right there." I shut the cabinet.

She kept talking, the link between us through the wires the only thing keeping her sane. "A patient killed May."

I looked up into the mirror. My face, stark white.

"He ate her heart," Sarah whispered.

I didn't hear her right. She was too quiet. My mind playing tricks. "He... he did what?"

"It all happened so quickly."

"Did you see who did it?"

"I didn't get a good look at him. I don't remember... I only remember what he did."

I swallowed my pills with a grimace. "He didn't hurt you?"

"No." There was no equivocation in her tone.

"They got him, right? The police?"

"He... I think he got away. I can't really... the doctor said I'm in shock."

I knew it was a bad idea before it came out of my mouth, but that didn't stop the words. "Do you want me to come over?"

She was silent for a moment, thinking it over, coming to the same conclusion. "No... no, it's okay. I've been alone all day. I needed to talk to someone. I couldn't sleep last night after... after it happened, and I just sat here all night and day, not sleeping."

"It's okay. I'm always here."

"I feel numb right now."

"Why didn't you call me yesterday? Or last night? Or earlier today?"

"I didn't want to be a bother."

"It's no bother." It never is.

"I… I can't see his face." She paused, and I saw her, scrunching up her face, the memories washing up over her. "All I can see is May's belly cut open. Him reaching in, and up. And the sound. Ripping. Popping. May's face. I don't think I can ever forget that."

I was already pulling my thick wool peacoat back on, still damp from the fog. "It's okay. Just give me like five minutes and I'll be at your—"

Through the phone I heard a loud thump. "What? Who are—"

"Sarah? Sarah, what's going on?

There was a loud scratch, like the phone being pulled over something, then distant struggling, and a sharp rap. Sarah's voice, distant now, terrified, screaming, "Chris! Chris, call the police! It's—"

The phone let out an eerie metallic shriek and went dead.

I stood there, in the quiet of my room, staring. Then, softly, "Sarah?"

I called the cops first. "Police? Please, you need to help!" I gave them Sarah's address, talking over the operator. I wouldn't let him get a word in edgewise. Wouldn't let him handle me. Put me on hold. Ignore what I was saying. I barreled through it, telling them everything I could remember, everything even remotely relevant. "Sarah Strauss! I'm a friend. I'm *her* friend. You have to help her! Her phone went dead."

"Do you know if anyone would want to hurt her?"

"She witnessed a murder! Two days ago, I think? She was telling me about it. On the phone! Just then. You should have some records of it. Sarah Strauss. S-T-R-A-U-S-S."

The operator said there was a car in the neighborhood. They'd check on her. Said it was nothing to worry about. Phone lines had been going out constantly since the weather turned. There had been blackouts, too: the city itself turning on us in misplaced anger over the coming storm. The operator told me to stay put. Someone would call me. Probably Sarah. I wasn't to leave the house. Wasn't to go check on her myself. Too late.

I ran back downstairs, out into the chill night. My crappy tenement in the Tenderloin was nearly falling down, and the damp wasn't doing it any favors. The fog seemed to have solidified. Before, it was a ghost, conscious but lacking in form. Now it was alive, solid, and malign. My motorcycle was chained up outside, but it didn't really matter. The thing was so old and broken down, no thief would ever want it. I unraveled the chain as fast as I could, my breath already coming quick and shallow. Sarah needed me. No one else would do it. Her family was on the other side of the country. I was what she had left.

My bike started reluctantly, the engine coughing and sputtering out its winter cold. It chugged toward Sarah's, even as my headlight could scarcely pierce the murk. There was no ground, no sky, no path in front of me, just an endless white void. From time to time, a yellowish glow would spread, and a car would wash past, disappearing shortly afterward. The only evidence was the muted sound of its engine, twisted by the fingers of winter.

I screeched to a stop in front of her place. A prowler was already there, the traffic stop lights glittering amber. I pulled up nearby and got off the bike. Sarah lived in a townhouse in one of the nicer parts of the city, shoulder-to-shoulder with other pastel Victorian homes. The front door was open, tendrils of fog invading the house.

One police officer stood on the porch, huddled in a long coat, his badge flashing in time with the lights on his car. He saw me as soon as I was off the bike, running for the house, his hand dipping into his coat for the pistol waiting there. "Sir? Sir, I need you to stop."

"I called you! I was the one who called you."

"Sir! Stop moving!"

I put my hands up, trying frantically to peer into the house. A moment later, another cop emerged. She was smaller, and something about her face calmed me down. "What's going on?"

"I called you!"

"Sir, just calm down."

The other cop's hand moved away from his gun, but both kept steely eyes on me. "Please, is Sarah in there? Is she okay?"

"Sir... there's no one home. Frankly, it doesn't even look like anything happened."

"But on the phone... someone came in!"

"We'd like you to come down to the station with us. Fill out a report. I think we can get everything sorted out there."

The haze stuck to me as I sat in the police station rattling off everything I knew, which was nothing. They asked the same questions again and again, rephrasing them at times. Maybe to get me to slip. Maybe to get at the truth. I gave them the same answers. The fog in my head wanted me to trip. It kept getting in the way of the story, turning everything soft and white, but this was Sarah. She had always been good to me, even when the rest of my family had already written me off.

The police listened to what I had to say. They gave me coffee as I huddled in the old peeling chair by the detective's overflowing desk. He wrote it all down. Until another detective came in. I knew the look on his face because I'd seen it a hundred times. Concerned a little, but undercut with annoyance. He pulled the detective questioning me aside and murmured something in his ear. The expression spread from one man to the other. The detective questioning me sat down again.

"We've got your report, Mr. Black. I wouldn't worry. Ms. Strauss probably just took a vacation is all."

They released me. Sent me back out into the cold with hollow assurances. Might as well have patted my head. And I knew, as sure as I knew anything: the police were in on it.

The parking lot was covered in freezing cotton. I sat on my bike, huddled in my coat, breathing out icy clouds. There was only one person who could help me. Who might listen. No matter what had happened between us, between him and Sarah, he wouldn't ignore this.

It took me a little while to find his apartment. I still wasn't used to the new place, but it wasn't bad all told. Much nicer than my tenement, Garth had a place on the upper floor of a well-maintained apartment building. I buzzed up to him.

"Garth? It's Chris."

"Chris? It's kind of late. Are you all right?"

"Can I come up?"

The long pause said everything. "Sure."

He buzzed, and I opened the door into the small lobby. The elevator went up to the sixth floor. Garth's apartment was at the end of the hall. He opened the door at my knock, looking rumpled and tired and small. He was in shirtsleeves, the tie gone, the expression bruised. The salty smell of a cheap TV dinner wafted out the door.

"Chris? What's up?"

He blocked the door with an arm.

"Can I come in? I can't talk out here."

Garth sighed and finally turned around, walking into the apartment. I followed. Boxes, most still half full, lined the sides of the room, with "living room" and "kitchen" scrawled on the side in Sharpie. He went into the kitchen, where the TV dinner I'd smelled waited in the breakfast nook. His wedding band flashed as he picked up the fork and prodded the gluey remains of his Salisbury steak.

"Haven't eaten those in a while," I said.

"Reminds me of when we were kids," he said. "Why are you here, Chris?"

I shifted, hot in his kitchen. I still had my peacoat on, the fog beading on every little strand of wool. "Sarah's missing."

He paused, staring at the unnatural white lump of mashed potato on his fork. "What do you mean, Sarah's missing?"

"She called me and there were voices on the line. Someone broke into her house and took her. Kidnapped her. Garth, I think—"

A clatter echoed through the small room as he threw his fork into the plastic tray. He looked about to shout, but instead barked out a bitter laugh. "You're amazing."

"What?"

Garth stood up, coming closer, looming over me the way only a big brother can. He had put on some more fat, more every year, but there was still muscle on his frame. "Sarah's missing? I'm supposed to believe that?"

"You don't understand! I was—"

"What? Try me, Chris. I've heard it all before. What crazy-ass thing do you believe now? What, was Sarah abducted by aliens? Killed by the fucking Zodiac?"

The words were worse than a punch. I leaned in close and got a whiff of that food rotting on his breath. "Don't make fun of me."

Garth turned away, deflating into the ring of flab over his belt. "I'm not. I've just… you know what you did to mom and dad with this shit."

I wish he'd just hit me. "That's not fair."

"No. It's not."

He stared at someplace in front of him, probably hoping that when he turned around again, I'd be gone. Garth wasn't listening, not really. He didn't understand that this time, this time I was certain. "Please, just listen. I was on the phone with Sarah. I heard her get kidnapped. Clear as day. I called the police—"

"—and there was nothing wrong, right?"

"No, they said they didn't see anything—"

"They never see anything, do they, Chris?" Garth slouched into his chair, looking grayer than he had in years.

"You're not listening. They said nothing was wrong, but I didn't see it for myself. They didn't let me in. They just took me to the station, got my statement—"

"Let me guess. Someone did a background check. Found your record, and all of a sudden they let you go."

"They let me go because—"

"Because you're crazy!"

"Don't call me—"

"Jesus fucking Christ! Why can't you just take your meds and be normal?"

As if he knew what the hell he was talking about. The words flipped a switch in my head. "I do take them for all the fucking good they do me. If this is… if this is all in my head, then they're not doing anything, right? And they make me walk around in a fog. I'm tired all the time… I can barely think… you don't know what it's like."

Garth had somehow gotten up and came over to me, gripping my upper arms. The tips of his fingers almost touched his thumbs.

"Chris. Chris, listen to me. It seemed real. It always seems real. Remember when you thought dad killed your cat and buried him behind the garage? Fozzie showed up a day later, remember? He'd just gotten stuck somewhere."

I remembered that. Fozzie, my little orange tabby. I had been told that my father killed him, and everything pointed to that. He'd come back grubby and a little skinny, but he was fine. My dad hadn't done anything to him. He was fine. The voices again, the voices yelling and lying. I managed to shake out a nod. "I remember."

Garth's voice was soft, tender. "Isn't it possible, just possible, that you're imagining this?"

The tears were filling me up and threatening to spill out my eyes. "It was so real."

"It always is."

I nodded again. It always was. As real as anything else. The strings connected. Everything operated with machine-like precision, but born in the sickness. The voices, whispering the true meaning behind it so I knew, just knew, it was what they said. So hard to tell, and there were too many times I couldn't. Sarah was fine. Who would want to kidnap her? She was a dentist. She was as innocent as anyone could ever be.

"Should I call her?"

Garth shook his head. "For now, Chris, just let it be. Go home and get some sleep. In the morning, everything will make sense."

"Yeah… yeah."

He guided me to the door. I was numb, the fog in my mind, the fog outside, and the feelings I knew were based on lies now. My own mind lying, telling me she was in danger.

"Hey, Chris?"

I turned around in the doorframe, huddling a little deeper in the damp wool coat.

"Sarah… is she… is she seeing anyone yet?"

"I don't know. I don't think so."

"Okay," he said, body deflating both with relief and self-hatred at even needing to ask the question.

I slouched back into the night. Always so real. Until someone showed me the crack in the facade. Showing me that I was, beyond the shadow of any doubt, exactly what they always said I was.

I went home and let the fog wash over my mind and take me to sleep.

My apartment hadn't been clean since I moved in. The next morning, I sat on a ratty couch I'd scavenged from the side of the road, eating cereal and staring at the front page of the newspaper. The headline blared, "BLIZZARD TO HIT BAY AREA." The picture showed a great Doppler pattern moving over the city, a giant eye made of clouds and snow. The article said the last one was a century ago, right around the great quake of 1906.

I flipped through the pages. The sugary cereal had turned the milk pink.

Nothing about Sarah, of course. Why would there be? The paper didn't report on what was only in my head. I flipped through, reading only to give my eyes something to do. It was almost restful, and when I was done, it would go into the yellowing stacks next to the couch. End of the month, I could stick them out on the curb for recycling.

Heart.

The word jumped out at me. At first, I wasn't even certain where it had come from. Focusing on the page, I saw it again. "The assailant allegedly ate the heart of his victim." The murder Sarah witnessed. No, the murder I *imagined* Sarah witnessed. Or was that real and the other fake? I scanned the article. No mention of Sarah, no mention of the dentist's office. Said the attack took place in a private residence.

I dug into the stack of papers next to the couch. Buried in the back of yesterday's edition, a small article on the attack that had to be the one at Sarah's office. No mention of any names, and no connection to the other attack. If someone hadn't been looking for it, they'd never have noticed. If they hadn't been me, they wouldn't have seen the connection at all.

Another article in the day before that one. Same thing, though the details were somehow even sketchier. Going through weeks of news, there was nothing else even close. Three murders, one the day before Sarah's, and one the day after. A serial killer hunting people in San Francisco and eating their hearts. Coming out of nowhere and killing three times in three days. The articles had no mention of suspects, no witnesses, and most importantly, no locations. Why would they hide the locations?

Because it's connected. Sarah's disappearance. The weird articles. The murders.

I smiled.

I might not be crazy after all.

One way to find out. Sarah's office was the only place I knew for certain a murder had happened. Go there first, look around, maybe find something. Maybe convince Garth that this was a real thing and he could get someone to listen. Someone who wasn't part of this thing.

Sarah's office was a quick drive away. The fog was thinner than yesterday, held at bay by the sun. I knew this was a momentary respite. With night, the grip on the city would be tighter, holding us down for the blizzard to swoop in from the Pacific. For now, in the diffuse daylight, I could at least pretend the storm was far away.

Sarah's name was stenciled neatly on the door: DR. SARAH STRAUSS, D.D.S. I was familiar with it, as she'd been my dentist for a couple years now, refusing to charge me too. I had good teeth, she said, but bad gums. My teeth never discolored, never chipped, never rotted. But my gums were sensitive, bleeding easily. Sarah said if I wasn't careful, my perfect teeth would fall right out of my skull.

Police tape webbed the door closed. Was ignoring that a crime? Plenty of time to worry about that later. I opened up Sarah's door and went into the darkened office beyond. It was unlocked, probably trusting that police tape would do the work of keeping people out. All the scents were still there: the drying flowers on the receptionist's desk, the sharp smell of the carpet cleaner, the antiseptic of the tools. The waiting room would have been cozy with the lights on. With them off, the mundane had become strange. The entertainment, fashion, and children's magazines were stacked on little tables next to the comfortable chairs, feathered out enough to see the titles. The silk plants next to the magazines were perversely bright and seemingly healthy. The only sound was the faint hum of the building's radiator.

I went behind the receptionist's desk, a semi-circle set into a nook. Clean, with a few pictures of a family. A man who looked like he was once athletic, now going to seed, and two good looking kids. The kind of pictures I'd never have. Erica. Erica Rosales sat here. She was a nice woman, always talking about something her kids had done. I liked hearing those stories. Calmed me right…

…my watch beeped.

Automatically, I went to the water cooler in the corner, filled a paper cup, and swallowed my pills. Right on cue, the fog rolled back in, reaching through the windows, winding through the dead hallways of the office. The volume went down on everything.

I couldn't quite remember what I was doing standing in Sarah's office. Slowly, it leaked back into my head, bit by bit. Each part seemed more and more improbable. Sarah was probably at home. Possible that thing with the police hadn't happened, right? Or if it had, she could have been on a trip. I shook my head and nearly laughed out loud.

I was here. Best to know things were all in my head, and I could get back to normal. The hall leading to the cleaning room, the x-ray room, and the small room in the middle where May, Sarah's assistant worked. Something was wrong with May. What was that? Right, she was the one who was supposed to be dead. I opened the x-ray room. The chair sat empty in the middle, the armature of the camera hanging beside it. The assistant's room was also empty, just the chair and the tools for the preliminary cleaning. I was almost ready to laugh when I opened the last door.

Blood coated the rug. Dried, crusted, soaked so far in the room stank of roadkill. Blood covered the chair, covered the walls, the little table where the tools were kept, spattering in the sink, on the lighted display for the x-rays, even little dots spotting on the ceiling. The murder in the room had sunk in. The act of violence seemed to be staring back at me as I entered. This place had become tainted. I knew it with a single look.

I wanted to run, but I forced myself to take it in. I knew I'd find this, even if I didn't. The murder had happened. I couldn't make this up. Wasn't in my head to do something like this. There were remnants of the investigation, an outline of a body—May's body—lying on her back by the chair.

It's over. Already happened. Nothing I could do for May. I could do something for Sarah. She was still alive. Somewhere. Taken.

By the killer?

I closed the door softly, absurdly praying the murder hadn't noticed me, and yet felt better almost immediately when the door was shut. I retreated back down the hall, past reception to Sarah's office. It wasn't very large, just enough room for her desk and a single visitor. Her degrees were on the wall, probably to comfort anyone who came in.

A floor-to-ceiling window looked down over the city and out to the bay. We were almost above the fog here. White tentacles reached in from the water to coil around the buildings. The streets were invisible under the smothering coat. Sometimes, the mist would flutter, marking the path of something rushing beneath it, like the surface of water stirred by a prowling shark.

There might be some clues in Sarah's desk as to what happened. I picked up the little statue of the wolf suckling the two young boys and turned it over in my hands. I'd gotten that for her. Never knew why; it just looked like the kind of thing she would like. And here it was, the only knickknack on her otherwise clean desk.

I went through her appointment book and flipped it to the day of the murder. Two patients, David Lister and Michelle Accette, that day. May had been killed here, probably while she was working. And if that was the case, one of these two people was probably the killer. Erica had to have been there, and would know which. She might even believe me. Might even be an ally in getting Sarah back.

I found Erica's address in the employment records and drove over there. The fog was getting thicker, choking me with cold and damp. I shivered in my coat, huddling like a wet bird. A block away from Erica's house, police and people gathered in the mist around a car crumpled inward from the front. It looked like it had hit a telephone pole, but there wasn't one where the car had stopped. The door was open, and the driver had his head back, a reddening cloth pressed to the bridge of his nose. A policeman talked with the driver, while another kept the five or six people watching from the curb.

I put my head down to keep the police from seeing me. I wasn't wanted. No way they would know I had broken into a crime scene to poke around. Still, something in me needed to keep them as far from me as possible. Until the fog swallowed them up, my shoulders were curled with fear.

The narrow townhouse Erica shared with her husband and two children was in the center of the block. It came out of the mist slowly, white tendrils clinging to the Victorian eaves. Police tape stuck to the door. I stopped in the middle of the sidewalk. Another crime scene. Another stop on the twisted path of the killer? Or a coincidence? Something my mind, on one of my bad days, would ascribe motive and meaning to that which had none on its own.

I parked my bike between two cars and went up the front steps, trying to shake the feeling that the place was as empty, as changed as Sarah's office. Just my mind playing tricks like it did.

The door was unlocked, and I slunk underneath the tape, just like I'd done with the office. The only sound in the house was the sizzle of blood in my ears. The place was dark, a diffuse blue luminance filtering in through the bay windows overlooking the street. A staircase in front of me led to the next floor, and a large living room opened up to my left. Pictures covered the walls, showing a happy family. Erica and her husband kissing, one of them holding a younger child, the son at ten in a baseball uniform, his father with a proud hand on the boy's shoulder. There were pictures over the course of their lives, and in the latest, the boy looked about fourteen and the daughter about ten. Their warmth would have sunk into the planks of the house, turning it into home.

There was no evidence of that warmth now. The house was dank and cold, and only a matter of time before the mist found its way in to infect it.

I knew it was a mistake as soon as I did it: "Hello?" I called out from the small foyer, next to the little hatrack and the wire basket of umbrellas.

The house swallowed up the word. Something heard it. Something deep in the house was holding its breath. Waiting.

I peered up the stairs. I could feel a presence, just behind the bend in the staircase, back pressed to the wall. If it leaned over, I could see.

I shook my head. Mind playing tricks again. The house was probably empty. Or the presence I felt was Erica and her family hiding from the murderer maybe. I was safe. I repeated it to myself, over and over.

Upstairs first. I climbed the stairs cautiously, trying not to pay attention to the smiling faces lining the wall. The silence was enveloping. At the top of the stairs, there was a narrow hallway, at the end of which a window. Outside, there was only the swirling fog. I could have been all alone here, cut off from the world.

But I wasn't alone. The hair on the back of my neck stood up. Whatever was listening, was watching, was up here.

"Erica?"

There was no answer. The house got even quieter, or maybe I couldn't hear anything over the pounding of my pulse and the shallow gulps of my breathing. The mist remained poised at the window. For a split second, I saw a face in the swirling white, but it was gone just as quickly. Tricks. Remember, trust nothing, no matter how real it seemed.

I knew which door to open before I touched the knob. The room was some kind of office, with a desk and computer, along with a few bookcases. The smell was stronger this time, the stain even larger. A taped outline of a large person, much too large to be Erica, lay in the center of the room. Other chairs had been thrown around, lying at crazy angles, and one even broken apart. The blood had taken over the rug, had dripped over the side, and flowed onto the hardwood. It had dried in long streaks, some smeared over the floors, others in delicate lines.

I stepped into the room to kneel next to the blood. I wasn't sure what I wanted it to tell me, but there was some kind of truth in it. The murder was still here, just like the site in Sarah's office. The pain still naked. Maybe I had become acclimated to the agony of death. Maybe finding Sarah was so important I could get over it.

The door slammed behind me.

My heart froze. I whirled around, losing my balance, and fell back onto the rug.

The woman would have been hidden behind the door when I came in. She was short and slender, but there was no fear of me whatsoever. Beautiful too, smooth brown skin, large almond brown eyes, and long, glossy black hair. She was dressed for the cold with a fleece-lined jacket zipped up to her neck, thick jeans, and heavy boots. She had to be a cop. No one else would be so confident.

"And who might you be?" She had an accent. Not Mexican or Chicana; I had lived in California all my life and could pick those out. It was Hispanic, but nothing I was used to.

"I'm sorry, officer," I said, picking myself up off the floor. "Miss Rosales is a friend of mine and I was worried about her."

The woman glanced at the window where the fog rolled against the glass and drifted down toward the street. It gave the impression of the house moving upward, into the thick storm clouds. She turned back to me with a little grin. "I'm not a cop and you know it. Now answer my question."

"Not a cop?"

The woman sighed. "Stop playing games."

"Are you one of Erica's relatives? Friends?"

"You know who I am, and I have a reasonable idea of what you are. So you should probably answer me before I get angry."

Angry? I took a step toward her, letting her see just how much height I had on her. Weight too; I might be skin and bones, but there was still more of that on me than on her. "Where's Erica?"

"Fine," she said.

The woman was still three feet away from me when her arm shot out as though to slap me on the chest. There was a loud *whump* and I was in the air, slamming into the far wall, cracking plaster, jarring bone, rattling teeth, knocking pictures from the wall. The second slap was the desk and computer as I hit both on my way to the floor. I lay there, gasping against lungs that refused to inflate.

She was to me in a second. My brain was scrambled. I felt like I'd been hit. Hard. Extremely hard. Nothing had touched me.

She grabbed me and pushed me up to the wall, hand reaching into my coat under my right armpit, then the left, then around my waist. "Gun?" she said. "Where's your gun?"

I shook my head. "No gun," I croaked, my lungs burning. I felt the blood flowing out of a hundred cuts, my bones cracked in a thousand places. A twitch of my head sent slivers of agony running the length of my body.

"If you move, you're a smear on that wall, understand?"

"Yuh... yes."

She nodded, taking a step back.

The pain started to fade. I touched my hairline, positive I would draw my hand back to see bright red blood. Only sweat. "What did you do to me?"

"Who are you?" she asked.

"I'm... I'm a friend of Erica's."

Her face slowly went slack. "You're not lying to me. You're not anyone, are you?"

"I don't understand what you mean."

The woman squatted down in front of me, taking my chin lightly in her hand, peering into my eyes. The look softened along with her tone. "You're serious. You really aren't anyone."

I coughed. "I'm a friend of Erica's."

She smiled at that. "Then I'm sorry for you and for her." The smile vanished and the tone turned serious. "I don't know what your stake is in this, but it's not too late. You can forget everything you've seen and walk away."

I swallowed. The pain wasn't as bad as it had been in the initial impact, whatever that was. "Please. Tell me where Sarah is."

The woman brightened, her voice eager. "Sarah? Is that the name of a victim? Murderer? Witness? Sarah who?"

"I don't understand."

"Did Sarah see this murder?" she asked, gesturing at the bloodstain on the floor. "Or was she the one who did it? I had assumed the wife—"

Outside, tires screeched. The woman popped up and ran to the window.

I hauled myself to my feet, relieved that nothing seemed broken.

"Shahmeran. Shit," the woman muttered.

I lurched to the window and peered down through the gauzy filter of the fog. A BMW, its hazards flashing red, was stopped in the middle of the street at the end of some black skid marks. A woman—Shahmeran, I guessed—was stopped in on the sidewalk, glancing left and right, before heading for the door of Erica's house. I couldn't see her face clearly, but her hair, a retro bob dyed purple and orange, would make her hard to miss. She wore a long beige coat with leopard print on the lapels, and I caught glimpses of long legs and high boots.

"You see her?" the woman said. "If she catches you in here, you're a dead man, do you understand me?"

"Wait. I don't…"

The woman opened the window, paused, and turned to me. "Walk away. Please." And she jumped out.

"Wait!" I reached after her, following her with my head and shoulders out the window. She landed on the pavement, looked up at me, and walked away. Anyone trying that jump would shatter both ankles, but she didn't have so much as a limp.

From downstairs in the foyer, a feminine voice called out, "I know you're there, Teotl! Did you think we weren't watching the sites?" The only emotion in her voice was a distant amusement. I knew for certain that the woman who had just left—Teotl—was telling the truth. Shahmeran was a predator and I was trapped in a house with her.

I ran to the desk and opened up the drawers. I couldn't leave empty handed. There was no way I'd make it back here, and then this would be a dead end. Sarah would be gone with no way to find her. I dug through the old bills, through the scratch paper, through the loose pens until I found what I was after: a little black book of names and addresses.

Shahmeran's heavy footsteps followed me up the stairs. Her tread was slow, an executioner approaching the block. I had nowhere to go, and she knew it. "You're not Teotl." Her voice came from the top of the stairs.

I nearly froze. How could she know that? Was she playing with me? Or was this something else I couldn't explain, a little piece of glass worming its way into my mind to make me doubt everything I saw and heard.

"Come out now and I won't hurt you," she said.

I opened the other door into a bathroom, went in, and shut it behind me almost silently. I could picture Shahmeran in the hall, her head cocked, multicolored hair shimmering in the dim light. Finally, she said with amused resignation, "Fine. Have it your way."

I opened up the other door, hearing the door into the office open. I was in the master bedroom. The bed was unmade, a glass of water half empty on the night table. I found what I was looking for next to that glass of water: a framed picture of Erica and her two kids, taken last Christmas.

I heard the door to the bathroom open, Shahmeran walking purposefully in my footsteps, stalking her prey. "You're frightened," she said. "Good."

She knew. There was no uncertainty in her voice, no sense she was fishing for a response. It sounded like she was stating a simple fact. Might as well have said, "It's cold outside." Other than the faint smile in the final word there was no emotion attached. These were the words of a stone killer.

The rational part of my brain insisted she was guessing. But she wasn't. She knew where I was. Knew I was terrified. And knew she was in no danger from me whatsoever.

I had to find another way out. The master bedroom had a single window, so I opened that. A two-story drop led to a tiny patch of dying grass. The cold would have packed the ground hard. It was either that or face Shahmeran.

I saw the look in Teotl's eyes when she told me what Shahmeran would do. No doubt there, either. And Teotl was a woman who could somehow fall two stories to the concrete and walk away clean. I sat down on the sill.

In the bathroom only a closed door away, Shahmeran spoke again. "Every minute you make me wait, the worse this gets for you."

And I pushed myself off. Forever, I fell into the white fog, swirling in eddies around me. And then I hit the ground. Red flashed over my vision as my leg buckled, and I hit the freezing mud. My right ankle throbbed from the impact. Broken. I knew it. Could Shahmeran follow me out the window and make good on her threats? I saw her doing just that, landing like a cat, a flash of color and death. Carefully, I pulled myself to my feet with the fence and put some weight on it. It twinged, but could support me. Just a little twist. I was okay.

I climbed the fence awkwardly, dropping myself into the neighbor's backyard, and limping in the narrow walkway up to the street. I extracted the picture and tossed the frame into the plastic garbage cans by the side of the house. Limping on the bad ankle, I pocketed the photo, and flipped through the pages, finally finding the one I wanted.

MOM. The address was 6225 Bailey.

I waited until dark, shivering in the deepening cold, before circling the block and retrieving my motorcycle. Shahmeran's car was gone, but I couldn't be certain she, or someone else, wasn't watching. My ankle was throbbing; the wait had stiffened it, and the walking had only started to loosen it up. The mist changed with the coming of night. It twined around the wires crisscrossing over every street, climbing buildings. Now it reflected the lights of the city back onto it, at turns gold, purple, blue, and red, reminding me of Shahmeran's hair. It was a man-made aurora, further showing us we were trapped inside the dome, waiting for the blizzard to come and pummel us.

The street sign said BAILEY STREET, almost lost in the shifting tendrils of green, yellow, and red. It was a working class avenue, the Victorian tenements packed shoulder-to-shoulder, each one probably holding one family per floor. Cars covered every inch of exposed curb. A small alley bisected the street. A homeless man, bundled up against the cold, leaned against the wall in a pool of gold light from the streetlamp, cradling a bottle.

I checked the numbers, finding 6225, and knocked. A moment later, I knocked again. I almost knocked a third time when the door opened a crack, the chain stretching across the opening. A tiny gnomish woman stood on the other side, peering out at me. I realized I had no idea what to say to her. I didn't even know her daughter that well, and yet here I was.

"Hi… I… uh… is Erica in?"

"Who are you?"

"I'm a friend of hers. Is she in?"

"She's gone!" And the door slammed in my face.

Gone? Gone how? Out for the evening? Arrested? Or gone like Sarah? I stared at the door for a moment and knocked again. This time there was no answer, and I could picture the old woman on the other side, glaring daggers through the door at me.

I walked away, crossing the darkening street. The alley was close by, a narrow space partly blocked with old battered garbage cans and in the back choked with trash. I leaned against the wall, staring at 6225 Bailey Street. Maybe Erica was out, and she'd come back soon. I could wait, and so huddled in the peacoat, let the dank wind its way around my bad ankle, worm into my bones and stay there. Across the street, my mirror the homeless man shifted and coughed. The sound was partly muted in the oppressive air.

I waited. The sun was gone, and now the damp hardened to ice. Breathing hurt. Standing hurt. I shivered inside the peacoat, wishing for this to all be over. Or even better, that this had all been some kind of product of my mind. And then maybe I could just go home, or Garth could put me in a hospital like he always wanted, and maybe then I wouldn't have to worry so much.

It probably was a mistake. All of it. What happened earlier. Maybe even the house, the two women, my ankle. Something I made up. Go home, forget about it.

The door to 6225 Bailey opened.

I straightened against the wall. A figure came out, partly hidden in the fog. It was a kid, about fourteen years old. I checked the photo, then squinted at the boy. It was hard to be sure from across the street, but it really looked like the same person. There were a few people on the street, going about their errands, not noticing me or anyone else.

I started to cross the street to ask about the kid's mother.

He didn't seem to notice me. He was walking toward the homeless guy, shoulders hunched, hands out. Almost like he wanted to tackle him. The boy's eyes were open so wide I could see the whites from halfway across the street. Every muscle was tensed, his fingers curled like claws.

I opened my mouth to say something.

The boy lunged at the homeless man, who let out a surprised grunt. The boy picked up the liquor bottle and shattered it on the cold pavement. An arc of blood glittered gold. And another. And another. Dripping down the walls, the sidewalk. The homeless man screamed. Gurgled. Was silent.

The feeling I had at the other murder sites returned, stronger than ever before. The eyes were on me, focused on the horror. The murder, the violence, knew. It knew and it could see everyone around it.

There were cracking and mushing and packing sounds. And then, with the rip of wet cloth, the boy pulled something out and held it aloft.

It was a bloody heart.

He stared at it.

And took a ravenous bite.

- 2 -

Frozen in abject horror, I watched Erica's son eat the homeless man's heart. This was the kind of thing my brain would have invented. This was the kind of thing I never wanted to see, would curl me up, squeeze the tears out of me. I wanted to call out, order the boy to stop.

All I could do was listen to the popping sounds his teeth made on the thick muscle.

Even as close as I was, the fog mercifully blocked some of the sights. The sounds though, those came from all around, until I was surrounded by the horrible mastication. Shut my eyes, and all I could see was that, only now the boy was huge, looming in the sky, eating a bloody heart the size of a streetcar.

There were other people on the street, going about their business. All we needed was one person to act, call the police, wrestle the boy to the ground. None of the people seemed to be seeing anything. They were in mid-stride, gazes focused on the middle distance. Every one of them frozen in place.

I ran to the closest one, a woman walking just outside the alley across from there the boy continued to eat the dead man. She looked right past me, face locked in the same expression of blank purpose. "Hello? Hello, can you hear me?"

Nothing changed.

I turned. The fog swirled around the other people, giving the impression of movement, but they were all perfectly still. Not dead. Not really alive, either. Statues with human flesh.

The revving of engines was the first familiar thing to hang onto. I turned to see bright headlights haloed in the thick white. The fog swirled aside as black SUVs pulled up into the middle of the street. I instinctively ducked behind a nearby car. Whatever was coming could not be good.

The doors opened, and men spilled out onto the street. Tall men, built like football players. They carried submachine guns, lined up and aimed, covering every section of the street. They were dressed warmly in black, dark sweaters, lean vests, cargo pants, and boots. Every one of them carried a pistol and knife on his belt.

A team of them converged on the boy, led by a weathered man, his head covered in a knit cap. "Stand back! Wait until it's left his body!" The soldiers kept their weapons trained on the boy as he ate the homeless man's heart unaware or unconcerned by the guns at his head.

The rest of the soldiers formed a perimeter around the two SUVs, steadily moving outward. The frozen people on the street never moved. Never saw what was right in front of their faces. One of the soldiers—and that's what they were, the way they moved, the tone of their leader—was edging closer to my position. His boots, visible under the car I was presently hiding behind, were creeping lightly over the asphalt.

I glanced behind me. The alley yawned, the depths disappearing in a mix of shadow and fog. The garbage cans at the mouth were the perfect hiding spot. It was a little over five feet away, a good foot farther than the man with the automatic weapon.

The boy howled into the sky.

"Back! Stand back!" shouted the man in the knit cap.

I bolted for the alley, hunched over as best I could, and dove behind the trashcans, hoping the soldier had reacted to the shout. The hail of bullets I was expecting never followed me. I knelt behind the cans, knees freezing against the chilled pavement, peering through a space between the dented aluminum. The soldiers had turned, weapons up, the ones farthest away already turning back, covering the street.

The heart was gone. The boy squatted by the homeless man's body, his chest torn open. Blood ran down the boy's mouth, sticking his shirt to his skinny chest. More slowly trickled down the hill. The boy stopped, staring at the corpse in naked confusion, then at his hands, gory to the elbow. "What... what's going on?" he said. Though his voice was quiet, the fog carried it across the street, coming to me from all sides.

"Don't move," said the man in the knit cap.

"Please... I don't..." the boy started to cry. None of the soldiers moved a muscle.

The fog began to glow gold. A minute later, the glow resolved into headlights as a BMW pulled up next to the SUVs. The soldiers straightened slightly, though none of them took their attention off of their surroundings. The back passenger side door opened, and a beautiful woman stepped out. She wore a long black coat, buttoned and hugging her slender body. Black ermine fur billowed at cuffs and collar. Sleek black leather gloves and high-heeled boots completed the outfit. Her skin was pinkish white, her hair snow. She was an albino. Her eyes hid behind a pair of mirrored sunglasses, but as she turned, I saw they were reddish.

"Mr. Barnes," she said to the man in the knit cap, her voice carrying effortless authority. "You have the fourth host?"

"Right here, Miss Cross."

She walked over to Barnes, her heels clicking on the street. Barnes nodded toward the boy, still sobbing in helpless horror.

"Hmm... A child this time. He'll never be credible."

Erica's son blinked away the tears, the blood staining his mouth making him look at once more childlike and feral. He stared at the albino woman in wonder. "Who are you?" His tone was plaintive. He wanted this woman to comfort him, to tell him everything would be all right. "What's happening?"

Miss Cross knelt in front of the boy. "Hush now. No questions, dear." She slid the glasses down her nose, her reddish eyes flashing, and muttered something under her breath. I could not hear it clearly, though as the whispers brushed my mind, they brought a twinge of pain between my eyes. The boy swooned, and as Miss Cross stood up, he passed out, slumping over the corpse of his victim. "Put him in the car, please."

Two soldiers hefted the unconscious teenager, opening the back of the SUV and dumping him inside.

"Mr. Barnes, if you please."

Barnes nodded. "You heard the lady. Get to work."

The soldiers fanned out, producing devices from their cargo pants. They looked like tiny *Star Trek* phasers, and the soldiers pressed the end to each frozen person's neck and hit a button. There was a soft hiss, leaving a small angry spot on the skin.

Miss Cross stood in the headlights of her BMW, one hand to her forehead, concentrating, whispering under her breath. "Six on the streets. Six more in the surrounding buildings. You'll find two there," she pointed to a tenement, "watching from a first story window. Another three there," to another tenement. "In the front rooms of the first two floors."

The soldiers ran to the buildings indicated, opening the doors with lock pick guns and rushing inside.

Miss Cross took her hand away from her head and sagged.

"Miss Cross?" Barnes said.

"What is it, Mr. Barnes?"

His voice softened. "Just wanted to know how you were holding up."

Miss Cross offered a rueful smile. "I haven't slept in four days."

"It'll be over soon," he said.

She put a hand on his arm. "Thank you, Michael."

He nodded, squinting at the surrounding buildings, his men emerging from their work. "What's the final tally for this one?"

"Twelve," she said. Then she touched her head, frowning. "No. Thirteen. There's another mind. I don't know how I missed him."

Miss Cross began to approach me, her gloved fingers tapping her temple while she muttered something under her breath. My headache returned, intensifying as the words began to resolve themselves into discrete syllables. Barnes followed close behind. "It's just fatigue."

Both of them drew steadily closer to my hiding spot. Whatever Miss Cross was doing, it was leading her inexorably to the moment where she would spot me, and they would stick that thing in my neck or just throw me in the back of the SUV with Erica's son.

"He's close," Miss Cross murmured.

Barnes scanned the surroundings. I was waiting for her to point one of her fingers at me and have Barnes level that submachine gun.

She took the hand away, straightening her gloves, and looked up, eyes hidden behind the mirrors of her sunglasses. "You'll find him there," she said, nodding to the tenement to my left. "First floor."

Barnes signaled to his men, and two ran for the building. Barnes touched his neck, where a throat microphone was almost entirely invisible under his dark clothing. "We have the fourth's tally. I need thirteen teams on my location."

Miss Cross turned and began to make her way back to the BMW. "That's everyone. I want you to make sure the boy is taken to Dr. Jeremiah, and that all of three's witnesses arrive safely."

"No problem, Miss Cross."

"Good work, Mr. Barnes," she said, getting back into her car. The soldiers flooded back into the SUVs. All three vehicles roared to life and drove away into the oppressive fog.

I emerged from my hiding place, determined to follow the convoy wherever they were headed. At that moment, one of the frozen people screamed, "He escaped!"

Another pointed at the corpse of the homeless man. "Someone call the cops!"

The people, once statues, were now reacting in horror to the murder that was already cold. I limped down the street to my bike, jumping onto it and gunning the engine even as that action bit into my bad ankle. The black SUVs had already vanished into the mist, and I had to move quickly or I would lose them forever in the coming blizzard. I took a few guesses, and then I saw them, the SUVs one in front of the other, making their way through the shrouded city. Miss Cross's car was no longer with them.

I followed, keeping several cars between them and me, but never too much. Let them outpace me and the murk would take them away entirely.

Erica's son couldn't have been the killer. Not of all of them. Kill his father, and then vanish, only to reappear and murder a homeless man? Kill May in his mother's office? From what Miss Cross said, it sounded like there were different perpetrators. That meant different killers using the same method, which made even less sense. The answer was wherever those black SUVs were headed, and so was Sarah's trail.

I followed the vehicles across the bridge into Oakland. The fog receded a bit behind us as we left the city. Looking back across the water, I could see the tendrils clearly, winding around San Francisco, choking it. The water lapped up against a rocky shore, a single winding road tracing the line of the bay. Warehouses, pockmarked with splotches of rust like dried blood, waited behind fences topped with looping razorwire. The street was otherwise deserted. Even the garbage collecting in the gutters was old and dead. There were no fresh newspapers, no wrappers still blowing in the stiff wind coming off the bay. It was unrecognizable lumps of brown and black, tamped flat by tires, dusted with salt, soaked in rain, until it became homogenous masses. Just the cancerous tissue of the city itself.

As the SUVs approached the street, the traffic lessened until on this one, it was utterly deserted. I paused at the corner, turning off my headlight. The convoy was easily visible, several hundred yards away, red taillights occasionally flashing.

The night was huge and empty. Other than me and the people in the two vehicles ahead, there was no one else around. Maybe no one else in the world. As the fog swallowed the city, it would slowly consume everything until there was nothing left. All except me, alone, freezing in the white.

I made the turn onto the street, following the SUVs. They followed the road, passing innumerable warehouses, some of which looked used, others that looked forgotten. The bay was completely black, except for a few smears of silver light from the moon, ending in a solid wall of white. In the swirling mass, faces would occasionally form only to dissipate into the roiling snowy barrier.

I turned back to the road, the warehouses streaking by on my left. The taillights ahead had vanished. I was on the strip alone. My heart seized as I throttled back, peering this way and that. The road bent ahead, a lot standing vacant. There was a building there once, the concrete foundation crumbling in the moonlight. The grass that had grown through the cracks in the asphalt had dried out and died in the cold. Even the graffiti along the side seemed perfunctory. Someone had passed through, many years ago, written an alias and moved on. This place wasn't claimed by anyone.

Past the lot, a small hill rose up on a little spit of land poking into the bay. On top of the hill was a large Victorian building. It looked almost like a castle, with an abundance of peaked rooftops and scalloped eaves, topped with a bell tower. The windows yawned open, occasionally with a bit of glass still clinging to the frame like the single broken tooth in the mouth of an old man. The walls were weather-beaten, the odd line of graffiti scrawled across the side. The trees grew wild around it, once shielding the landward side from whatever used to live there. Now, the cold had stripped the branches, leaving bare claws to scratch the sky. A single road split off from the street I was on to wind up to the front door.

Beyond the building, there was more city spread out, old and crumbling, just as dead. I knew before getting any closer, that all this was just as abandoned. Any tenements would be devoid of life. Parks would be empty, reclaimed by dying vegetation. These were the bones of the city, where no one living dared go.

I saw the flash of red between the dead trees up on the little hill and pulled the bike over to the side of the road, turned it off, and hung the helmet off the handlebars. I moved along the shore, on a dirt path running parallel to the large rocks, the ocean slapping against them hungrily. Something skittered beyond my sight and plopped into the surf.

I made for the building. The path terminated at the base of the hill, with more of the large stones forming the coastline making a natural wall. The message was clear: no one was ever meant to go up this path.

I climbed the rocks, my fingers freezing against the slippery surface. Off to my right, farther out onto the little peninsula, the waves grew rougher, hammering at the rocky slope. I had no doubt that falling off down there would result in drowning, the same thing that had kept Alcatraz as the most secure penitentiary in America. My ankle protested, but I ignored it. I crammed my numbed fingers into the crevices in the rock, hoisting myself up ever so slowly. The biting wind swept in from the water, plastering the salt spray against my face and neck. The grass on the hill was dead. Sinking my frigid fingers in for handholds, I tore out chunks of it before I forced them into the saturated soil and hauled my body in.

For a moment, I rested, ankle throbbing away the pain. Back against the ground, face up to the sky. In any part of the bay, the sky reflected the lights back down, creating a city night where it never got truly dark. Except fog had swallowed San Francisco and the sky over Oakland was muted as well. Now, the full moon had taken over, giving me a sky as black as it was supposed to be, and bigger than I could have imagined. The stars were beyond counting. Only the edge of the great wall of fog was visible, a few tendrils reaching into the dark.

Soon there would be nothing but white overhead.

I got to my feet. Sweat mingled with ocean on my skin. I knew I was cold, but I didn't quite feel it as much as I might have. Adrenaline, probably. Pursuing two carloads of armed men into this forgotten place had fortified me.

The ground was covered in a sludge of wet leaves. I crept from tree to tree, making my way toward the lone structure. A faded sign out front proclaimed this building to be the San Pablo Sanitarium. The driveway had mostly been reclaimed by dirt and vegetation, though fresh tire tracks marred it now. The hospital was not quite as dark as it had initially appeared. Behind some of the windows glowed a faint and fitful luminescence.

I was still, watching the hospital from behind one of the last trees before a section of open ground led right to the building. Here, for the first time since the murder, I felt the chill in the air. One step, pressing through a membrane, and the cold settled in. I shivered violently, behind one of the trees, gathering myself in preparation to move closer. I was almost ready when the tiniest bit of movement drew my eye.

In the shadows by the front doors, a man shifted almost imperceptibly. I peered into the dark, and slowly, the figure resolved. He was a large man, around the same size as the bruisers in the SUVs, the ones I could only assume were soldiers. There was no uniform, merely a paramilitary costume of dark, functional clothes and body armor. There were plates on knee and elbow, a vest, a helmet, and goggles. Under that was something like fatigues, covered in tools and pockets, bolstered against the cold with gloves and a ski mask. He cradled a submachine gun in his arms and when he was still, he was nearly invisible.

In the other shadowed areas, in a sunken door leading into a subterranean level, in the shadow of a tree behind a side entrance, there were other soldiers. They were only visible in the subtle shifts of their bodies, or the occasional frosted breath. I was certain that if I saw three men, there were more I hadn't seen. Outside or inside, crouched behind one of those broken windows, just waiting for someone dumb enough to break in.

Who would want to break into an abandoned hospital?

Other than me?

I couldn't make it in. Not without help. Garth hadn't believed there was danger before, but now I had something. The murder on the street, the soldiers, the frozen people, the injections, the albino woman, and the armed guards outside an abandoned building. And when he told me I was just being crazy, I could show him. First the pills, that I'd been taking them, that I was perfectly on schedule. And then I could show him the San Pablo Sanitarium. No way he could deny that.

Sarah could be safe. I pictured her hugging Garth, and felt a little lurch in my belly. I forced that away. It was good and right she should do that. It was the way things were supposed to be. Even then, her blue eyes were on me, the way they seemed to be whenever we were in the same room.

I crept back, wincing when I stepped on the ankle wrong, taking care to keep the tree trunks between me and the guards. I kept expecting to hear the click of a radio, followed by the chatter of a machine gun. Even during the short and awkward climb down the rock wall followed by a jump onto the dirt path, I was certain it would happen at any second.

I ran back to the bike, muscling it around and even rolling it a few yards before finally relenting and starting it up. I resisted the urge to gun the engine and rocket away. I knew the buzzing of my engine would draw those black SUVs out. Run me down, drop me into the bay. And who would investigate? One conversation with my brother would tell them what I was. And the story wrote itself: a simple motorcycle accident with inevitable, albeit tragic, results.

It wasn't until I was far along the winding road that I opened the throttle. Racing along the bridge, the fog bank grew larger and larger. At first, it was merely a hill. Soon, it eclipsed the sky, wrapping arms around the bridge. The air around me softened, and wispy tendrils flowed around and dissipated. Then I was in it. Sounds became muffled and ghostly. Vision narrowed. Lights became indistinct, catching the particles in the air to turn into little auroras. Cars loomed out of the white suddenly, and I was forced to ease up, cautiously making my way up the divider between the traffic.

Leaving the bridge and making it to the narrow streets of the city was a challenge. The mist wound around the wires, crisscrossing every street like grapevines. I turned down once familiar routes made strange by the all-consuming fog. Garth's building came out of the white like a dream. I pulled my bike perpendicular to the street in the little area between driveways and buzzed Garth on the intercom.

"Hello?" Garth's voice was sharp. He had been awake. What time was it?

"Hey, Garth, it's me."

"Come on up." The intercom buzzed.

I went into the lobby, the fog still clinging to me. It wanted to pull me back out into the night. That's where I belonged. I'd return soon, and this time with someone to help. The ride on the elevator seemed to take forever, and I almost ran to Garth's door.

He opened it, and a sunny expression immediately wilted when he saw me. "You look terrible."

"I was outside," I said, waving vaguely. "We need to talk."

"Yeah, come in." Garth stepped aside as I walked inside. I turned and caught him shivering.

"You okay?" I said.

"I'm fine. You brought the cold in with you."

"Oh. Sorry."

"Don't worry about it. Sit down, I'll put some coffee on."

The apartment hadn't been cleaned up any more than it had been the other night. Garth had not unpacked a single box from that time to this. I couldn't blame him. Soon as the last box was unpacked, that was the end of it. Made it all real.

I sat down on his sofa while Garth went into the kitchen. Soon after, the aroma of coffee began to warm the room up. Garth emerged from the kitchen to settle into a chair nearby.

"You don't look so good." Garth said it lightly and I frowned.

"I'm taking the pills," I said to him.

"Good. I was worried."

I shook my head. "None of it was made up. None of it is in my head."

"What do you mean?" Garth said.

"It's there. I found it. I know where Sarah is."

Garth leaned forward. "Where?"

"There's this hospital on the other side of the bay. I can take you there. We can go right now."

"And you saw Sarah go in? You saw it all?"

"No. No, I didn't see her go in. I saw them take Erica's son."

"Erica?"

"The receptionist at Sarah's office," I snapped. If he had paid even a little attention to her work, maybe he wouldn't be in his present situation. "She witnessed the murder along with Sarah.

Now she's missing too. I think they're all in this hospital. Under guard."

"What kind of guards?"

"Three men with machine guns were outside. There's probably more inside."

"How did you find this place?"

I paused. I knew how it sounded. I could hear it in my head, see Garth's disbelief. The knowledge writ large on his face that my stupid brain had made the whole thing up. "You have to believe me. It's going to sound crazy, but I promise you, it's not. It's real—"

"You said you were taking your medicine."

I nodded.

"Then I believe you," Garth said softly.

I closed my eyes, feeling the tears welling up. Hearing someone else, especially my skeptic brother, say this about something even I doubted at times was a gift. "I went looking for Erica to talk to her about the murder in the office. I thought maybe she could shed some light on what happened. Instead, her house was another crime scene. I went to her mother's place, figuring maybe Erica and the kids were staying there. Her son was there, but before I could talk to him, he killed a homeless man."

I looked up to check Garth's expression. I expected to catch the eyeroll, the smirk tugging the corner of his lip. And right on the end of it would be another rant about the meds I was already taking and probably a final push to get me back into a hospital.

But Garth was looking at me with clear eyes, sitting forward in his seat, nodding along. "What happened then?" was all he said.

"There were men. Soldiers. They swept down on the area. I thought someone else would react, but everyone was frozen in place."

"What do you mean, frozen in place?"

"Exactly that. They stopped moving in the middle of what they were doing, and it was like they couldn't see or hear anything."

"Why weren't you frozen?"

"I don't know."

"Go on."

"Then a woman came. She was... she was albino. And she talked to Erica's son, and he fell asleep." I shook my head, a bitter chuckle escaping. "It sounds crazy. I can hear it."

"I believe you. Go on."

"All right. She knew who was on the street, and who was in the buildings around, I guess. And she had her men inject something into the necks of everyone there."

"She never saw you?"

I shook my head.

"Incredible," Garth said. "And they went to this hospital?"

"Yeah. I followed them there."

"That's some story."

"You don't believe me."

"I do. It's a lot to swallow is all."

He got up. "Let me get you some coffee, all right?"

I nodded, relaxing a little, taking off my coat and folding it over the arm of the chair. A moment later, Garth sat a cup in front of me, pale with milk. "Thanks," I said.

"What are you going to do now?"

"Go in there. Get Sarah out. Somehow."

Garth nodded. "I'm going to call in sick to work tomorrow."

"Why?"

"Because you need someone looking out for you, and it would make me feel better."

"Sure thing, Mom," I said, hiding the smile behind a sip of coffee.

"Okay. I'll be back in a bit," Garth said, heading into the bedroom.

I inhaled deeply at the top of the cup. The coffee smelled delicious, the taste putting a little lightning back into my limbs.

I put the cup down and sniffed again. Whatever smelled good wasn't the coffee. My stomach groaned loudly. I tried to remember when I ate last. A while ago. I put a hand on my stomach, and it let out another snarl.

The scent pulled me toward the kitchen. A snack was probably a good idea. Keep my strength up for the hospital. My stomach was steadily gurgling now. The scent driving me was clean and sharp. Something really good, though I couldn't identify it specifically. Probably something I'd had a long time ago. Maybe something Garth picked up that our parents used to buy. Whatever it was, I knew it would hit the spot.

I wandered into Garth's kitchen. There were a few boxes on the formica counters, clearly labeled in black Sharpie. I opened up the fridge, but it was still a sad, nearly empty bachelor fridge. Another sniff pulled me over to the pantry. The food, whatever was giving off that heavenly smell, was in there.

I opened up pantry and almost cried out.

Garth lay in the middle of the pantry, a bullet hole through the center of his forehead.

The smell, the wonderful, hungry smell, was coming from my brother's body.

I stood there, his body wobbling in the tears springing up in my eyes, trying to think. Had he ever been at the door? Had I imagined the whole thing?

"Garth?" I called out. I wasn't sure what to pray for. I didn't know which one was worse.

"I'll be right out!" my brother called back from the bedroom.

Not my brother. Something else. Something using his voice, wearing his face.

I pulled a butcher knife off the magnetic strip by the sink and crept toward the bedroom. I was silent on the carpet, and step by step, I could hear Garth's voice speaking softly. At his bedroom door, barely open a crack, I paused. Once again, uncertainty took me. This was my brother, and what I was about to do was crazy. I listened to the words he spoke. If he was calling in sick, I could calm down, go back to the pantry and find that the body had vanished into the fog.

Garth was not speaking English. He wasn't speaking any language I recognized. It was a soft and lilting tongue he spoke with the rapid confidence of a native. Garth didn't know any other languages. He'd almost failed Spanish in high school and retained none of it. Whatever that was, it wasn't Garth.

I nudged the bedroom door open. Garth was sitting on the bed, back to the door, speaking into the phone. I took a few silent steps and put the knife to Garth's throat.

He finally spoke English: "I'll call you back." Garth hung the phone up and placed it on the bed. "What are you doing?"

"Don't try to talk your way out of this, whatever you are. I found my brother's body."

"I don't know what you think you saw, but I'm right here."

"I know what I saw."

"Do you? We were just talking about your pills—"

"I'm not crazy, goddamn it!"

Garth—the Garth-thing—moved the blade from his throat smoothly with one finger against the flat, and got to his feet. "I never said you were. No one said that. It's just that you're clearly a little confused. How could I be here and in the other room?"

"I know what I saw!" I shouted, the tears welling up again.

"Do you? Look, let's just go get Sarah. You said she was in that hospital? That's the important thing. Let's do that."

I smeared the tears over my face. Garth had backed up to his nightstand. One hand had snaked down and slid the drawer open, and now was reaching inside. While he tried to placate me, he was reaching for something.

"We need to talk about this rationally."

I was already lunging for him when he brought the black pistol up, a silencer screwed to the end of the barrel. I slammed into him, sending us both sprawling into the wall, and then to the floor. He was under me, struggling to get up, to get the gun. I grabbed at him, trying to use my weight, negligible as it was. He reached for the pistol as I tried vainly to pull him across the carpet. He sat up, punching me in the face hard enough to send me sprawling away.

Garth lunged for the gun as I fought to shake the cobwebs. My hand closed around the knife. Garth had the gun in his hand. I brought my fist down.

He screamed, and I noticed then that the knife was buried in his leg. I pulled, but it was stuck through the meat on the inside of his thigh, driven into the floorboards of the apartment. Face ghastly white, the thing looked less like my brother. He brought up the gun, slowed now by the blade through his body.

I was slow too. Fatigue, pills, and the fact that there was still part of my mind crying out that this was my brother. I fought that, focused on the rage. My brother was dead in the other room. This thing was his murderer. This thing had kidnapped Sarah and was trying to kill me. Only room for one of us on this earth.

I lunged for the gun, grabbing the thing's right wrist. It hammered into my ribs with punches, each one slightly weaker as the pool of crimson grew underneath its leg. I cracked an elbow across the Garth-thing's face, both hands now wrestling for the gun. I peeled its fingers, and it cried out again, releasing the pistol.

The gun fell into my hand, handle hot from the thing's palm. I pushed away, landing hard on the floor, the gun up and pointed at the thing's face. It was pallid, covered in sweat.

"Don't move. Don't you move." I'd never used a gun in my life, but I could point one.

The Garth-thing sucked in short gasps of breath, focused not on the gun pointed to its head, but on me. "Please. You have to call an ambulance. It's okay. We can tell them it was an accident. But you have to call someone."

"Cut the act. Who are you?"

For a single, horrible moment, I saw Garth in the thing's eyes. Scared and betrayed and alone, facing death from the one place he always imagined but hated himself for doing so.

And then the expression washed away. The eyes went hard, staring not at me, but through me. "You're already dead. We all are."

"Who are you? What's your name?"

"They take those first. I'm a spy, nothing more."

"Spy for who?"

"My master is only an observer here. He's the least of your worries."

I brought the gun up. "Who?"

The Garth-thing let out a held breath, its eyes falling from me to the floor, where its blood was forming an ever-widening pool. It had been beaten before, but now it was truly defeated. "Do you believe in God?"

I shook my head.

"Good, because there is no God. Not anymore. Just nine pretenders to the throne." It inhaled a rattling, empty breath. "I work for one of them."

"Is that who you were talking to?"

"His spymaster. A Familiar. Not a lowly Servitor like me." Death was close to it now, drawing the shades over its eyes. The Garth-thing looked for me, but couldn't see anything. As it spoke, the words grew softer and softer, carried by the last breath it would ever draw. "You're between the Twins and the Priestess... in the path of a wendigo... you're a dead man, one way or the other... just like me."

My brother's body was cold and white on the floor. The blood stopped spreading. I had never seen so much in my life outside of the movies. It was dark and red, reflecting the overhead light in the room, and the man sitting in it, forming a picture of my brother still and cold underneath a crimson lake.

I don't know when I consciously noticed it, but by the time I did there were dozens of wisps of smoke rising from the pool of blood. The room stank of copper, but now it was burning, leaving behind a cool and clean scent of fresh rain. I looked at the bloodstains on my hands and clothes, turning into wispy white threads.

Garth's face began to lose definition. His nose shrank into his face, his lips vanished, the contours of his face smoothed into ivory. His eyes sank into his skull, the eyelids melding together, the flesh filling in. The mouth disappeared in the same way. Garth's hair retracted into the dead thing's skull. Lying in front of me was a faceless mannequin.

The blood had almost entirely vanished into smoke. Now the creature was as well, more cottony lines spinning upward and turning into that clean rain smell. The knife clattered to the floor, perfectly clean.

Soon, there was nothing in the room at all.

I stared at the empty place on the floor where that thing had been, wondering if I had imagined it, knowing I hadn't. My body ached from the fight. The blade was there, sticking into the floorboards. It had happened. It was real.

My watch went off. I jumped, for a moment forgetting what the sound meant. Time to take my medicine. I almost laughed. The shapeshifter with my brother's face, the albino, the frozen people, the murder. All of those things, coming to me when the drugs were in my system, smoothing out the broken chemistry of my malfunctioning brain.

I fished the pills out of my pocket and went into the bathroom.

If it was fake, if I was making it all up, that meant the pills were useless. All they did was fill my head full of fog. Make me slow.

And I had to be fast. Sharp. Nearly killed me fighting the Garth-thing that had turned to smoke. If I was going to help Sarah, I had to be at my best.

I flushed the pills down Garth's toilet and left his apartment.

- 3 -

The first snow started to fall at dawn. I never returned home. Instead, I found an ATM and withdrew enough money to last a couple days and ate at an all night diner. The food tasted gray and I could only finish half. I spent the rest of the night waiting on the steps of the library, a boxy building on Larkin that looked like a Civil War fort. The mist rose from the streets to coalesce overhead in the big gray thunderclouds now covering the city. This happened late into the night when the air was so cold it burned my lungs, and by the time the sun rose, it was invisible behind a thick curtain of frowning sky.

The cold did not bother me. My ankle throbbed a bit, but the constant activity had done it some good. My face and ribs ached from the beating I took at the hands of the thing in my brother's apartment. Those would heal.

I tried not to think about Garth, dead in his pantry. I had the vague sense I shouldn't be the one to call the police. So for the time being he would have to stay there. I wondered what the cops would say when they finally investigated. The murder weapon was in his apartment, my prints wiped off the handle. The gun was probably untraceable, but on the off chance there was something to find, maybe the cops would find it.

I really was the only one Sarah could count on.

So I sat on the concrete steps and waited until the night faded away into the shadows. The security guards showed up before the librarians. When they finally unlocked the door, I headed inside. The librarians were in their alcove, taking off heavy coats and chattering about the bizarre weather. They spared me a single concerned look as I limped into the back.

My watch beeped, reminding me that it was time to take my medicine, medicine that had been flushed out into the Pacific Ocean. The final reminder of how far off the path I had gone. I touched the buttons; they were sticking. I hadn't touched them since Garth bought me the watch, already having programmed the alarm. I had a tendency to forget even then, or more damning, to pretend to forget. With the watch, I no longer had that excuse. And now it no longer had a purpose. I forced the recalcitrant buttons in and turned off the alarm. I had the dim sense that was the last time the watch would ever go off.

Going into the abandoned hospital in the daytime would be impossible. Those soldiers would kill me in seconds. I had to wait for night to fall again and give me some cover. Until then, there were things to look into. Something about the weather bothered me, and not just the oddity of it. Whatever it was niggled at the tip of my brain. And there was the word the thing with Garth's face had used: wendigo.

The stacks had copies of the *San Francisco Times* stretching back since the paper was founded. They were being kept in large folders to protect them from the acids in fingers while waiting to be scanned. It might take all day to find whatever it was I was looking for, but I had all day to look.

I staked out a small wooden desk, clicked on the little green-shaded lamp, and fetched the first stack of folders. They were heavy, but history was like that. I set them down and started paging through the older issues. The papers were yellowed, but otherwise in remarkable condition. I was able to look through the history of San Francisco in its own words.

The news had mentioned that a blizzard had hit the city once before. Something like a hundred years ago. I started with that. Paging back through the yellowed sheets, I found a notice of the quake of 1906. The city had almost been destroyed. The pages chronicled the destruction with an undercurrent of lurid sensationalism. Showing the damage for the sake of showing it. After the earthquake, fires from ruptured gas mains raged out of control, eating 25,000 buildings. In a touch of old-timey insanity, firemen tried to create firebreaks with dynamite, causing even more destruction.

I found a single reference to an earlier earthquake that some scientists thought triggered the later and far more destructive quake. I reached farther back, seeing images of the city sitting on the precipice of destruction. San Francisco had always been beautiful, a gold rush town bolstered with Victorian architecture perched at the edge of the endless Pacific. Even then, right before the apocalypse came.

Looking backward into the months previous, I found an article on the earthquake. It was small, as these things went, localized in Golden Gate Park. It knocked down a few buildings, cracked the Nesbitt residence in half, and did some damage to one of the wings of a local hospital. There wasn't much commentary on it at the time; its importance only coming into context with the big earthquake in April.

One article mentioned something that seemed out of place. The damage to the hospital had resulted in the closing of the wing. This would not have been necessary, the article explained, if not for the weather. I paged back a few more issues and found what I was looking for.

A blizzard had washed over the city. This was the one the news mentioned in passing. It lasted the better part of a week, and the earthquake had hit in the middle of it. I went back a few days and found the headline. The article explained, in slightly archaic English, the snows descending on San Francisco. I checked the date.

A hundred years ago. Exactly. To the day.

I paged through the neighboring articles, searching for stories I knew were there, even as I feared finding them. The first cries of "maniac" surfaced shortly thereafter. Sifting through the rest, I found the trail leading back through the pages. Stories of a madman loose on the streets of San Francisco. Some thought the monster in question was none other than Jack the Ripper, having crossed the Atlantic and the continent to arrive here and continue his work. Despite striking five times, the so-called Frisco Cannibal was never caught. He murdered all over the city, and while Jack confined his attentions to working girls, the Cannibal was indiscriminate. He killed his five victims and vanished, forgotten in these old stacks of newspaper.

Another thing repeating itself.

I looked back through the papers. They wouldn't reach another hundred years into the past, but I couldn't shake the feeling there was something much larger at work. I turned the page to an article about the courthouse being dedicated. A picture showed a gathering of city dignitaries. In the corner, a beautiful woman whose chalk white skin was unmistakable. Miss Cross, looking the same as she had last night.

I knew it wasn't a coincidence. Exactly a hundred years from that day to this one. Same players. Another Frisco Cannibal. Did that mean there was another city-breaking earthquake on the horizon as well?

I sat silently in the stacks trying to comprehend the enormity of it. Nine pretenders to the throne, the shapeshifter had said.

Some strange cycle, every century. And now here I was, in the middle. Only as long as it took to get Sarah. After that, maybe I could forget what I'd learned. Pump myself so full of pills I could get back to the haze I used to hate but now longed for.

Then there was the word the shapeshifter had used. Wendigo. I moved on to reference books, digging through dictionaries and encyclopedias, finally finding it in a book of folklore. The wendigo was an evil spirit of the north in some Native American traditions. It comes with the snow, forcing others to commit horrifying acts of cannibalism.

The Frisco Cannibal.

It almost didn't matter if that were real. The fact that something believed it was real was horrible enough. But I had already seen things that I couldn't explain, so it was not unthinkable that some cannibal spirit of winter was murdering people in my city.

I left the library feeling worse than I had before. Night had rolled in, and the snow was falling gently, collecting only in gutters as slushy ice. The sidewalk was slick. I found my bike and gunned it toward the hospital on the other side of the bay. Once again, leaving the local environs allowed me to look back on my city swallowed in storm. The barrier was no longer a thick sheet of fog marking the boundaries of the storm. Now the clouds sent fat gray feelers over the bay and into the neighboring cities. Snow fell intermittently from these arms, making them appear almost as the tentacles of a great kraken surfacing from the depths, shedding water.

Crossing over the bridge and looping back toward the San Pablo Sanitarium, I watched the clouds spread across the sky. Before I was even within sight of the hospital, I knew they already made it there. When I arrived, the blizzard would come with me. It felt right, even as snowflakes drifted onto my shoulders to turn to glass and then to water.

Snow fell along the deserted street lined with warehouses.

The garbage in the gutters was covered in graying sludge, a few drifts collecting where no one would ever disturb them. The ocean lapped against the rocks, the water choppy with whitecaps. The stand of trees hiding the San Pablo Sanitarium came into view.

Sarah would be with me when I came out of there. I didn't want to think of the rest, but it came anyway. If Sarah wasn't with me, I wasn't coming out at all.

I cut the engine of my bike and got off, walking it forward. The guards would hear the coughing buzz of my engine from far off. I was already starting in a hole. No reason to make it any more difficult. Most of the lots lining the left side of the road were fenced in, the gates bound shut with rusting chains. Loops of razorwire and lines of barbed wire stretched across the top, as if the rotting shipping containers were worth stealing.

Walking through veils of falling snow, I went from lot to lot. Finally, a little over a mile from the sanitarium, I found a gate whose chain had no lock. I unwound the chain, big bloody flakes of rust coming off on my hands, and opened the softly squealing gate. The area beyond was a gas station, now long since closed down. All of the grass growing through the cracks in the sidewalk had died. The windows into the minimart were broken. The pumps were sagging. I wheeled my bike into the shadowed area between the fence and minimart, where the old air pump was rusting away into the ground.

I walked along the street toward the hospital, staying on the sidewalk alongside the abandoned warehouses. The air was chill, but I scarcely noticed. The snow was comforting. I felt hidden amongst it, and in that was power.

My shadow flung out in front of me, suddenly far darker than it had been. I whirled around. Headlights on the street, coming closer, flaring against the snowflakes. I dove down a side street. It didn't take a guess to know those were more of the SUVs from the other night, on the same errand. There were no walls to press up against, only the permeable cover of fences, so I dropped to the frozen sidewalk. The sidewalk was perfectly flat, the snow not yet forming drifts to hide behind. I was a small dark lump against the bare ground.

I looked up as the first black SUV pushed through the curtains of snow. Then the second. And a third. And a fourth. None slowed. None stopped. None turned down this street, spitting out a team of armed men. I got up, creeping to the corner and watching the disappearing caravan. Four? Seemed like a lot. The previous night had only needed two.

I padded closer, breaking into a jog a half mile out, worried there would be more SUVs coming. This might be a bad night to go in, but if the timeline from a century ago held, there wasn't any time to waste. Besides, Sarah needed to be home safe as soon as possible.

I climbed the rocks as I had done the previous night. A palpable anger flowed from the roiling water into the glassy skies. Everything was gathering around this place. I couldn't put my finger on exactly what it was, but I could sense it as clear as anything else. The old brick hospital rising up from the little hill through the trees was the source. It wasn't the eye of the storm; that was a place of preternatural calm. Instead, what I sensed from there was a cold rage radiating outward. And yet, I wasn't afraid.

I crept closer. This time the ground was dotted with small, crunchy drifts of snow. The soldiers were right where I had left them. Were they the same men? Maybe they were something else, like the thing that had killed my brother, some automatons who could stand for days in the freezing cold without any need for relief. I waited there, watching the man at the front and the man tucked in the side entrance. More movement caught my eye. There were now two men at the front, the second as much of a shadow as the first. Another man threw a tiny shadow over the open ground by the corner. More SUVs, more security.

The vehicles were parked by the hospital, all facing the road, ready to move quickly. Whoever ran this place, were they expecting something? Or was it time to leave? The two entrances I could see from my position at the edge of the bare trees were guarded. I couldn't cross in front of the sanitarium without the men at the door seeing me. I glanced around. There was only one way around the place where I wouldn't be seen.

I retreated through the trees to the edge of the rock wall where it dropped to the path and climbed halfway down. I knew if I thought about it too long, I might lose my nerve, so I just moved. Inching sideways along the rock wall, around the far side of the little promontory.

The bay was infamous for its deep and freezing water swarming with sharks, Alcatraz's final and most foolproof line of defense. The wind coming off the Pacific whipped the gray water into a frenzy. As it splashed up onto my feet and ankles, it felt as though the bay were trying to drag me down.

Though it would not have been a long walk, I was moving inch by inch, finding openings between the rocks. They were all salt-slick, simultaneously scratching my hands and threatening to squirt me off and into the bay. I worked along it, certain I was almost there, but when I glanced back, I saw I was not even halfway.

Above, I could only see the sky, scratched by a few bare branches overhanging the water. The gray clouds were pregnant with moonlight, shining in patches, a beautiful cancer over the city. In places, the water threw the reflection back in blinding silver light. I turned away, licking the salt from my dry lips, blinking it from my eyes, and kept the desperate climb.

My ankle started to betray me as the shore curved. It had held up for a long time. Now the strain was growing, like a bubble balancing pain on all sides. There was no way around it, either. I needed all four limbs to do this. I gritted my teeth and kept moving.

Finally, when my arms were noodles, my ankle was broken glass, my eyes and hands were stinging, I was probably where I needed to be: behind the sanitarium. It would be stupid to assume there weren't guards on the seaward side, so I peeked up over the rocks very carefully.

This side was almost like a resort, or had been before the sea got its fingers into it. What had been a series of wooden sunbathing chairs had almost completely fallen apart, and a cabana was little more than a rotting collection of boards and nails. A few trees, similarly bare, were between the shore and the hospital. There were entrances, and I waited, trying to probe the darkness for what I already knew was there.

Double doors led inside, and sure enough, in the shadows, I saw the soldier shift, the moonlight momentarily glinting off his submachine gun. Movement by the southeastern corner drew my eye. Another soldier, his face a blank mask behind the balaclava and goggles. Between us, the snow was falling, and here even more heavily. A flake landed on the back of my hand and stayed there unmelting, freezing cold and comforting. The soldiers didn't see me, or if they did, gave no sign. Between night and snow, I had some cover.

Until lights flashed from the front of the hospital. Slowly, the sounds muffled by the curtain of falling snow, I heard more vehicles pulling up to the hospital. Radios clicked from the soldiers, and they shifted in their posts, heads craning involuntarily. I clambered over the side, and inched to what had been the cabana. The falling boards and wispy shadows should be enough cover for the time being.

I scanned the upper windows of the hospital. If there were snipers up there, I couldn't see them. Down at ground level, there were the entrances I'd seen. No way in. On the road, another set of headlights flared against the snowfall. Another vehicle. More, gathering at the hospital. The brightening headlights splashed illumination across the ground.

I saw it, partly hidden by a largish drift of snow: one of the windows opening into a basement level was broken, a bit of snow hanging on one brittle and jagged tooth of glass. From where I was standing, three men could see me if I broke cover. The one by the back door, the one at the side entrance, and the man on the corner. As I got closer, the man on the corner would lose sight of me, followed by the man at the back door.

When the SUVs had arrived, there was the barest moment when the men were distracted. That was my only chance. I would have to take it. Sprint across open ground and dive into the hole. Hope I didn't hear the chatter of their guns, feel the bullets chew me to pieces.

I shut my eyes, steeling myself for the run.

Something kissed my forehead. And again. Again. Cold and soft, gentle and comforting. I opened my eyes. The sky had turned inside out, the clouds overhead were thick. The moon was hidden behind the great gray tendrils and now snow was following in ever-thickening sheets. In seconds I could scarcely see the two closest men.

Finally, something going my way.

I broke cover, moving as quickly as I was able on my stiffening ankle. I ran in a loping shuffle over the freezing ground, falling to my hands and knees before the wall, and crawling the rest of the way to the broken window. The wet ground soaked through the knees of my pants and crept into my palms, though I scarcely felt it. As thin as I was, there was enough room for me between the hanging triangle of glass still stuck in the frame.

Inside it was almost pitch black, stinking of dust, rot, and mildew. Shapes loomed out of the dark, and though my mind desperately tried to give them arms and faces, I fought the impulse. Snaking through the narrow window, my balance shifted, my stomach lurched, and I was falling the six feet to the ground. I tucked and rolled, slamming into the floor on my shoulder. It hurt, though not as much as it could have.

I got to my feet, wincing as the weight came down on the bad ankle. Testing my shoulder found it worked fine, but there was a persistent buzzing that would turn into a deep ache over the course of the following day. A narrow shaft of moonlight fell into the room from the broken window. The other windows were more intact, covered with a smeared layer of grime. Ahead of me, I could barely make out a doorway, the door long since gone, and a long hallway. At the end, some diffuse light barely made it to me.

I crept to the doorway, putting my back against the wall, trying to let my starved eyes adjust. Outside, I could see the snow had stopped falling as quickly, though even now flakes were drifting into the room to settle into smaller drifts collecting against the sagging frames of old shelves. It looked like I was in a storage room, the walls bare brick, in places picked out with spidery graffiti. Anything of value had long since been looted. All that was left were the remains of the shelving, holding a few rotting bundles that might have once been bedclothes.

The hallway leading out had doorways on either side, most yawning and black, a few still had doors long since warped to the point that they no longer closed. I couldn't tell where the light at the far end of the hallway was coming from, but it was bright and yellow in contrast to the soft silver of the moon. There was artificial light in this place, though there was no way they still had power.

I padded down the hall, trying not to let my feet scrape on the dust-covered cement floors. All around, there were shallow pools of stagnant water, some frozen solid. Along the walls, generations of kids had scrawled their aliases, symbols, and messages. A pentagram covered the wall next to me as I paused.

Footsteps.

I cast about, taking a couple steps back into an open doorway. The room was darker than the first, and the shapes looming large in the darkness could not be identified. I turned away from them, trying to ignore the persistent feeling of something large and dangerous in the room behind me. I stayed just beyond the threshold, peeking out as the footsteps drew closer.

The first people walking past the hall were soldiers, armed and armored like the men outside. Behind them were men and women in medical scrubs carrying stretchers between them. On each stretcher was a person, dressed in normal street clothes, unconscious. There were four of them, followed by a man soaked in blood to the elbow, on his shirt, covering his face, and dribbling from his mouth. Two more soldiers brought up the rear. They disappeared from sight, and I heard more footsteps, then a door opening and closing.

Two of the soldiers marched back. I waited in the darkness, listening to my own breath. The door opened and shut again, and the men and women holding the stretchers and the last two soldiers walked by. I waited a little longer, and one man in scrubs followed the others. I did a mental count of who I saw, and was pretty sure that everyone conscious had left. Then, I went to the corner and peered into the hall.

It was no different than the last, bare brick almost entirely covered in graffiti. Lights were strung up at regular intervals, cords tracing the corner of the wall and disappearing out of sight. I could hear the muffled hum of a generator deeper in this place's expansive basement. Ahead, where the men had come and gone, the doors were heavier. Made of metal, they were not warped, but spots had been rusted into their skin. There were even little windows in the door, smudged over the lattice of chickenwire.

I went to the first. A handwritten card had been carefully placed in a small holder on the front. It read simply, "HOSTS." I peered into the window. There were five cots lining the walls of the room. Five people, dressed in bloody clothes, mouths and hands stained with blood, lay there. IVs dripped into their arms. New IVs, clean and sterile, at odds with the rest of the rotting building. The bloody people were held onto the bare wire mesh of the cots with leather restraints lined in sheepskin. I opened the door.

They were all unconscious. I recognized Erica's son immediately, and right next to him was Erica herself. Five cots, five murderers. I almost ran to them, unbuckled the restraints, and tried to wake them. Then I remembered what the kid had done to the homeless man. I took a deep breath. I would save them, but not before I found Sarah. She was the most important. Sarah first, then see about these others.

I closed the door carefully and went back out into the hall. The next five rooms, two on one side of the hall, three on the other, were illuminated with one of the bright lights, throwing my dark shadow against the wall. Each door had an address printed out carefully on a card. 1537 Paper St. Marlowe and Rutledge. Bailey and Downs, where the kid killed the homeless man. 1634 Racine, Sarah's office. 2342 Neff, Erica's house. These were all five of the murder sites.

I opened the door to 1634 Racine. Six people lay on cots, strapped down with IVs dripping into their arms. They all wore white garments, something halfway between hospital and christening gowns. A smudged and cracked mirror stretched along one wall. I caught a glimpse of myself, pale and frozen, snow in my hair and on my shoulders.

Sarah was in the farthest bed. I ran to her, kneeling on the dusty concrete floor. She was beautiful, and a part of me hated that was the first thing I thought when I saw her lying there. It was impossible to see anything else. From the moment we met and she gave me the first genuine smile I had received in years, to all those moments when we were each other's closest friend, her beauty haunted me. And in isolated instances, when a hug would linger, a look would last, I could almost believe she felt the same way. She was paler than she had been, her normally fair skin becoming more like ivory. Her Hitchcock blonde hair fell through the exposed wires of the cot. I took her hand, the wedding band hard against my fingers.

"Sarah! Sarah, wake up! It's me, Chris!"

Sarah stirred, her eyelids fluttering. A small groan came from somewhere deep inside her. It seemed as though she was fighting to the surface of the bay, the black water trying to drag her down.

"Sarah!"

I shook her gently. The tapping sound of her body against the cot made me stop. Should have been a rattling of wire mesh. The tapping didn't stop when I did. I looked up. Footsteps, in the hall.

Panicked, I got up and ran for the door. The footsteps got closer and closer, accompanied now by a persistent high-pitched squealing. I hit the corner right as the door opened inward, putting me between the battered door and the bare brick of the walls.

The first thing through was a metal cart, the wheels the source of the squealing sound. It was piled high with IV bags fat with clear liquid. The man pushing it was smaller than me, short and slight. From the back, I saw the bald spot peeking through his graying curly black hair, the collar of his pinstriped shirt, and the labcoat. The tapping sound was his expensive shoes on the cracked floors of the sanitarium.

"How is everyone?" he asked the room, gravelly voice echoing off the hard walls. "I hope you're hungry. This is the last bag before…" His voice trailed off, attention on Sarah, eyes fluttering, heavy arms fighting against the restraints. "Didn't get here a moment too soon, I see. Don't worry, you'll be back in dreamland—"

I lunged for him, grabbing the collar of the labcoat and planting my elbow in the small of his back, driving him face first into the mirror. He smacked into it with a grunt, struggling for a second, but I had all the leverage in the world. He was older than I was, his loose skin deeply lined.

"Don't you move, you son of a bitch," I growled.

The doctor went slack in my hands. In the mirror we were facing, I loomed over the twinned doctor, teeth bared. The doctor shrank away from me, brown eyes rolling crazily in their sockets, trying to see me. Finally, he looked into the streaked mirror I was mashing him into. He seemed to calm, the fear still there, but under control for the time being.

"Easy. Easy! You don't have to do this. I'm sure you and I can come to some kind of arrangement."

"Be quiet and I won't hurt you. I'm taking one of these people out of here."

"I can't let you do that. You know as well as I do the wendigo could choose any one of them. Unless… did your master find a way to know which one?"

"I don't know what you're talking about. I'm taking the blonde woman and going."

"Unfortunately, son, you're not going anywhere."

"I got in just fine."

"It's not the getting in that's the problem. It's the getting out."

Motion caught my eye. I looked up, into the old mirror. Staring back at me were a pair of brilliant green eyes, like a cat's. Not mine.

The face pushed into view, distended and skeletal, a pattern of bone white and tar black. The thing's smile was horribly human, its teeth perfect exemplars save for the elongated canines on the upper and lower jaw. The face came through the mirror, the smudged and rusted surface rippling like water and dripping from its all-too-human features. It reached through with a three-fingered hand, the glittering black claws first stretching, then permeating the mirror.

I let go of the doctor, staggering backward. It emerged fully into the room, carrying with it the stench of ammonia.

"Please tell me you have Familiar back-up son, or else your master sent you to die."

"I don't have a—"

The demon jumped forward, grabbing me with one claw and slamming me into the far wall. I cowered there, on my ass, as the demon took two light steps, its long tail whipping about behind. It leaned in close, grinning, inspecting me with eyes carrying the cruel glint of intelligence. I knew then that I was a dead man. This thing would tear me apart, suck the marrow from my bones. Take me to the other side of the mirror where no one would ever find my body.

"Wait, please," said the doctor.

The demon paused, watching the pulse in my neck.

The doctor removed a walkie-talkie from his belt. "He might know something important. I'll contact Miss Cross and see what she wants done with him." He clicked the button on the side. "This is Dr. Jeremiah. We have an intruder with the potentials."

The voice crackled over the walkie. "Has the intruder been subdued?"

"One of the thraxians has him. Have someone inform Miss Cross."

"Right away, Dr...." There was a pause, and when the voice returned, it had turned urgent, and there was indistinct shouting in the background. "Dr. Jeremiah! Kill the intruder! Secure the potentials! Now, goddamn—"

The building shook, dust raining onto us. Jeremiah looked up, the fear blooming over his features far worse than anything I had managed to inflict. Even the demon cocked its head, the alien amusement falling away for a moment.

"Oh god," Jeremiah whispered.

The building shook again, feeling like a wrecking ball had slammed into the side, but when the shaking from a blow like that should have subsided, the trembling only increased until it sounded like a train, getting closer and closer. Freezing dust kept falling until a chalky fog filled the air in the small room. Outside, over the cracking and groaning of stone, I could hear the rapid chattering of guns.

Jeremiah turned to run. The demon's head whipped around, its tail lashing the air. I had been forgotten, but there was nowhere to go.

And then the room opened up.

With the cacophony of fracturing stone and howling metal, a fissure chased itself up the ceiling, webbing outward, splitting again and again. The ceiling then cracked like an egg, cement dust raining down, as the brick and mortar were literally peeled back by invisible hands. Above, I saw the night sky looking down, and for a moment, my terrified mind manufactured a broken window where the moon shone down on me. But there was no roof anymore. The asylum had been ripped in two and even now was still being torn open, the walls cresting like waves and falling to either side. All around, the walls, floors, and ceilings of the once abandoned hospital were an angry slurry.

At the mouth of the rift, I saw a man, his arms parted, shouting incomprehensible words into the screaming wind. He was tall and thin, a brown leather trench coat flapping around him. Gunfire ripped into the air from a pair of soldiers in a section of the sanitarium that had once been the first floor. The man in the coat threw his right arm upward, more of the bizarre words tumbling from his lips. Spears of rock and debris shot from the ruined building, impaling both soldiers through the chest.

Jeremiah had turned stark white. "Kisin," he whispered.

The demon loped toward the man in the brown leather trench coat. He paused for a second, straightening his tie as the abomination charged through the shifting destruction, claws bared.

The man, Kisin, merely made a clutching motion, muttering something I could not hear. Cement and rebar exploded from the ground beneath the demon, wrapping it up, and constricting.

Sarah.

I forced myself to remember what I was doing there. The world might be insane, but Sarah was still there. Sarah still needed my help. I pushed off the ground, running to her side, ripping the IV from her arm. Her eyes opened, her voice, thick and groggy, "Garth?"

The word felt like one of the rock spears the soldiers were still impaled upon. Outside, there was more gunfire, cut off with rumbling and screams.

"No, it's me, Chris."

Relief spread over her face. "Chris. Thank god." She embraced me and for a moment, though the world was in chaos around us, I was calm.

"Come on, Sarah," I said, trying to get her to unsteady feet while the sanitarium rattled and shook.

"What's happening?"

"I'll explain everything later. We have to run."

Jeremiah screamed into the walkie-talkie. "Shahmeran! Kisin is here, at the hospital! Now!"

Somehow I was running, even though every step on the bad ankle hurt worse than the one before, as I was shouldering Sarah's negligible weight. The wall behind us had collapsed, and unlike the clean ramp down which Kisin was striding, this was a wall of broken brick and torn rebar. I boosted Sarah up the wall and followed her. My foot gave under the cracking wall, and I nearly slipped when I felt an ice cold hand gripping my wrist. I looked up to Sarah's face. She hauled me up, her gown dirty.

At the top, I turned in time to see that Kisin had reached Jeremiah. Kisin grinned, though there was no humor in his face. He spoke English for the first time in my presence, his accent Mexican. "The wyrm cannot help you now."

Jeremiah opened his mouth to say something, but it was cut off with a surprised cry, as Kisin raised his gloved hands and whispered, tentacles made of brick, concrete, and rebar emerged from the walls and floor, wrapping around Jeremiah's limbs. Kisin opened his palm, and Jeremiah never had a chance to scream as he was torn apart.

From this vantage on what had once been the ground floor of the hospital, I could see into all of the bottom level. Kisin, somehow, had exposed everything. The people in the six rooms were all sleeping peacefully in their cots, unaware of the trail of horror the brown-coated man had tracked in. Soldiers were impaled and splattered all along Kisin's path in endlessly creative ways.

In the center of the room, he threw his arms up and out, almost like a man conducting an orchestra. His voice rang out. Hard, solid words in no language I recognized, their power thudding through my bones. Rock mouths opened from the debris in the floor beneath the beds, and with horrible cracks, bit through each of the sleeping people.

He looked up, his large brown eyes meeting mine. I had never seen a man look so haunted. Blood from hundreds of murdered people flowed in rivers through the wreckage to pool around his expensive shoes. His voice carried right to me. "No one escapes."

Another word, another gesture to guide his symphony of rock and stone, and hands burst from the concrete at our feet, grabbing our ankles. Graffiti, still legible, wound over the knuckles of these rock hands. I cried out, the sprain grinding under the implacable grip. I looked down, and Kisin was ready to finish us off.

Behind him, the demon had freed itself from the crushing trap, tracking its black blood, already freezing in the chill air. It dragged itself toward Kisin, its tail severed and legs broken. As Kisin started the sweep of his arms and the sentence that would kill us, the demon grabbed his ankles, claws biting into his flesh.

Kisin screamed, and the rock hands holding us exploded into plumes of dust. I grabbed Sarah's hand and ran. Behind us, the remains of the San Pablo Sanitarium finished the last bit of destruction and crumbled, leaving a bombed out collection of rubble. For the first time I ran down the driveway toward the street. The SUVs that had once held the soldiers were destroyed. One had been ripped in half, the other looked as though a colossal bite had come out of the side.

We hit the street right as headlights shone from the turn up ahead. There was no choice; we had to run toward them and hope they didn't see us in the swirling snow and cloud of dust.

"Chris! Chris, what's happening?" Sarah gasped.

"I'll explain, but we have to get out of here!"

The headlights were coming up too fast, burning down the street toward the broken sanitarium with desperate speed. I hurled Sarah and I down a side street and were still. My battered ankle throbbed. The SUVs sped past, tires hissing on the fallen snow. I grabbed her hand and pulled, running as fast as I could for the motorcycle. Brakes squealed, gunfire opened up, and there was a loud smash. A moment later, a deep sibilance, like the sound of continents sliding past one another, reached me. I kept running, biting back the pain, to the gas station, grabbing my bike and handing the helmet to Sarah. I stomped on the starter, and only as I was rolling out of the station, did I look back at the asylum.

Through the haze of snow, I could see the bright lights of muzzle flash. The ground roiled and surged, grayish tentacles tattooed with graffiti rose and fell. There was something else amidst the ruin. A shape, coiled maybe, colored like a sunset, thrashing amongst the spears of rock.

I gunned the engine and burned the other way, as far and as fast as I could, heading inland, as far from the storm as I could manage. Sarah had her arms wrapped around my waist, her hips close to mine. It was hard to concentrate; she was only dressed in the slight gown. I tried to forget it as I pulled off the freeway for a gas station.

Sarah took the helmet off. She was shaking, but not from the cold. "Chris, please."

I nodded, trying to think of a way to phrase things that didn't sound like I had in the past. "The murder you saw was one of five. It's a cycle... it happened a hundred years ago, and it's happening again."

"What?"

"They're real. I found them in newspapers of the time. Every hundred years, a blizzard hits the city, and for some reason it brings this... I don't know. Mania? People, normal people, kill. There are five, and then it just stops." I shook my head, watching the snow touch the asphalt and turn gray. "I know this sounds..."

"I believe you."

I looked up. "You do?" I had a sick lurching feeling; that was exactly what the thing wearing my brother's face had said. I didn't think I could handle losing Sarah as well.

She nodded. "I saw everything too. I didn't know… that, but I saw the man… I don't know. But I know this is not something normal." I nodded. She had seen it too. Not just taking my word for it. She had seen Kisin bring death from the ground as though he were conducting an orchestra. She knew, maybe not the reasons, but knew that we were in a place were the crazy was sane.

"I don't know why this is happening. There's an albino woman, Miss Cross, and I think she needs the witnesses for something. Something to do with a cannibal spirit of winter. And I think there's a group that wants to stop her. I wish I could say that in some way that made sense."

She smiled. "Thank you for saving me."

I colored, turning away. "There's one more thing. Hold on."

Hunching my shoulders, I went into the minimart in the gas station, and got the bathroom key from the dead-eyed attendant. It was secured to a scratched and dented block of wood. I beckoned Sarah over. The snow had started falling more heavily since we arrived, and she looked like a ghost in her white gown. I unlocked the door into the small and stinking room. Sarah blanched for a moment.

"I'm barefoot," she said.

Her feet were muddy, and probably cut in a few places. "Sorry," I said.

She shrugged, joining me by the sink and the small, cracked mirror covered in red graffiti.

"What are we doing now?"

"They injected something in all of the witnesses," I said. "Some kind of tracking device, I think. Let me see your neck."

She stretched her neck, moving her long blonde hair out of the way. Her skin was smooth and perfect, and even though she wasn't wearing any perfume, she smelled like flowers. I ran my fingers over her neck trying to ignore the gooseflesh in my arms.

She shivered, and I knew it wasn't the cold. I found what I was looking for in the meaty part, away from the big veins: a small nodule just beneath the skin.

"Is that it?"

I looked up, our eyes meeting in the mirror, and nodded.

"Get it out."

"Do you trust me?"

She nodded.

"All right." I cracked the mirror with the wooden block attached to the key. Another hit smashed the glass, the silvery shards falling into the sink. I fished one out. "Hold still."

She winced when the glass bit into her skin and the bright red blood welled up. Somehow, she smelled even better. I wanted to cover the cut with my mouth, kiss it, and let it flow onto my tongue. Instead, I found the nodule, and plucked it away as she hissed in pain. "All done."

She put a hand to the bleeding wound. I took off my coat and shirt, handing the shirt over and putting the coat back on. She tore the shirt into strips, leaving little bloody fingerprints all along it like a crime. She quickly bandaged her neck, and the wound had already slowed to a trickle. "Need help?" I asked her.

"I know a dentist isn't a medical doctor, but I'll manage," she said.

I looked at the tracking device, washing it off in the sink. A tiny grilled button was hooked up to a crystal. It didn't look like I imagined that technology to look. It went into the toilet and was flushed out to sea along with my pills and everything else I didn't need.

"Aren't you cold?" I asked.

"No."

"Me neither."

"Where are we going now?"

"We'll find a motel somewhere close by. Get some sleep, and maybe figure out what to do."

I got back on the bike and drove a few more miles down the road, thinking I could get out from under the storm. Eventually, the snow would stop falling and there would just be clean night sky overhead. But every mile down the road was another mile under a relentless blanket of freezing white. Finally, I turned off to a little motel tucked in the brown hills, its red neon light blazing through the snowfall. I checked in, giving the clerk a fake name and paying in cash.

We got into the room. Sarah looked down at her feet. "I need to clean up. Then we can talk, okay?"

I nodded.

Sarah disappeared into the bathroom, and the shower started up. I took off the coat and sat there in my undershirt, looking down at my bony arms and waiting. Too much had happened. It was crushing me, and the only thing I could do was silently bear it and try not to think.

The shower shut off and Sarah came out of the bathroom wrapped in a towel, her hair hanging in lank strands. "I don't have any other clothes," she said, "but that gown... feels wrong. Something they put me in."

"I wish I could tell you who they are." The weight gave, and I had to say something. "Sarah?"

"What?"

"Garth..."

"He's dead, isn't he? They got him."

I nodded, tears blurring my eyes. "How did you know?"

"I saw your face when I called you his name," she said, streaks falling from both eyes.

"He was already gone before I knew what was happening."

She sat next to me. My eyes should have gone to her legs,

stretching from under the towel, or to her breasts, peeking out from the top. But they went right to the wet strip of my shirt around her neck where the blood bloomed like a flower.

"I wish… I wish…" I said, but the rest of the words were a sob, and after that I couldn't stop. I could only think of Garth, cold and dead in his pantry.

Sarah held me. "Oh god, Chris, I'm sorry. I'm so sorry." And she was crying too. Both of us, crying for Garth, far too late to do anything for him. I don't know how long we were like that, but when I moved away, wiping the tears and snot, my face was wet from her shower.

"He didn't believe me," I said.

"What do you mean?"

"When I told him you'd been kidnapped. He thought…"

Sarah's eyes, red and wet, went stony. "I know what he thought."

She had always been so nice. She had never seen the worst of me. "I am crazy, Sarah. I know I've fought against it. But I am."

"No, you're not."

"Yes, I am. There's something wrong with my brain. The chemistry or something. I hear things, abusive, shouting voices…"

"And what are you hearing now?"

"Nothing."

She touched my face. "You're not as crazy as he made you feel. You always knew, somewhere deep down when it was true."

I closed my eyes. "I really wish that were true."

"You found me," she murmured. "No one else did."

And I felt her lips on mine, opening my mouth, arms twining around my shoulders. For a moment I surrendered to the fantasy, before I had to push her away. "Sarah, we can't. You're…"

"It was over. You know that, right?"

"You're still wearing the ring."

Sarah pulled the ring off her finger. I expected it to stick, but it came off easily. "It didn't feel right. Even after what he did, I couldn't quite take it off." With a click, she set the ring on the nightstand. "Chris…"

She didn't have to say anything else. She leaned to me, and this time I didn't stop. Not when I kissed her, or unwrapped her, or when she whispered my name into my mouth. I had fantasized about this moment for so many years, hating myself each time. And even though she was as soft and sweet and beautiful as I could imagine, I couldn't stop thinking about the blood dribbling sluggishly from her neck.

We were quiet in the aftermath, dozing in each other's arms. The sun came up, the room going from dim blue to the diffuse gold of the curtains. Her fingers touched my ribs, counting them one by one. "The first thing we're going to do is get some food in you," she said. "When was the last time you ate?"

"I forget sometimes."

"Yeah, I know. That used to worry me more than anything else."

"Well, I guess you can keep an eye on me from now on."

"Yeah," she said, sliding her body over mine and kissing my bottom lip. When she got up, shedding the covers, I couldn't quite believe it. Sarah, with me. I put a hand on her back, just to make sure I wasn't making it up. She was there.

She pulled the gown over her head. "Well, first thing is new clothes. I don't care what, but it has to be better than this. Then food."

I nodded, getting up and pulling my clothes on. "The cycle is over. I think if we lay low for a day or two, we can go home."

"Good."

I headed to the door, smiling back at her. "Now, what did you want to ea—" The question died as I opened the door.

Directly into the faces of the albino and the purple-haired woman.

- 4 -

The purple-haired woman—Shahmeran—was as fast as a snake. She was on me in a second, hand closing over my throat and lifting me off the ground as though I weighed nothing. "I thought you said she was alone!" she hissed to the albino.

Miss Cross stepped into the room, bundled in her fur-lined coat. Behind her came two men holding pistols and dressed for the cold. I recognized one of the men from the other night, Barnes. Their guns were on Sarah, who was backing off, hands up, terrified.

"I did say that," Miss Cross said. "He does not appear to be here."

"Then what the fuck am I holding?" Shahmeran said, wiggling me. I tried to suck air through my collapsed throat and got nothing. I clawed at her hands, but her skin was hard and dry, yet somehow slick. My fingers slid right off. Shahmeran barely looked at me. She had strong Middle Eastern features, a prominent nose, arched eyebrows over brilliant emerald eyes, and a large, predatory mouth. She was beautiful in a strange and abstract way. Shahmeran then did something strange: she put her tongue through her teeth, tasting the air. "I know him. He was at the Rosales house."

"You're certain?" Miss Cross asked.

"The scent is the same."

"Well, we can add that to the list of things to ask him." Miss Cross removed her sunglasses, revealing her red eyes. Her chalky brow furrowed. "I can see him with my eyes, but it's as though you're holding nothing at all. Curious." She stared at me, then through me, her lips moving as she whispered under her breath.

I felt the words brushing over my flesh, flinching where they touched. Miss Cross recoiled as though stung. "There he is. The wasp in the apple."

"I'll go ahead and crush him then." Shahmeran's grip tightened. I felt her fingers in my neck, digging into the muscle, popping capillaries. My vision irised in, the black pressing all around. All I could see was Shahmeran, and she was growing ever more distant. Soon, all I could see were the orange bangs.

"Let him go," Miss Cross said from somewhere far away.

"What? Why?" Shahmeran's voice was underwater.

"Do it."

And I fell to the floor, pain blossoming across my neck as I desperately tried to breathe through a crushed throat. Sarah was beside me, holding my shoulders trying to comfort and be comforted.

A pair of black granny boots stopped right in front of me, the hem of Miss Cross's long black coat swaying slightly. "Sarah Strauss and Christopher Black, I presume," she said.

"Who... what... are you?" I croaked, looking up at the albino woman. Shahmeran seethed behind her, and the two men had fanned out, their pistols still trained on Sarah and I.

"My name is Rose Cross," she said. "As to what I am, I'm a woman."

"I saw you. In the newspaper. A hundred years ago."

"I look very good for my age."

"How do you know us?"

"That's a complex question. You, Miss Strauss, I got to know after David Lister used some of your tools to remove the heart of May Fong and then eat it. I had a file created on you after that. Thirty years old, recently divorced. Your husband was unfaithful with several women, most notably a co-worker. You have parents in Albuquerque, New Mexico, and a sister in Boston. Your only close relatives in San Francisco are your ex-husband and his younger brother, Christopher."

Rose Cross sat down on the bed, her gloved fingers lacing together. She continued speaking to Sarah, as though I didn't matter. "We didn't have much time for anything more than bare bones, if you'll forgive the pun. We have no way of knowing who the wendigo will take, and so you were no more or less important than any of the other witnesses. However, since I have been tracking your mind, I have learned a few other things." She cleared her throat, and continued somewhat awkwardly, "I hope you'll forgive the voyeurism. We're going to be colleagues for a long time, so I would like to do this with a minimum of bad blood."

Sarah was still holding me. "What?" she asked through tears.

"You're the last potential," Miss Cross said. "We had no way to know who the wendigo would choose. Now we do, because it no longer has a choice. You've become incredibly valuable."

"Wendigo?"

"You'll understand after the rite." She paused, regarding the expression of disbelief on Sarah's face. "I could keep telling you things about yourself. The origin of the scars on your body and your mind, but we don't need that. You understand what I can do." She smiled. Then she turned to me, and the expression hardened. "As for you, young man, you're in a great deal of trouble."

I wanted to say something, but could only cradle my bruised throat.

"You, I only learned about through her. Lovesick mental patient brother-in-law. Quite the knight in shining armor. Tracking her all the way from the Rosales home, apparently." She rose from the bed, straightening her coat. "Sorry it has to end this way for you."

"So you're going to let me kill him?" Shahmeran stepped forward. Where Rose Cross was dressed entirely in black, contrasting with her dead white skin and red eyes, Shahmeran was a riot of color.

She wore a long coat over a minidress, tights, and go-go boots, almost as if she had come from the sixties.

"Don't be silly," Rose said.

Shahmeran spun on her companion. "What? He found the hospital. For all we know, he was the one who led Kisin there!"

"You think he's a spy for the Priestess?" Rose asked with an amused grin.

"I think it's something we should consider."

"If it pleases you," Rose sighed. She turned on me. "Let's see what you know." Her red eyes locked with mine, and she began to whisper under her breath. Once again, I felt her words. It reminded me of Kisin, only Rose's were more subtle. They penetrated me, thrumming my mind like harp strings. They seemed to recoil, touching, then dancing away, touching again, forcing themselves to grip. They burned ever so slightly in my head. Rose winced, continuing to whisper. Finally, there was almost a pop, and Rose fell backward.

"His mind is like broken glass," she said, rubbing her head in annoyance.

"Let me kill him then!"

"No!" Sarah screamed. And suddenly she was on top of one of the men, grabbing his weapon. Three gunshots, deafening in the small room, hit Shahmeran in the chest. The woman barely reacted, even as three smoking holes had appeared in her minidress. I heard thumps as the bullets fell from her chest to land on the carpeted floor.

The soldier threw Sarah off of him and leveled his gun at her. Shahmeran's green eyes went wide and she lunged, lightning quick. The gun went off, but Shahmeran had it in hand and effortlessly yanked it from a man twice her size.

Rose spoke a single word, and I knew everyone in the room felt it thrumming through them. I had the vague sense I should drop something, though the word did not hit me as it did everyone else. Both pistols fell onto the carpet.

"Damn it, Rose, stay out of my head!" Shahmeran shouted.

"I'm sorry, but our last possible host was almost shot. I wasn't thinking of your feelings."

Rose advanced on the man who had fired the shot. I looked over at Barnes, still by the door, leaving his pistol on the carpet where it fell. He was willfully staring straight ahead into the middle distance.

"What the hell were you thinking?" Rose asked the other soldier.

He opened his mouth to speak, but she spoke first, a short, powerful sentence that burrowed through everyone in the room. Rose turned away, continuing to speak, this time in English. "You were thinking, 'Miss Cross is in danger.' Sweet, but unimportant." Behind her, the soldier's eyes rolled back in his skull and body went completely limp. He fell to the ground like a rag doll and lay motionless. "You should have been thinking, 'Miss Cross ordered me not to fire my weapon at Sarah Strauss under any circumstances.'"

Rose looked at Barnes, still standing ramrod straight in military posture. Her attention turned back to the fallen man. "One hundred years. If the ritual fails, that's when we can try again. You'll all be dead by then. Never think I will hesitate to hasten the inevitable." She sighed. "Mr. Barnes, please collect the weapons."

Barnes immediately scooped both pistols off the carpet, holstered one and trained the other on me.

Rose Cross turned her attention back to me. "You found the asylum, and yet you seem to have no connection to the Priestess, no connection to the Serpent, nor any of the others. Can you really be exactly what you seem? Just some sad, twisted little man who stumbled into all of this?"

My voice was nearly shattered from Shahmeran's grip, and every word was agony. "I know about the Twins."

"See?" I didn't even see Shahmeran move. She was suddenly in front of me, lifting me by my neck. Fresh pain burned long her fingers. I struggled, even though I knew it was completely useless. She was stronger than any human had a right to be, her skin harder and smoother than stone. As I looked down at her cruel face, her eyes seemed to change. The pupils split vertically, the brilliant green spreading until it became as cold and dead as an emerald. "He knows too much."

"Chris!" Sarah screamed, running to me, attacking Shahmeran who showed only mild annoyance at the woman raking fingernails over her face.

Rose spoke a single word, and Sarah collapsed onto the bed. For a moment, I was terrified until I saw the even rise and fall of her chest. "Michael, please?"

Barnes threw Sarah over his shoulder and walked to the door. "Shahmeran, please put him down."

"Sorry, Rose. He knows too much. He needs to die."

"He knows a name, nothing more."

"He might know more. If one of the Priestess's men got their hands on him—"

"They won't," Rose said, putting a light hand on Shahmeran's shoulder. "Now load them into the car. Miss Strauss is going to the ritual site. You will take Mr. Black to the townhouse."

Shahmeran threw me aside with a flick of her wrist. I hit the wall and fell to the floor. "Why are you letting him live?"

"He's perfect, don't you see that? The mortal authorities need their killer, and here, right in our laps, a former mental patient."

I tried to get up, but between my ankle and the battering my body had taken, it was difficult. I croaked, "There are no witnesses left. They all died at the sanitarium."

Rose smiled without humor. "And do you think it would be difficult for me to manufacture some? I could make your own mother believe you assassinated President Lincoln if I so desired."

Shahmeran lifted me effortlessly. It took a moment to get my feet on the ground, her powerful hand staying on the collar of my coat. "You're sure?"

Rose nodded. "I need to assist with the final preparations. Put him under guard and join me as soon as you can."

Shahmeran shoved me. "Walk. Try anything and I'll tear you in half."

Barnes was first, carrying Sarah over his shoulder, then Rose, and finally me and Shahmeran. Two BMWs were parked outside, four more soldiers standing by them. "There's a body inside," Rose said. "Take care of it."

The soldiers never blanched. They went inside, and a moment later, two came out carrying the dead man between him while a third popped the trunk of one of the cars. The dead man tumbled bonelessly in, and they slammed it shut. Barnes unlocked the other trunk, and carefully laid Sarah's sleeping form in the back. Rose, Barnes, and two men got into the car with the body.

"Get in," Shahmeran said, standing by the open trunk.

"What?"

"One way or another, you're getting in this trunk."

I was beaten and we both knew it. I climbed in, the cramped space forcing me to spoon with the unconscious Sarah. Shahmeran loomed over us. In the neon glow from the motel's sign, I concentrated on her lapels, the leopard print turned from tawny to bloody. "Stay quiet," she said. "You're not going to make it out of this alive, but you do get to choose how you die."

I wanted to say something, but only a cold, wordless hatred blazed at her.

"Watch your head," she said, slamming the trunk.

The car started, a rumbling at once distant and immediate. It crunched up the gravel driveway from the motel, to the smooth and sloping road leading onto the freeway. I couldn't sense where we were headed by touch alone, but assumed it would be back into the heart of the storm. After the hospital, after the flight from the bay, we were worse off than when we started. Sarah was back in the clutches of whoever these people were—if they were even people at all—and now so was I. The only comfort was that they didn't seem to want Sarah dead. At least not yet. Not until the ritual sometime in the next eighteen hours.

I'd be dead by then. The thought came suddenly, easily finding a home in the dark and cold place I had fallen into. Shot in the head by one of the soldiers maybe, buried beside the man whose brain Rose Cross had effortlessly turned off. I'd just be part of a rash of disappearances some later conspiracy theorist would rant about. My bones, buried under a hill, or dropped in a weighted bag to the bottom of the bay, would never be found. Or maybe Shahmeran would get her wish and rip me apart with her bare hands. I had no doubt she could do it, and had done similar in the past. She was a killer, and her casual threats carried the weight of a promise. Then I'd be something to be cleaned up with mops and buckets, any recognizable remains having been smashed to a pulp.

I shuddered. Sarah murmured, shifting in my arms.

"Sarah?"

She murmured again, this time more forcefully, almost like she was desperately trying to warn me, but couldn't.

I stroked her hair, whispering softly into her ear. Trying for comfort, but not finding much in either of us.

Finally, "Chris?" The word was so soft, I thought I'd imagined it over the persistent hum of the road beneath us. "Chris?" She said it again, and I could be sure.

"Sarah. It's me."

"Oh god. Oh god."

"It's okay. I'm here." It sounded stupid as soon as it left my mouth.

"Chris... can you hear me? Am I talking?"

"I can hear you."

She let out a sigh that turned into sobs. I held her, and she gripped at my hands around her waist, as though I had some kind of strength to give. "I was calling to you. It's been hours. You couldn't hear me."

"You were knocked out. Rose Cross, the albino, she did something to you."

"Did something?" She swallowed. "I felt it. I was me, and then, she was in my mind. At first, just pressing inward, and then she was everywhere. I tried to think, but the words vanished. I saw memories, clear as day, but they weren't... brought up by me. I didn't move from memory to memory like I would. It was someone else, directing them, and I knew who because I could feel her. She was so strong, able to hold my mind hostage without trying. And then, she eclipsed me completely, like it wasn't even my mind anymore. It was hers, and I was only watching. She threw me down into a hole, a big, black hole, and I could talk again, I could scream. For you. But you couldn't hear me. No one could."

I held her tight, hoping my presence could comfort her because there were no words I knew that could.

"Where are we?" she said finally.

"In the trunk of a car. They're going to separate us. They're taking you to a ritual site."

"Ritual site?"

"I don't know what they meant. I'll find it. I promise."

"I know." I could tell she wanted to believe me. "Where are they taking you?"

"Somewhere else. Doesn't matter."

"Did they hurt you?"

"No. I'm fine. Don't worry about me."

"Why us, Chris?"

"Bad luck."

"More than that."

"Very bad luck."

We both chuckled. Gallows humor was the only thing that could reach us now. Once someone puts you in a trunk, there is almost never a happy ending to that story. So we were left with each other as the storm howled outside and the road crunched underneath. The car ride lasted a million years, and we spoke the whole way, though soon meaning was gone, replaced with babbled nonsense to one another. We tried to have every conversation we never got around to when we were in the light, and ended up having none. I wished the ride would never end, just so I could be with her a little longer.

When the car finally stopped, my stomach wrapped up in knots. The trunk opened, and Shahmeran was there, snow falling onto her sunset hair. "This is your stop, Black. Say your goodbyes."

I hugged Sarah close, leaning over to kiss her. She leaned into me, her kiss as desperate as mine. "I'll find you," I murmured into her mouth.

"I know."

Shahmeran yanked me away from Sarah one handed, my collar wadded up in her hand. "That's enough of that." The ground seemed to spin, and she set me on my feet, but never let go. With the other hand, she slammed the trunk. The last I saw of Sarah was her huge blue eyes staring up at me in abject terror. I wished I could find some way to comfort her, but Shahmeran, the monster shaped like a woman, would never let me.

She tapped the back of the car, and it started back up, driving off into the snow, soon fading from view behind a wall of white. I repeated the promise in my head. I would find Sarah, even if I had no idea how.

Shahmeran poked me in the back, barely a touch but I went stumbling forward several steps, hissing in pain as I came down on the bad ankle. I caught myself on the columns of a cement fence. Perched above us on a berm was our destination, a rich townhouse. The landscaping on the slope was still visible, slowly dying under a layer of frost. There was nothing to distinguish this house from any of the others on the street. I limped up the stairs, conscious of Shahmeran shadowing my steps.

The door opened as we stepped onto the porch.

"Ma'am," said the man at the door, a bruiser in a designer suit openly carrying a submachine gun.

Shahmeran didn't bother acknowledging him. At another time, I might have called the house cold. It looked as though it should be, with the bare checkerboard tile of the entryway, the scalloped wooden staircase spiraling up the back wall, the end table displaying what had to be an antique vase, and the chandelier overhead. But with the wind picking up off the freezing Pacific and the swirling drifts of snow, anything was warm.

"Upstairs," Shahmeran said. Probably only to see me walk on the ankle that was obviously bothering me. I acquiesced, supporting myself heavily on the bannister.

The staircase went past several paintings, all sharing a similar motif. In the lowest one, a single church stood against a wide Midwestern sunset. Native American warriors formed a loose cordon around two red-haired women in white gowns. One was partly translucent, her bare feet several inches off the ground. Their arms were raised against a creature of spinning wheels, burning from within with a white flame, eyes all along the rings of its body. Beneath it was a crying child, lit by the thing's fire.

In the next, a shadowy wolf tore into a group of armed men with muskets out in some Southwestern desert. The red-haired women were there again, and again one was translucent and appeared to be floating, though this time both were dressed in deerskin dresses like Native Americans. They carried antler daggers, and behind them, an Indian man lay on a rock, bleeding from a hundred cuts.

The next painting was in a dark forest. A pale woman screamed from within a tree that looked as though it had grown around her body. Angry faces marred the bark at various points. This time, the red-haired women were nude, one kneeling beneath the tree, the translucent one floating about her shoulders.

In the final picture, the red-haired women were armed and armored. One carried a bloody broadsword, the other a shield. White cloth billowed from gaps in their armor. They stood on a rocky outcropping underneath an angry sky, ready to do battle with a huge dragon-snake, a purple beast with an orange hood, gazing down on them with hateful green eyes. A woman, chained to a stake, waited behind them, terrified. Her Persian features seemed familiar. I turned, seeing them again behind me, along with the colors of the beast.

"Yes, that's me," Shahmeran said. "Keep moving."

I turned around, pulling myself up the stairs. "What are you?"

"Unimportant."

We reached the top of the stairs to find a carpeted hallway running the length of the townhouse. Another staircase went up.

"Keep going," she said, nodding to the stairs.

The second staircase was as long as the first. The paintings were similar here, though they almost seemed hidden in this secondary staircase. The first was of a man, tied to a rock while the two women stood out on a breakwater. A massive shape approached through the water, a fin like a sail knifing through the gray ocean.

The next was in a moody swamp. The two women, now dressed in long dark gowns, stood on the prow of a boat, lit only by a few men carrying revolvers and lanterns spilling a tiny amount of golden light into the greenish black. In the bottom of a boat was a terrified girl, tied hand and foot. Rising from the water ahead was a long-nosed hunchbacked hag, her black hair falling in greasy shocks over a misshapen skull. Her skin was pea-soup green, her fingers long and clawed, her teeth sharp.

The final panting was in a snow-covered pine forest. The two women were dressed in warm clothing that vaguely looked like something my grandmother might wear. The men with them wore cold-weather military uniforms, but there was no rank insignia and they carried old Thompson submachine guns. Lying in front of them was a sledge with an unconscious white-haired man. A huge bear, with ridges of skin almost like horns, snarled at the assemblage.

The top floor was smaller than the other two, the ceiling rather low. Shahmeran opened the closest door, and we were in a cozy living room. A single small window, too small for me to fit through and too high to jump from, looked out onto the street. It was almost totally white out there, the blizzard descending upon us for good.

"We can be alone up here. Sit down," Shahmeran said, indicating the sofa. There were several chairs around as well as the sofa, all big and comforting as pillows and arrayed in front of a small fireplace. The art here was landscapes, with smaller bric-a-brac on end tables and the mantel. The rest of the room was bookcases and afghans, the kind of place to curl up and read out a storm. That was probably not my fate.

I obeyed her. "Who are the Twins?"

"Sisters of Atlas," she said, turning her back on me. "I don't believe it, Black."

"Believe what?"

"That a nobody really could have made such a nuisance of himself."

"Your boss said—"

Shahmeran whirled. "The Twins are my only master, and Rose doesn't speak for them, no matter what she thinks. And Rose never cleared you. She can't read your mind. You could be one of the Artisan's automatons or one of the Wolf's spies for all I know. Even if you don't know you're a threat, you are."

"I'm not—"

"These plans are older than me, and I'm not going to let you jeopardize them. So it's a shame you tried to escape and I was forced to kill you."

It took a moment for the words to sink in. "Wait, no—"

"Let Rose find another patsy." Shahmeran was on me in an instant, lifting me off the ground with one hand. "Shall we begin?" She threw me, this time using the strength of her arm rather than a mere flick of her wrist. I slammed into the door, which splintered, sending me sprawling into the hallway, my breath crushed out of me.

Shahmeran stepped to the other side of the broken door, pausing to be framed in the meat of the wood. Her expression was a combination of pity and disgust. I clambered to my feet, swaying drunkenly. Everything hurt, so at least I no longer felt the ankle as much as I had. She took her eyes off me for a moment, delicately opening what was left of the door to join me in the hall. I reached over to an end table, grabbing a bust, and as Shahmeran came through the door, I brought it down on her head.

The bust crumbled into chunks. Shahmeran shook the white dust from her hair. "Even in this form, you're going to have to try harder to hurt me." Her hand closed on my collar.

With a toss, I hit the wall and tumbled down the staircase to the second floor. I wanted to lay there, see how much of the pain would bleed away, but Shahmeran's heels were already on the stairs above.

I pulled myself to my feet. Upstairs, the indestructible juggernaut in a minidress; below, a man, maybe men, with guns. My only hope was a window, the way I had escaped her the first time we'd met, in Erica's house a million years ago. I limped down the hall, my bones rattling. Shahmeran took her time, each step thudding into me.

I was halfway down the hall, close to the staircase that would lead right to the man with the machine gun.

"Don't misunderstand. I'm impressed." Shahmeran was at the bottom of the stairs, only a few paces from me. I tried to run, but it was like moving through mud. Three quick strides and she was on top of me, grabbing my shoulder and spinning me around effortlessly. "Not with your acumen." She punched me, and though I knew she was using only a tiny fraction of her strength, blood poured into my mouth as a molar came unmoored and fell onto the carpet. "Nor your survival instinct." This time she used the back of her hand, holding me steady with a wad of my coat collar. More blood bubbled from my lips, and the world seemed to get smaller. My weak gums gave up some more teeth. I wanted to fall to the ground, but she kept me up. "Just your ability to take a punch."

And with that she hit me again, this time in the eye. I heard a crack, and felt the sensation of flight. Another crack, and nothing. I opened my eyes. The left one was stinging and dark. Touching it, my hand came away bright red. I staggered to my feet. Black crept in on the edge of my vision, trying to envelop me like the storm taking the city. Another ruined door was right in front of me.

"Probably time to end this," she said from the hallway.

I turned to run. The blackness swept over me. I opened my eyes, not realizing I had closed them, and I was falling to my knees. The walls were blurry and everything was agony. I could barely make out shelves of books, and a break in the wall I hoped was a door. I could not walk; it was more of a barely controlled forward fall. The darkness hovered in, always threatening to turn out the lights completely.

I hit the clear area, hands scrabbling over it. Dimly, I could see crimson marks left. Bloody handprints. Mine. I found the knob, turned.

And the lights went out.

"Still some fight left in you. Good."

The words came from the room I'd just left, and they pulled me to the surface. I was on all fours, my blood tapping a carpet below me. I spat out a mouthful of red, another tooth swam in the blood, and hauled myself to my feet. I found that it was a desk that had helped me. A blurry and dark desk that seemed so far away even as my hands were on the surface.

In the other room, I heard Shahmeran's steps coming closer. Another hit from her would be last thing I'd ever feel. And Sarah, abandoned to whatever fate awaited her at the ritual site. My hand closed around something. My eyes tried to focus on it, and I felt a lurch as though I was on a boat, and I wanted to throw up. It was a letter opener.

A pathetic weapon, but it was all I had. I stumbled to the corner of the room and waited, holding off the dark that kept trying to drown me. Shahmeran came through the door. "Black?"

I jumped on her back, fighting the gorge as the seasickness returned with a vengeance, wrapping an arm around her neck.

She reached up to grab me, and I forced myself to line the letter opener up. I touched her eyeball with the metal, and she froze. "Your skull is rock, but how tough are your eyes?" I asked her, blood and missing teeth making it sound like mush.

"Don't do anything foolish. I can still—"

My hand twitched. It was taking all my concentration to keep the hand steady, so that was more a matter of losing focus for a single second. She let out a strangled cry. "Where did you take Sarah?" I demanded.

"To the ritual site. The eye of the storm."

"Always comes back to eyes, doesn't it?"

I jammed the letter opener into her eye. I felt rather than heard the pop as the little blade sank in. She screamed, somehow resisting the urge to clap her hand over the blood and bits of eyeball now flowing down her cheek. "Where, goddamn it?"

"The center of the murders! The blizzard will be all around it!"

I fell off her, dropping the bloody letter opener onto the ground, staggering away in horror. Half her face was nothing but red, and there was more on her shoulder where I had just been. She had one hand pressed over the empty socket, the other eye screwed shut. "You son of a bitch! You're lucky these things grow back! I'm gonna kill you!"

I stumbled backward, hitting the far wall right as the door opened. "Ma'am?"

It was the doorman, shocked into paralysis by the sight of Shahmeran on her knees, blood pouring from her face. "Look out—" she said, but I heard nothing else.

I kicked the door as hard as I could, slamming it into him. The submachine gun clattered from his hand. I dove for it, my head feeling like it was ready to come apart. My hand closed around the handle. I grunted as the doorman kicked me in the ribs, something cracking very far away. I rolled, coming up on my back. He loomed over me, hand out.

I squeezed the trigger, and he fell back, his chest exploding in red. Clambering to my feet, I lurched to the door. Two more men were charging up the stairs, and I killed both of them. I staggered past the bodies, their blood running down the paintings of the red-haired women. As I moved, the staircase seemed to get longer, disappearing into the ultimate darkness of the underworld.

The door opened above me.

"Still there, Black?" Shahmeran called down.

I stumbled off the last step and to the front door. The chill wind hit me in the face, freezing the blood to my skin. I held onto the railing with one hand and the gun with the other. Everything inside of me felt like it was shifting around, and with each shift, a new agony threatening to drop me. All I needed to do was find the center of the storm.

Wind howled down the streets, chasing thick flurries of snow. I couldn't feel any of it, and was grateful for that. Let the bone deep chill numb the pain and hope I could stay awake long enough to find the eye of the storm and somehow save Sarah.

Shahmeran emerged from the house when I was halfway down the block. She stood straight, scarcely noticing the eye I'd taken out of her skull. Even through the sheets of driving snow, I could see her, a swatch of crimson like a blade.

I could only limp, stumbling every few steps. The blizzard had driven everyone off the streets. I was alone. The black at the edge of my vision stayed there, the cold keeping it at bay. The pain in every part of me was far away, like it belonged in the body of someone else, and I was just taking care of it for a while. I couldn't tell if my vision was still blurry or if the winter storm really had leeched the world of its color and focus.

I turned a corner, knowing Shahmeran couldn't be evaded for

long. Her missing eye and the storm might hide me for a little while, but it was a losing game. And after what I'd done, a quick death was too much to hope for.

The townhouses had given way to tall buildings disappearing overhead into roiling banks of snow. I dropped down the first alley I saw, knowing it was hopeless but hoping nonetheless. My steps felt light for the first time since I'd jumped from Erica's window. The walls were shifting, probably a lingering effect from the beating Shahmeran had given me.

No, I wasn't hallucinating it. I was flying.

Straight upward, the ground growing hazy as wind pushed eddies of snow beneath me. Shahmeran passed by the mouth of the alley, never once looking up. She was soon gone, hidden behind the solid white of the blizzard. I didn't know what to think beyond the momentary relief of escaping that creature.

Until I reached the top of the building. There were eight people up there, and I floated over and down in front of them.

Standing in front of the others was Kisin, the man from the sanitarium, his long hair and coat whipping around him from the wind. Teotl, who I had met at Erica's, flanked him, bundled in her coat, looking miserable and half-frozen. Another man stood by her, olive-skinned and heavyset, dressed in a designer suit topped off with an overcoat. Five more men carrying assault rifles and dressed for the cold were arrayed behind them.

Kisin said something in a language I didn't recognize.

Teotl looked at me sadly and nodded, saying something quietly.

Kisin spat out a word, and Teotl repeated what she had said, louder this time.

The roof of the building was under my feet now, and my injuries felt like they collapsed in on themselves. I could barely stand. Kisin walked forward. "Now, tell me where it is and I won't kill you."

"Fuck you," I said, bringing up the gun.

Kisin spoke a few powerful words, ripping through the gun. The surface of the metal liquified, reaching back at me in tendrils of oily black. They wrapped around my wrists and fingers, pinning my hands in place, forcing my bound hands to my head. Then the metal flowed from my hands to wrap around my skull, cocooning me in a cordite-stinking hood and manacles.

- 5 -

I felt wind, the bone-biting wind of the blizzard. My head was pounding inside the metal prison, but I couldn't even cradle it. The ground fell away, and my stomach lurched. I fought the gorge, knowing if I vomited I would drown.

My eyes opened suddenly as my feet touched the ground. Had I passed out? I felt hands on my upper arms, yanking me roughly down the sidewalk. A car door opened, and they shoved me inside, where I guessed I was between two of the large men with guns. An engine turned over, and I felt motion. I heard talking, in the same unidentifiable language as before.

The car moved quickly, and I imagined the streets of San Francisco, empty save for drifts of grayish white snow. It was difficult to tell if we were going up or downhill, with every turn rattling through my cracked skull. The pain was enough to keep the darkness at bay, or else I passed out and dreamed the agony. There was no difference to me one way or another.

The car finally stopped, and the men got out, yanking me into the howling wind. I stumbled to my knees, and was hauled back up. My head felt like it was breaking open. I was dragged through the wind, and then my footsteps were on wood. On the little bits of exposed skin at my wrists, I felt the stinging needles of seawater. Then, suddenly, the wind stopped, and I could hear my footsteps echoing hollowly off far walls, muted by the prison of metal over my head. More staggering, and rough hands pushed me down into a chair. My skull gave me a final stab of pain.

I felt rather than heard the words. The metal around my hands and head liquefied, though the temperature didn't change. The outside was frigid from the snow. The inside was still warm from my face, covered in a layer of breath and sweat. When droplets moved from one side to the other, they grew thick and sluggish, the transparent going cloudy. Or they smoked briefly and ran quicker, tapping the concrete floor of what I now saw was a warehouse.

The chunk of metal flowed off me into an unrecognizable lump, then flew away to clatter across the floor, coming to a stop next to boxes covered with a tarp. The lights were on overhead, boring into my head and burning along the cracks I imagined Shahmeran had put there with her vicious beating.

Kisin stood in front of me, his coat open, revealing an immaculate designer suit. His black hair fell around his shoulders and his skin was the palest possible shade of olive. He stared at me, radiating pain in his gaze even in a moment of rest. Teotl stood behind him, head turned away. The other man, the one I didn't know, was closer to Kisin, watching me with narrowed and piggish eyes. The others were scattered around the warehouse, standing sentry at the doors out.

I stirred, and the unnamed man wrinkled his brow, putting his left hand out, palm down, and suddenly I was completely paralyzed in the chair. It was not that my muscles would no longer respond, but that something powerful and invisible had clamped me in place.

Kisin reached into his coat and removed a sheaf of paper, which he unfolded and set in front of me. It was a map of the city. "Now, where is it?"

I looked up at him, my head rebelling against the light and

motion. "Where's what?" My words were slushy, blood still falling down my chin, the missing teeth making the words whistle.

Kisin sighed. "Huracan?"

The man I didn't know—Huracan—brought his hand up, waving it vaguely before freezing with a single pointed finger at my cheek. His hand stiffened, the finger tracing a path down my face from ten feet away. I felt the flesh along the path tear itself in half. Blood spilled in a gout down the front of my coat, slowing to a trickle. I screamed.

"Don't fuck with me," Kisin said. "Where are the Twins making their new Familiar?"

"Familiar?"

"Huracan?"

"No, wait... wait—"

Huracan moved his hand to my chest, his fingers curling into a clawed rictus. I felt my ribs moving. Pain exploded as I heard and felt a horrible crack all along my left side. My breath was squeezed out of me by fists of cold fire.

Teotl shouted a single word. It was hard to see, with blood blinding one eye, and the newly broken ribs making it hard to sit up straight. She walked across the black crowding into my vision and got right in Kisin's face, speaking in a low voice, using that strange language I couldn't identify. He listened to her, the muscles in his jaw growing as he ground his teeth. Finally, he said something back to her, and she nodded.

Teotl approached me, dropping to her knees to look me in the eye. "You remember me, right? From the Rosales house?"

"Yeah. I remember you," I said, sucking in burning breaths between every word.

She pulled a small handkerchief from her jacket and dabbed at the wound above my eye. I winced. "Who did this to you?"

"Shahmeran."

"I'm sorry."

"You... you tried to warn me."

She didn't say anything. The pain from my broken body receded slightly as I was able to focus on the first kind face I'd seen since Sarah.

"How did you get this far?" she asked softly.

"They took Sarah. So I went to my brother's place, only it wasn't my brother anymore. It was something wearing his face."

"One of the Serpent's mimics?" Kisin said in disbelief. "That bastard really does have eyes everywhere."

Teotl half-turned with a glare.

"Mimic?" I asked.

"Shh," she said, turning back to me. "Tell me what you found."

"The abandoned hospital... the San Pablo Sanitarium. I found it. They were keeping all the witnesses and the murderers there. I was going to save Sarah, then he... your friend... Kisin showed up. And killed everyone."

"Not everyone," Kisin said to the room at large.

"He had to do it," Teotl said to me.

"Why?"

She shook her head. "I can't explain."

"What about Sarah? She was there. He was going to kill her!"

Teotl was still, and I could see the decision across her face. Was she going to lie and deny it? "Yes. He was going to. But she doesn't need to die, not anymore. If we can get her away from Shahmeran, away from the Twins, Sarah can live. But we need you to tell us where they are."

My thoughts felt scrambled. I could barely latch onto a thought before it flitted away. All I could think of was this nice woman finally talking to me rather than at and around me. Even before all this, that was a rare kindness.

"Tell us!" Kisin shouted, advancing on me with his hand raised, sending a shock through my body and rattling off a domino wave of agony through the cracked bones.

Teotl stood up and whirled on him. "Calm down! Calm down or he's dead and we deal with the Twins having a Familiar who can kill the lot of us."

They were silent, glaring into one another's eyes. Teotl was far shorter than the lanky Kisin, but it was clear she didn't fear him. The promise of violence was there, and I was grateful for once I wasn't the target. Finally, Kisin turned away, waving a hand dismissively. "Fine."

"We know two of the locations the wendigo chose," Teotl said, pointing to two dots on the map. One was over Erica's house, the other over Sarah's office. "We need one more before we can plot the rest, and when we know that, we can find Sarah."

I stared at the map, feeling Teotl's gaze on me. All the thoughts came at once, whether I could trust them, what was happening to Sarah, what could happen to me. None of it made any sense, just a slurry of shouts and hisses in my breaking head when all I could really hear was the shifting of my bones.

"1537 Paper Street," I whispered.

Kisin stepped forward. "That's here," he said, and whispered a thrumming word as a black dot appeared on the map. "And that means," and the same word and another dot appeared. "The last must have been here," he spoke the word once more with a flourish at the end. A final dot appeared, then lines connected each one, forming a pentagram over the city.

In the center, a final dot appeared. "The ritual site," Kisin said.

Teotl said something, but the words were very far away. Someone else said something, and I couldn't tell if it was in English, Spanish, or that language they kept using amongst themselves. Then there were no more sounds other than the distant howl of the wind and the throbbing of my pulse.

I opened my eyes. My lap held a small puddle of blood already scabbing at the tops and corners. I lifted my head, wincing as that drove a fresh spear through it. The warehouse was empty and the lights were off. I sat in the middle of the room, on the lonely wooden chair, little drips of red on the concrete floor.

Left for dead. How much did that really matter? They were going to save Sarah. There was a thought to keep me warm, and I could just stay here for a little while. They said they would. They also kidnapped and tortured me. The memory was so faded, it almost didn't register. Trying to put the thought together was agony. What should have been clear was lost in the muddle of shifting ideas and pain. I grasped at the one thing I could: Sarah. Her safety was what mattered, what put me on this path to begin with.

The doubt was quieter this time, though no less convincing for it. Had I made this up? Were the injuries all over my body from something else? A fall, maybe? Police or someone else subduing me? Was I in a hospital somewhere, my sick brain coming up with some elaborate scenario to make it all okay, make me not crazy? And I realized something, through the haze of anguish ripping me apart: it didn't really matter.

If Sarah was safe, then the only person hurt by my actions would be me. And if she was in danger, like I thought she was, I was the only one who could possibly help her. The choice between Sarah and myself wasn't a choice at all.

The old me, the me who took his medicine, who watched vigilantly for signs, who used every coping tool the hospital taught, was gone. The pills were flushed, the watch was silent, the reality accepted. This was the me Sarah needed.

I failed the first time I tried to get up, falling back to the chair heavily. Some more of my blood dribbled off my face to make more dots along the floor. On the second try, I got to my feet. The ground was lurching under them, but I was almost certain that was an artifact of my broken skull. I staggered toward the door, running into some stacked boxes. My stomach turned over and emptied out my mouth. It was mostly a thin red liquid.

I retched twice more before making it to the stairs leading to the door. I hauled myself up the stairs, my breath aching and shallow in my chest. Two more steps to the door. I opened that into the shrieking wind.

It came sweeping in off the roiling Pacific, streaking into the city. Sheets of ice and snow hit me in the face, sending me stumbling backward. I grabbed the doorjamb and hauled myself onto the wooden pier where the warehouse sat. Across the bay, I imagined I could see the San Pablo Sanitarium, but really there was only a mass of shifting white, the wall of the blizzard enshrouding the city.

I pictured the map in my mind, the single point in the center of the pentagram. It kept shifting, as bits of it seemed to follow the fault lines in my skull. The site was impossibly far away. Even at my best, I didn't think I could make it. Didn't mean I wouldn't try.

I staggered into the streets, the blood dripping from my face and body, but that soon stopped. The sticky strands had frozen into crimson icicles. The wind howled and beat against me, snow clinging to my body and clothes. My head wanted to split apart, my body wanted to fall to pieces. I couldn't feel the cold over the burning agony in every part of me, though I tried to ignore it as I trudged up toward the ritual site.

Everything has a price.

The one thought that came through everything, through the wind and the snow, through the blood and the pain, was that, clear as crystal. I knew it, even when things had been slightly more sane. I knew it when I started looking for Sarah, when the cops and my brother had dismissed me as crazy. I hadn't let myself think it. But I knew, all along.

I never thought it would be this high.

Stupid. It had been this high for the thing wearing Garth's face. It had been this high for the men I killed at the house where Shahmeran had cracked my skull. It had been this high for all those people at the hospital and for the people whose hearts had been ripped from their chests. The thought I was dancing around came to me on a burning stab through my head. I was paying the price. I was dying. Every step I took was one closer to the last one, a number that was now horribly finite. Stepping out my life.

I could barely see two feet ahead. The storm was a constant rushing wall of frozen white, fading to gray and finally the black at the edges of my vision. Still encroaching at every corner. I would never see completely ever again. The black would come in and engulf me, and I wouldn't wake up.

My pace grew slower, as though my body knew it was running out, and this was some way to prolong a worthless life. I had no idea where I was. Everything was washed out in the howling white. I knew only that where I was going was far, far away.

And as my foot hit the pavement, I realized I didn't know where I was going. I searched for it in the burning recesses of my brain, but could find nothing. I knew it was there. There was something keeping my legs moving, keeping me sucking in breaths that tasted like raw meat.

I made a promise to someone. I would keep it. I had to.

Later.

My body could barely move. Every breath was shallower than the last. I needed a little rest. I could find somewhere to curl up, let my ruined body try to heal for a few precious moments. Then I could get up and do whatever it was I was supposed to.

I fell to one knee. I couldn't get the other leg under me to rise. The breath squeezed out of my chest on the broken ribs. I fell to the sidewalk, the snow enfolding me in soft, warm arms. The wind blew overhead, but it was gentle and soothing. More snow piled in on me, and I waited to feel better.

The word came out of the wind. Though I couldn't hear the unfocused shrieking of the blizzard, I heard the word, ripped as it was from the heart of the storm. "Rise," it said.

I obeyed without realizing I was doing it, sitting up in the drift of snow.

I saw the foot first. The skin was pale and bluish like a dead man left out in the cold, stretched thin over an almost human limb. The edges of the figure seemed to blur into the air, as though it was wind made flesh. I looked up, from the impossibly thin legs to the spindly and starving thing looming above me. Even hunched over, it was easily ten feet tall, its jagged spine poking up through the strained skin. Its arms were spidery, its fingers even more so, the nails long and curved into vicious claws. Its face was almost human, with baleful glowing yellow eyes, a sunken nose, and a wide mouth overflowing with carnivorous teeth. The only hair on it was a few wispy strands coming from its skull. It stared down at me with naked hunger, and though I should have been terrified, I was not. I knew it was real, more real than anything I had ever seen before, but it would not hurt me.

"You've miles to go before I let you sleep," it said.

I whispered one word, the only thing my tortured body could manage. "Wendigo."

"Yes." It licked those razor teeth, its tongue leaking a drop of blood. "Those whores want to bind me to mortal flesh. To make a Familiar of me."

"Sarah," I breathed.

If it heard me, it gave no sign. "I won't be controlled. Not on their terms." It reached down to me with one of its almost-human hands.

I took it. The flesh was ice cold, yet somehow comforting. It pulled me to my feet. I flinched, ready for the pain of my broken body settling into a new shape, but the ache was far away. "Stop the ritual and walk with my blessing. Now and forever." The last word turned into the howl of wind as the wendigo's body blew away into the storm. I could feel the thing all around me. It was with the blizzard; it was the blizzard. It was there, hungry and cold.

As I looked into the snow, I realized that the black had receded from my vision. The world flooded back into my ruined synapses, and I could behold the storm in all its terrifying fury. And I smiled.

I took a step, my feet suddenly light on the ground, the wind at my back. I lifted my foot, and felt the ground spinning below me. I was moving with the storm, a part of it somehow, the blizzard carrying me closer to my destination. I should have felt the agony of the broken bones, but in the storm I didn't. I felt safe and powerful for the first time.

Until I didn't. There was a lurch, and the pain returned with burning fingers. I was trudging through the snow again, the wind my enemy. Ahead, through a momentary break in the swirling white, a SWAT van blocked off the street leading into a residential area. Houses on one side of the street along with Victorian apartments on the other. No police were visible, but they didn't have to be. The red and blue flashed, lending the snow an otherworldly aura.

The Twins needed their privacy. The people issuing the orders to block the streets probably had no idea why they did it. A sudden compulsion to cordon off several city blocks, insuring that anyone crazy enough to be in the teeth of the blizzard would stay away.

I turned down a narrow alley following the natural slope of the land. The three story apartment along one side blocked the worst of the wind, although snow still piled up drifts that by now were man-sized. The fence on the other side led to single and two-story townhouses, each with small yards in the back.

I shuffled further down the freezing alley. The pain no longer troubled me as much. It wasn't that I couldn't feel it. On the contrary; my steps crunched through the broken bones, spearing up through my chest and into my skull. But the pain no longer incapacitated me. I fed on it. The burning spurred me on, just like the cold seeping into my body and the gnawing hunger in my belly. The pain no longer nourished the black in my vision, but drove it back, bringing heightened clarity.

I hoisted myself over the fence. The agony exploding from my chest and the bile springing into my mouth should have dropped me into a snowdrift to fall into a bloody sleep. I made it over, clumsily, tumbling into a small backyard. Everything, from the little birdbath to the plastic big wheel, was covered in a layer of rime. The back door was sliding glass, mostly frosted over.

I limped to the back and peered inside. The tableau was a family enjoying an evening in. The door looked into a kitchen area, where a fortyish man was coming back from the refrigerator carrying an open beer. Farther in, and a woman and boy were sitting around a television, laughing. The screen was showing a commercial, and not a particularly funny one. The people were frozen in time, mid-laugh, mid-step.

I went to the side fence, bracing myself on a pipe coming up out of the hard soil. The next backyard was cramped, with no evidence of children. The windows here were a little smaller, and I put my face to one. The ice was thick on the pane and I could dimly make out a few shapes within. All were motionless, caught in the midst of whatever it was they had been doing. I climbed over several more fences, and each glimpse into another house revealed the same thing.

Rose Cross.

The same trick she had used at the crime scene, freezing all the witnesses to be tagged by her men and later collected and thrown into the San Pablo Sanitarium. Only now it was an entire neighborhood. How far had she reached? How far could she reach?

I moved along through backyards until I was certain the police would be invisible beyond the storm. A path led up a small slope, the ground buried under crunchy snow. I followed this to the gate, unlatched it, and was back out on the street.

The wind was louder here, building a crescendo to a fever pitch. The sky wasn't falling; it was all around me, swirling and hissing and angry. This wasn't just a blizzard, this was the blizzard of blizzards. Some kind of end-of-the-world storm to wipe my city off the map.

Direction was almost gone in the oppressive din. The ice whipped into my face. I knew the edges of my cuts would be frozen solid, the bloody flesh underneath livid with cold. I staggered down the street, no longer even bothering to huddle into myself. I was not warm. I would never be warm again.

The white seemed to thicken. It was a solid wall, rushing past, the snow sweeping sideways on the roar of wind. I touched it. My hand sunk in only gradually, buffeted by wind and ice. I stepped forward, and for a moment, I knew my body would be thrown into the sky to fall somewhere far away, hopelessly battered beyond recognition. The wind flowed around me, exerting pressure but never pulling me away. And I was through.

The eye of the storm was maybe a half mile wide. At the edge, the snow and wind shredded everything in its path. Though there were large drifts of snow piling around the edges of cars and the walls of houses, there was no snow falling. Even the sound of the blizzard was muted in here.

In the absolute center of the eye, I saw them.

Even though there were many things between us, my eyes went directly to them, standing dead center. They didn't look exactly like they did in the paintings, in those, their features had been slaves to the prevailing style of the time. Here they were delicate-featured porcelain dolls, beyond beautiful. One was perfectly solid, the other stood by her twin, body translucent, and then she was gone, a ghost flickering in and out of our reality. Their red hair was wild, their arms outstretched into the flashing heart of the storm. They both wore flowing snow white gowns, their feet bare on the frozen ground. Blood dripped from their left eyes like tears. The solid one held a curved dagger and was calling into the sky. I felt her words as jagged blades cutting across me. I recoiled from them, wanting to block the words out, but couldn't.

Sarah was by them, standing still, dressed in a new christening gown. She swayed slightly, a glassy-eyed zombie.

Rose Cross was nearby, head bowed. Her pale lips moved as she whispered whatever incantation was keeping the neighborhood paralyzed.

Shahmeran stood farther away. Her left eye was now covered in a gauze patch, blood still flowing freely down her cheek and staining the leopard print lapel of her coat. She glared outward with the remaining eye, waiting, maybe for me.

Farther out was a loose ring of twenty men. Dressed for the cold, all in black, they wore the body armor of SWAT police, carrying submachine guns and shotguns, pistols and knives on their belts. Their guns were leveled, and they were no more than a single pace away from taking cover behind streetlamps, telephone poles, or parked cars. They had two armored SWAT vans at either end of the formation, parked perpendicular to the street. Behind each were BMWs, noses pointed outward.

I pressed myself against a car and caught a flicker of movement. One of the demons from the sanitarium lurked in the shadows across the street. It hadn't seen me, and merely lashed its tail back and forth, maybe in anticipation or annoyance or some emotion I didn't have a name for. Two more were hidden outside the ring of men and had no doubt there were even more I hadn't seen. Maybe on the other side of mirrors.

Sarah was a hundred yards from me and guarded by an assortment of human and monstrous beings. On my best day I couldn't take one, and this was not that day. I was unarmed, and though I no longer felt like I was dying, I knew I was. A single bullet would end any dream of rescue, to say nothing of what the demons or Shahmeran would do to me.

One of the Twins continued her dark incantation, the other one flitting in and out of reality, providing an ecstatic dance in counterpoint to the words. As I watched, helplessly trying to think of a plan that didn't end with me splattered all over the street, the ritual was gaining power. The wind's howls were growing in volume, steadily losing the muffled quality they'd taken inside the eye. And there was something within the wind, a voice that sounded almost human.

I was running out of time. Sarah was in a trance, and next to a crazy woman with a knife. If I was to get to her, it had to be quickly. Pressing my back against the car, I started to move. About fifty feet away, one of the demons waited in the eave of a Victorian roof. His claws bit into the wood as he peered out over the street. Getting closer to Sarah meant getting almost underneath him. The only other option was to go into the middle of the street where twenty men could tear me apart with gunfire.

I was pressed up against the side of a compact car, right by the wheel. Snow had filled in the gap between car and sidewalk, and the core had probably frozen solid, gluing the car to the curb. The sidewalk was narrow, with two-story Victorian townhouses bowing under the snow collecting in every nook and cranny, like stubborn food caught in teeth. The demon was on one of these, three houses away.

I was a swath of dark color, with my black coat and blue jeans. The snow was too thick along the railed stairways to the doors to provide any color. The only way I wasn't silhouetted was along the cars. So I crept along the line of vehicles, keeping as much of me against the car as I could, my eyes fixed on the demon lurking on the side of a bay window.

It kept its odd mask-like face focused on the road, its barbed tail periodically flicking. It wasn't a rational thought, but I hoped my attention wouldn't draw its. See that head turn, our eyes meet, and have it leap lightly to the sidewalk and drag me to Shahmeran.

I edged ever closer to the thing, almost beneath him. I wished for the eye to collapse and flood the place with snow, give me the cover I needed to get closer to Sarah. But the storm couldn't hear me, not over the pounding words of the Twins. As I paused by the side of a car, something caught the corner of my eye. I turned, staring directly into the car's sideview mirror. A shape moved past it, far behind, something large and multi-limbed, trailing writhing tentacles. I turned, but there was nothing behind me, and in the mirror again, nothing.

Mind playing tricks, but something told me it was all too real.

I had made it to the edge of the ring of men. The closest held his submachine gun at the ready. He was next to the BMW, a few steps from the van blocking the street. He was larger than me and probably much stronger. He was also armored, wearing a vest, arm and kneepads, and a helmet and goggles, looking as inhuman as the demon.

I could rush him, knock him over, get at the pistol on his belt. And then I'd be armed. Then only nineteen more men, three demons, one Shahmeran, and three witches between me and Sarah.

But there weren't any other options.

I steeled myself, hoping whatever blessing the wendigo had given me would be enough to do this one last thing. My bones shifted again as if to give me the jolt of pain I'd need.

And right at that moment, a bass rumble snarled beneath the high-pitched shriek of the wind. The ground under my feet shimmied, and chunks of snow and ice fell from the eaves of a nearby house.

The van right next to me was flung a hundred feet into the air, turning end over end.

"They're here!" Shahmeran screamed, but it hardly seemed necessary. The armed men scattered into cover, some weapons already chattering. The street where the van had been was torn apart, a fist of solid rock having punched through the concrete, now flowing back into the stone.

The van crashed back down to earth on its roof, crushing the BMW, the parked car right next to me, and the soldier I had almost charged. I jumped backwards, falling into a snowdrift while bits of metal and glass rained down on and around me. Gasoline and blood leaked out into the snow. The demon above me skittered along the side of the building, as yet unseen by the attackers, and ready to flank them.

More gunfire ripped through the air. I got up, shaking the snow off of me, searching for the soldier, thinking I could get his gun, but the body had utterly vanished in the web of smashed and tangled metal.

Striding up the street was Kisin, his hand out as though to say stop, speaking those low and powerful words that tore through everything solid. Teotl was by him, walking purposefully forward, completely unafraid. Huracan was on the other side, the air shimmering in front of him like heat coming off asphalt. Their soldiers were dressed warmly in white, AK-47s barking as they advanced from car to car.

Kisin spoke a word that I felt in my guts, and the ground rippled like a wave, throwing cars out of the way and dropping men to the ground. Several soldiers were exposed and quickly riddled with bullets from the attacking force.

"Hold them back!" Shahmeran screamed. "Don't let them interrupt the ritual!" She stood in the middle of the street. I had already seen her resilience, and was not surprised when a few bullets found her, ripping her clothes and staining her skin, but never harming her.

Kisin stopped in the street, just short of where he shattered it. Bullets whined off the asphalt close to him, while he raised his hands, as though pulling a strong note from the brass section. The ground rumbled, giving up a wall of stone. He walked along it while it undulated to keep up, deflecting any bullet that came close. Teotl advanced past it, fearless. Bullets chattered off her, but seemed to do nothing at all.

Huracan stayed back, several soldiers moving up to support him. A demon leapt from the shadows, tearing one of the soldiers open, stinging another with its tail before pouncing on a third. Huracan turned to it and made a flicking motion. The demon's head came off its shoulders with the sound of heavy cloth ripping in two.

Sarah was in the line of fire, behind the Twins, but clearly exposed. A stray bullet would end it all and there were far too many of those for comfort. Men were dropping to the ground, some dead, some screaming for help. I had to go.

I hauled myself to my feet and ran along the street, ducking as low as I could manage, each step sending a fresh bolt of agony through my body.

I turned in time to see Teotl hold one hand up, and four of the Twins' men fell, shredded with phantom gunfire.

Shahmeran faced Kisin in the center of the street, and though there was chaos and death all around them, they seemed to see no one else. "Leave now, Kisin. I won't tell you again."

Kisin smiled sadly. "You know I won't do that."

Shahmeran held her arms out, closing her remaining eye. Bullets still whined off her occasionally. A purple shimmer seemed to be coming from her, from her chest, arms, head. It was ghostly, growing and changing and coalescing. Soon it had surrounded her body and yet kept growing. It had taken a definite shape, long and serpentine, stretching out, and coiling back onto itself. A head formed in one end, the huge and terrifying head of a giant snake, an orange crest stretching down its neck. Its right eye was a baleful green, the other had been poked out of its skull.

By me.

The serpent thing was Shahmeran, and as it bared fangs the size of my arm, I wanted to hide from this thing and never come out again. It was more than fear, it was an atavistic dread of a creature that had once preyed on all of humanity. It hissed, rearing up in front of Kisin.

And somehow, the man showed no fear.

"I know," hissed Shahmeran, her voice a great sibilant echo.

Kisin responded with his earthquake words, arms in great motions, conducting his invisible orchestra. The ground exploded beneath Shahmeran, vomiting water from ruptured lines and stinking sewage, both of which began to freeze immediately. Hands of rock gripped the monster while she flailed helplessly in the earth's grip. The explosion rippled outward, throwing me off my feet into the stairs of one of the townhouses. A shot of pain went through my broken bones, and for a moment, I was certain that my spine had gone. I moved, and found I still could. Good enough for now.

Bullets whined off the asphalt in front of me. I looked up. One of the Twins' soldiers was advancing, submachine gun raised. He fired again, and I jumped for the gap in the cars ahead of me. The bullets followed my path. I didn't know if he saw I was unarmed or just didn't care.

Across the street, three of the black-clad soldiers and one of the demons huddled behind another car while bullets chewed into the metal all around them. Huracan stepped forward, his brow furrowing, and lifted up the car, sweeping it all the way across the street, killing all four beings and taking the head off the man who had been shooting at me.

There was a clean path to Sarah. Shahmeran was tangled up. Most of the soldiers were dead. If there was a demon left, I couldn't see it. I broke cover, sprinting for Sarah. The storm had opened up, and above, a yellow eye, the same color as the wendigo's, shone down on her.

Teotl screamed something, and Huracan, brow furrowing, focused on a car. Jagged spears of metal came off it, floating in a phalanx in front of him. He turned to Sarah and the Twins.

I seemed to be moving through thick mud, every stride barely eating up any ground at all.

One of the fallen soldiers raised his gun.

Huracan gestured, the spears flying at the Twins.

The soldier pulled the trigger, a burst of bullets chattering off the cars, a single one finding a home in Huracan's arm. He yelped in pain, and the spears spun off target. Most clattered to the street, but a single one flew on a new, false path.

Impaling Sarah right through the heart.

- 6 -

I don't remember covering the rest of the distance to Sarah. I only remember seeing her shudder once and fall bonelessly to the ground, and then I was holding her freezing body, helplessly watching the blood spread over her chest. It frosted over almost immediately, growing brittle and flaky. Her face was as pale as the snow, her eyes closed, hair falling across my arm.

Gradually, I became aware of the woman standing behind me. "One hundred years!" she moaned. She didn't look any older than nineteen, but the power and authority in her voice was undeniable. The words faded and reverberated at turns, feeling as though they wove around and through me. She stared down at Sarah's body, eyes impossibly blue, the left one rimmed in red where a bloody tear streaked her porcelain cheek.

The translucent one flickered into view at the other's shoulder. "We're lost." Her voice was like her sister's, but even more disjointed, a whisper felt rather than heard.

I turned away from the creatures. They looked human, but they weren't.

Sarah. I had gone into this place to save her and I had failed. Because of me, Sarah was dead. And with her went my last connection to the world. Now I wished for the haze of the drugs to wash over me, numb me, make me not care.

"Is this one of ours?" The solid Twin knelt in front of me, peering up in confusion. She could not have been more baffled had I been some kind of talking animal.

The other one passed through her sister, their faces momentarily becoming one, then going from almost solid to a wispy outline as her face stopped inches from mine. "The creature Rose spoke of?" The ghost twin moved off, examining my face and neck.

I could still hear the sounds of battle, the gunshots, the screams, the cracking of earth, and the hissing of the snake thing, but I couldn't care. I wanted to be alone, to hold Sarah. I wanted her to be alive, for everything to be a big bad joke. I knew it wasn't. Her skin was too real.

The Twins never strayed from my face. The solid one was angry. "Why have you come here?"

The ghost one was curious. "Why have you interfered?"

I closed my eyes, feeling a tear leave a freezing path down my cheek.

"Matters not," said the solid one. "We should kill him."

"Sister," whispered the ghost.

"When Shahmeran finishes with—"

"Sister. Look."

"Oh. Oh my."

I opened my eyes. The solid one was gaping at her wrist in naked wonder, the ghostly one close by, having already drawn her attention to it. A tiny drop of something had frozen mid-splash. My tear.

"This one is consecrated," whispered the ghost.

"But how?"

"We have the luxury of neither choices nor questions, sister. The wendigo is coming and he needs a skin."

A moment of wordless communion passed between the Twins, and the solid one put her arms around my shoulders. She was small, scarcely over five feet, and slender for it. Her skin was almost as pale as the white dress she wore. When she spoke, the ghost followed it almost immediately. "Precious boy," she said.

"Bless your presence."

The tears fell from my eyes freely now. The Twins were merely wobbling shapes in a smudged and murky world. Sarah was gone. "Please. Please just go away. Leave me alone."

"We can't walk away," said the ghost.

"And neither can you," said the woman.

It was too much. I shoved the solid one away, setting Sarah on the snowy street. "Leave us alone!" I stood up, ready to fight these women. I could hear my tears hitting the ground as solid bits of ice to shatter.

The Twins smiled in indulgent amusement. "This one was dear to you?" asked the ghost.

"Sister? Lover?"

"Wife?"

I couldn't answer them. Sarah was all those things to me at one time or another. It was wrong and horrible, but it was also wonderful. Now she was nothing.

"She was to receive a great gift," the solid one said, coming to my side, and looking up at me. She was almost childlike, but the crushing power behind her eyes said exactly what she really was. I thought to what that thing with Garth's face had said. A pretender to the throne.

"You were going to kill her!"

The solid one giggled. The ghost, floating at my shoulder, put her arms around me. They were solid, then gone, then solid. "Never. She was to be flesh of our flesh."

Stifling the laugh, the solid one said, "We wanted to give her eternity. Power."

"And now these gifts fall to you."

"And one more."

They parted from me, gesturing forward. Shahmeran was still in the grips of Kisin's earth. As a sharp rock tore a massive rent in her scales, a cut opened along the Twins' bellies, staining their white dresses. It wasn't as serious as the wound on the snake, and though they winced with it, they did not seem surprised. Teotl was locked in combat with two demons. She was unhurt, though they looked covered with wounds caused by their own wicked claws. A few firefights still rattled between cars, though most of the men were dead or dying.

They were gesturing at Huracan. He was bleeding freely from the gunshot in his arm, but was still up and fighting. He picked up cars, one by one, and smashed them into Shahmeran.

"Revenge," they said.

Revenge. The man who finally killed Sarah. Take it if I wanted it. The man who stole everything from me without knowing or caring about what he had done. Was that even what she would want?

I knelt by her body. I couldn't ask what she wanted. She was past caring. At least there was that. No more fear, no more pain. Sarah was at peace. I had my answer.

I bent over and brushed a kiss over her forehead. Goodbye.

I stood up. "Fuck you both."

The solid one smiled. "We weren't giving you a choice."

"Precious boy."

The storm opened up right above me. I expected the clouds to part and to see the clear blue sky. Instead, it was a yellow glow. Not the sun, but something far more feral and hungry. It was the heart of the storm, a ball of angry clouds roiling and twisting, spitting off jaundiced lightning. The snow fell now, the once large ring of peace having shrunk to be only large enough for me.

"You betrayed me!" The voice was in the howl of the wind and the crackle of the lightning, the rage palpable in the electric chill.

I tried to shout a denial, but the words were swallowed. The wind snaked down from the sky, ripping me off the ground and dragging me up toward the unblinking yellow eye. "I ask that you stop the ritual and instead become my prison?"

It kept pulling me upward. Thirty feet, forty. Then a hundred. More. The ground was still visible through the driving snow. Not because it had thinned, but now it seemed the storm focused my perception rather than blocked it. The people below were tiny. I could still see the struggling serpent, but the clearest things were the two pale faces of the Twins, gazing rapturously upward.

And then, the wind pulled me into the yellow eye.

The storm raged above, all around, and below me. The amber glow came from the wendigo's eyes, crackling with lightning, each one now bigger than a car. Its blue-gray body was huge, roiling with storm, freezing over with ice, and fed with surging funnel clouds like colossal veins. It opened its mouth to speak, displaying teeth of ice and a tongue of storm. "I should have let you die!" it howled.

The wind tore me upward, solidifying into freezing gray. And then it was a hand, coiled around my body. The face of the wendigo, half flesh and half storm stared down at me, light flashing off its jagged teeth. "Bound into your flesh until someone slays us. Is that what you wanted?"

The wendigo's plaintive scream hit me through the chest. Sarah was dead. How dare that thing say anything? "I tried to stop it! What do you want from me? I'm just a man! You want me dead? Then kill me! Kill me!"

The fingers coiled around my body blew apart, turning into wisps of charcoal cloud. The wendigo was in front of me now, as he was in the snow. No longer a titan, he was ten feet tall, floating across from me in the icy winds, still glaring with impotent rage. "I cannot," it said. "You are consecrated. Sacred to me, like it or not."

"You're this whole storm! Break free!"

The wind was howling, but it was no longer angry. It had become mournful and frightened. "This started two centuries ago when they bound me to this pattern," it said, a claw pointing downward at the upturned faces of the Twins. "The trap is set and I had no choice but to come." It turned its attention back to me, and I smelled ozone. "You were my one hope."

"There has to be a way out!"

"There is only one path. At the very least, your skin is a preferable prison to the girl's. Your heart reminds me of my own, and we have the rest of time to truly become one."

The wendigo regarded me as the storm swirled around us.

And then it plunged its claws into my chest.

I cried out, the howl of pain merging with the storm. I could feel the spidery fingers digging through my chest, severing nerves and tendons, slicing through muscle and bone. The hand was icy, leaving trails of frost burning through my body. With a sucking crunch, the wendigo yanked its hand free, letting my blood rain down where it would freeze into ruby crystals before hitting the street. In its hand was my heart, still stuttering a terrified tattoo. As I watched, frost spread from the fingers, coating the organ, stopping it, turning it blue-gray and hard. I think I was still screaming, but my throat was raw and bloody, my lungs exposed to the raging storm. The wendigo regarded its prize.

And he ate it like a nice apple.

I had seen that exact expression on the face of Erica's son when he ate the heart of his victim.

The wendigo polished it off in two ravenous bites, licking frozen blood from its claws and picking little bits from between its teeth. When every last shred was gone, it plunged its hand into its own chest. The flesh gave way, turning to bits of angry cloud. It pulled the hand out a moment later, holding another heart, this one snow white, shining with crystalline ice. It reached out, planting the heart in the empty cavity where mine had been.

The wendigo began to fade, its flesh turning into the raw stuff of the blizzard. The muscle in my chest regrew before my eyes, the skin expanding in a healing web. The rest of my injuries were suddenly gone, cured in ice. My bones knit together, my wounds closed, my teeth burst back through my gums, strong and new. The strength flooding into me had made me whole, and more than whole. Powerful.

And then the clouds surrounded me, wreathing my body in freezing tendrils of gray and white. As they solidified, I saw my limbs, now naked, turning into slender mirrors of the wendigo. I felt something in my mind, like the voices I knew, but this was a constant. It was cold, it was ancient. And it was angry.

I gloried in the icy rage spreading through me in a comforting haze. My vision was so sharp, I could make out facial expressions in the people far below. Yet more importantly, the blood pounding through their veins was eerie music. Every heart was a glowing beacon, from the strong hammering ones to the ones pumping their last shuddering beat.

The storm stretched around me, but it also was me. I had the sense that if I just knew what muscle to flex, the blizzard would obey. Like reaching out an arm, like speaking a specific word. I could blanket the city below in ice, freeze everyone. My stomach rumbled, and though my mind knew what I craved was wrong, I still wanted it.

First, I would deal with what was below. I rode the wind to the street, landing lightly beside Sarah's body. She was covered in a fresh layer of snow, her eye sockets filled with fluffy white.

Shame her heart is destroyed. The voice growled through me, more definite than any voice I had ever heard. The wendigo was in me now.

Touch her and—

You'll kill yourself? There is no you, there is no me.

The Twins approached, one padding through the snow, the other through the ether, somehow holding hands. They looked so tiny. Exhausted and beaming, they had the expressions of new mothers.

"Coldheart," said the solid one.

"Our sweet Coldheart."

There is only us.

"She is dead."

"But her murderers are here."

"Kill them."

I don't know if the words were mine or the wendigo's. "Go to hell." I don't think it mattered.

The Twins gazed quizzically up at me. I slashed at them with my claws, ripping into the solid one. A set of ragged cuts ran from her shoulders over her breasts and down to the wound in her side. As I did this, I felt the fire burning down my chest all the way to my abdomen. Looking down in horror, I saw wounds tracing the path of my claws on my body, far deeper than the shallow ones I put on the girl now staggering backwards, her white dress stained red.

"You can't kill us, Coldheart," she gasped.

The ghost was by her, trying to comfort, but she was fading from existence, her moments of solidity fewer and farther between. "Our pain is yours, tenfold," she said.

"If you die, I die," I said.

"Yes."

"Visit your rage upon our enemies," the solid one said.

"Take your revenge," said the ghost.

I turned to the battlefield. Shahmeran was in poor shape, desperately holding off the three intruders. Huracan was badly wounded, still throwing things at the colossal snake. Teotl seemed to be trying to get hit, but the serpent's thrashing avoided her. Kisin was the most brutal, turning the ground to instruments of pain. With each grievous wound opened on Shahmeran, a lesser version sliced into the Twins.

You want to weaken them? Kill their Familiar. Kill the snake goddess.

I never had to run. My body became a chill wind, and I was on top of the writhing serpent, clouds coalescing into my bloodless flesh. I tore into her back, and the keening wail of the Twins joined the storm. I smiled.

"Are you crazy?" Shahmeran hissed.

"You hunted me like an animal!" I screamed back, my claws raking into her back. Unlike the bullets which had bounced off her harmlessly, my claws slipped between her scales, tearing them out, her steaming blood welling to the surface. She undulated, a rock spear shattering off at the base, and I went flying, slamming into a steetlamp. It broke in half and crashed into a nearby house.

I was barely hurt, standing up, and getting ready to cut into the creature. "I'm going to kill you."

"We don't have time for this, you psychopath!"

I poised for the sudden jump onto her, when my body was no longer mine. I felt something warm and powerful spreading through me. The wendigo's voice was silenced, and I could only scream. My body turned of its own accord. The Twins were coming closer, the solid one limping as she bled into the snow, the ghost growing more translucent by the moment. Their arms were linked and they each held out a hand as a beam of pure sunlight bored into my chest.

"Whatever vendetta you had with her is over now," said the solid one.

"You are both flesh of our flesh."

"No! You need... you need to die!"

The energy coated my skin, reaching into me. It was not pain exactly, more of a horrible disconnect, like I was coming apart at the seams.

"No, we don't."

"These are our enemies."

"They are yours now as well."

I fell to my knees. The energy relented, the Twins now close to me, close enough to hurt. "No," I murmured in the wendigo's ragged voice.

"Coldheart," said the solid one, putting a soft, pale hand on my shoulder.

"My name is—"

"Names have power," said the ghost.

"Guard yours well."

"We will call you what we wish."

"I can't do this," I said.

"You are reborn, Coldheart."

"Resistance causes only pain."

"Pain for you," said the woman.

"Pain for us," said the ghost.

"We can give you anything you could ever want."

"We ask only that you serve."

I regarded both of these strange creatures. "And if I refuse?"

"There is no refusal," said the woman. It wasn't gloating, nor was it threatening. She was stating a fact, something I knew even as my rage had hurt only myself. "Not for you, not for us. You are ours now, like as not."

"Then I guess I accept."

"Good. First, a gift."

The ghost pointed her flickering hand, now more ephemeral than real. "That killed your dear one." Huracan was crawling away from Shahmeran, leaving a thick streak of blood over the snow.

"He is yours."

I could not kill them, but I could kill this man. Instinctively, I was wind, and then I was standing over him. He stopped, looking up from my feet to my face in horror. Only a few hours ago, I had been in an identical position, seeing the wendigo for the first time.

"Please. No."

"Yes," I said to him. My claws went into his back, just to the left of his spine. I dug under his ribcage, finding his heart with ease, closing around it while it pumped in panic, tightening the grip and tearing it from him with a flick of my wrist. I brought it to my face, my stomach snarling. Frost grew from my fingers to chase lines over the organ, encasing it in a crunchy rind. And without thinking, I ate it in two quick bites.

It tasted like nothing had before. Every one of my senses luxuriated in it, imparting pure bliss. My hunger still lurked, but for a moment, all the pain, all the misery was gone.

I want another.

"Now the others," the solid one called.

And as the ghost vanished into the ether, she screamed, "All of them!"

Shahmeran was in bad shape, impaled on multiple spears of rock. I allowed myself a grin. Teotl and Kisin had paused in their torment of her and were staring at me in horror. They exchanged some words in that bizarre language, and Kisin turned back to Shahmeran, bringing up another shard of stone to tear into her scales. She made a horrible, sibilant sound.

I was the wind, and I was in front of Kisin, my hand closing around his neck. My long fingers overlapped my thumb behind his neck, a strange feeling I reveled in. I lifted him easily off the ground the several feet it took to look him in the eye. "Release her," I said.

Kisin did nothing.

I remembered the feeling I'd had when taking the heart. I thought of it then, the tasty morsel, ready to be eaten. Kisin's own heart thundered in his chest. He feared me. Not like before, when he'd ordered Huracan to torture me. Now the power was mine. Ice crept from under my fingers to coat his neck. Kisin was choking, his eyes already rolling back in his skull. Time to finish it. I reached for his chest.

And something hit me, sending me sprawling, and making me lose my grip on Kisin. I turned, finding Teotl advancing.

"You," I said, straightening. "I watched you fight. Anything hits you and you reflect the force back. But what happens if I never touch you?"

I thought about embracing her. I was around her, colder than ice, swirling and roiling. She fell to her knees, skin turning blue, teeth chattering, curling into a pathetic ball. I felt the temperature as an extension of myself, another limb, and willed it lower and lower. The storm closed in around her shivering body, ready to bleed the life from her.

Good. Now take her heart.

My stomach snarled. She was helpless, shivering and chattering. I remembered what she'd said to me at Erica's house. I remembered her at the warehouse. She was moments from death, when the cold would turn to warmth and she would go to sleep forever. And I relented.

No.

Why not?

She goes free.

I stared down at her. She stared back, shivering and terrified of the monster I had become. "If you want to live, run."

She got unsteadily to her feet, nodded to me, and ran.

I turned to Kisin. His heart I would eat with relish. Shahmeran had freed herself from the spears and was slithering forward by my side, leaving an impossibly long slick of blood. "You're a dead man, Kisin," she hissed.

"Perhaps," he said, "but it will be my mistress that kills me for what I allowed to happen here today." He spoke a single, rumbling word, and sank into the earth. Shahmeran struck once, but she was too late, her jaws smashing a dent into the surface of the street.

The intruders were beaten, either fled, dead, or bleeding in the snow. I had turned the tide. I had won the day, and I was the one who had taken the most powerful scalp. I let the storm surge around me, announcing my victory.

You like the power.

I'd give it up for her.

For now. Soon you'll find you can't live without it.

I didn't want the wendigo to be right, but it was. The feel of the storm around me, the strength coursing through my limbs, the knowledge that there was literally no one who could ever hurt me again, was intoxicating.

I concentrated on myself and felt the storm leave me. As I opened my eyes, clouds billowed off me to disappear into the sky, leaving behind my human body. I ran my tongue over the new teeth, checked the wounds that were now closed. I had never felt better in my life. Even the cold didn't bother me, and when I took off the peacoat, crusty with my blood, the feel of the winter wind on my skin was a caress.

Shahmeran was returning to her human shape as well, bleeding from a hundred wounds as she sat down on the snowy street. Bodies were everywhere. A single soldier I recognized as Barnes was going from man to man, checking pulses. He comforted his own men, giving them medical attention as he could. Kisin's men got a bullet in the head.

The ghost twin was gone, leaving the human woman. She was in bad shape as well, but beaming. I felt her eyes on me constantly, like a proud mother. She could not stop smiling when she found me looking, and invented excuses to put her tiny arms around me.

Soon, armored vans arrived, collecting the bodies of the dead. These were followed by work crews.

I left with the remaining Twin and found my new life.

- 7 -

It had been three weeks. *Three weeks into an eternity of slavery.*

After the carnage in the middle of San Francisco, they took me north. First we returned to the house where Shahmeran had beaten me. Doctors tended to all of us, first the Twin, who everyone referred to as Hope when not merely calling her Mistress. Her wounds no longer bled, a wispy bluish substance webbing them closed. Shahmeran was next, and her wounds were already healing as well. Under the smooth pale olive flesh, snake scales had formed a protective coating and skin was slowly regrowing over them. The doctor looked under the eyepatch and seemed to be happy with what he saw. She didn't speak to me, which was just fine.

The doctor looked me over, and found nothing. The wendigo had regenerated me entirely. The doctor called me sir, and treated my requests like orders.

I was given a room with its own bathroom and a change of clothes. They were designer labels, brand new, and though they were not precisely my size, they were close enough to be comfortable.

Rose Cross found me soon afterwards, and the tutoring began. We left Shahmeran in San Francisco for the time being and drove north and east. I watched the blizzard, already beginning to fade away into the atmosphere, disappear behind me. Going north, and at least for a little while, the weather grew milder. We rode in a limousine, Rose and I, while she spoke and I missed Sarah and the storm.

I asked Rose where we were going. Northwind, she told me, the manor house of the Twins. When I asked where it was, she smiled, explaining it existed between realities, and we had to go somewhere where the barrier between was weak. These places moved around, and sometimes it could be very difficult to find the way home.

Rose Cross taught me everything I needed to know for what would happen that night, these three weeks later. Hope rode with us to Northwind, though she spent most of her time in a seeming trance, sometimes speaking with things that weren't there. She would occasionally give directions to Rose, who would then convey them to the driver. Every window and mirror reflected alien worlds and bizarre monsters. Rose explained that either Twin's mere presence was enough to get glimpses into other worlds, a side effect of their mastery of Diablerie.

I don't know where we were when we crossed over exactly, but the sky was no longer the one I knew. It was ribboned with all the colors of the rainbow, perpetual night, yet almost as bright as day. The trees grew tall and straight, and though they were close to pines, the smell was all wrong. The small creatures I saw were not quite skunks and squirrels and owls and raccoons, but strange amalgams of the mundane and fantastic.

"This is between worlds. Half ours, half something else," Rose explained.

We drove through the enchanted snowscape. Occasionally, off in the woods, I caught sight of small structures like standing stones or wigwams, partly frosted in a light layer of snow. The road wound up to a small hill, on top of which sat a manor house. Not entirely Victorian or Georgian, it combined both to create something unique and beautiful. Later, I would find sections that mimicked an Iroquois longhouse, and others where the walls were deerskin. Behind the manor a moon shone, but it was much too big to be ours. And beyond it were two others. This was Northwind.

Rose taught me what I needed to know about my new life. About the Twins and their organization. About their enemies, from the Serpent to the Butterfly. About the League of Magi and the Twins' seat of power in Pemhakamik, their word for North America.

Three weeks after I had become a Familiar, I was in my room, easily the most luxurious place I'd ever been. The furniture was all burnished and antique, the quilts were embroidered, the art was stunning. The place looked and felt like a full-sized dollhouse of such immaculate detail. Everywhere I looked was a painting, scalloped wallpaper, an antique clock, a rifle, the skull of a strange animal, or any number of other things.

Anything I wanted I merely mentioned to Rose, and it was waiting for me the next time I returned to my room. Books to read, a TV, clothes, all of it. I either ate in my room or in one of the many dining rooms with Rose. The first night, when they revealed my meal, a raw beef heart, I nearly laughed. Until my stomach growled and I tasted it and after that never wanted anything else.

Three weeks of that, and learning about the people in the world I might have to kill.

That night, I was ready for my final initiation. When I returned to my room from a tutoring session with Rose—she gave me her schoolteacher smile and told me I'd do fine—I found a white suit waiting, all laid out on the bed. It was perfectly tailored to me and one of the most comfortable things I'd ever worn.

As I tied the tie, there was a knock at the door. I opened it to find Rose, smiling warmly. "You look very handsome," she said. A blood red silk evening gown clung to her slender body.

"You too."

She offered me one chalk white arm and I took it. Her skin felt feverish, but that was because mine was freezing. I just didn't notice anymore until something called attention to it.

She guided me down the endless halls. I knew I had seen only a fraction of Northwind during my time here. It was much bigger on the inside than it appeared, but in my new life, that was the least of the wonders surrounding me. She picked a door and opened it. They were gathered around a fireplace, where several logs blazed away, covering the room in liquid gold.

The Twins were on either side of the fireplace, Hope on the right, and Faith, far more solid now that we were closer to where she actually was, on the left. They wore purple now, each one holding a broadsword. Their Apprentices, those other than Rose, were close by. Ash Wednesday, the heir, was by Hope. Where the firelight touched his skin, runes appeared. The Machinist stood on the other side, her dress showing off the tattoos covering her arms and shoulders.

The other four Familiars were arrayed around the room, ready to accept another member into the ranks. I had seen their gifting in those paintings back at the house in San Francisco. Another painting was being prepared, this one of the wendigo choosing me. Shahmeran, still wearing a patch over her eye, was glowering. Blackthorn gave me a friendly smile, her pixyish face cheerful.

Rose let me go, and I remembered her instructions. Go to the fireplace, between the Twins, a couple steps away. They smelled like rain and expensive perfume. *They smelled only of blood.* Their power was palpable, the feeling of reality straining to keep them contained. Creatures all around, ready to burst in at their command. *They are the gatekeepers.*

Their words were ritual. A call and response, a statement from one, then the other, then spoken in unison.

"Today, you become a fist of Pemhakamik," Hope said.

"Today, you become our creature," Faith said.

"Are you ready?" they both asked.

I had my own responses, as scripted as a wedding. "Yes, Mistresses."

The Machinist handed me a silver goblet of wine, the firelight glowing on the tattooed stars along her temples.

"For your vigilance. For your vigor. We shall keep you close," the Twins said.

"From the unreal, lead me to the real," I said, drinking the wine.

Ash Wednesday handed me a book with the dragonfly symbol of Diablerie embossed on the cover.

"For your loyalty. For your love. We shall lift the veil from your eyes."

"From the darkness, lead me into the light." I accepted the book.

The Twins brought up the swords in a V, resting them on my shoulders, each blade crossing in front of my throat and kissing my neck.

"For your fortitude. For your faith. We shall let you know forever."

I closed my eyes, letting them know my life was theirs to take if they wanted it. "From the mortal, lead me to immortality."

"Rise, Coldheart. Sweet Coldheart. And take your place as protector of Pemhakamik."

I opened my eyes to the smiles of everyone in the room. They surrounded me, patting my back, shaking my hand. Accepting me into the family. Ash Wednesday told me that anyone who could take an eye from a Familiar while still mortal was a man worthy of respect, a comment Shahmeran didn't seem to find amusing.

I was with them. Bodyguard. Assassin. All the voices that had once tormented me were silent. There was only one voice now.

And I knew its name.

Dante
Ascending

CHEVALIER TOWER STOOD AT THE CORNER of Avalon Street and 142nd Avenue for as long as anyone could remember. A thirteen story tenement, it had probably been built sometime in the late 19th Century, and its weathered brick had lasted the test of time as the neighborhood around it crumbled. Its name was in a copper nameplate by the front door on the Avalon side, turned as green as the Statue of Liberty.

The dull brick tower loomed over the neighborhood, a good six stories taller than the tallest of other buildings, a lonely sentinel that could see all the way to New Jersey on a clear day. The other tenements its size were razed to make room for larger, stockier apartment buildings, leaving Chevalier Tower as the sole remnant of an earlier age.

Its loneliness was exacerbated by its isolation, even at ground level. Set back from the street, it was buffered by a small parking lot on the Avalon side. A sidewalk separated that from a fenced in basketball court on the 142nd side. The rims were rusted, and only the oldest people in Brooklyn could remember a time when there were chain nets hanging from them. The paint on the court was faded, the asphalt cracked, and no one ever played on that court anymore. Even the neighborhood's few skateboarders shunned it. On the other two sides were vacant lots, overgrown with green, a single rusted out car parked near the back of one. Chevalier Tower's closest neighbor was the apartment block on Avalon, a squat and ugly building put up in the late '60s.

The reason no one came near Chevalier Tower or played on the basketball court was the same reason there was only a single tag on the side of the building, spraypainted in spidery black. ASH. Everyone knew that stood for Avalon Street Homeboys, and could be found on buildings, mailboxes, and dumpsters, always in small, sparing text, for five blocks in every direction. Less like an ostentatious threat and more a solemn warning. Other buildings in the neighborhood had tags, but they were always individuals. Other gangs stayed the hell out of the ten square blocks ruled by ASH.

Chevalier Tower was their headquarters. They came in and out at all hours. The strangest part was the composition of the gang. Most were black, most were men, but not all. There were women, there were Hispanics, Caucasians, and Asians. It was tough to get an accurate count, but it was a known secret that ASH's manpower was within.

Virgil Alves had grown up in the shadow of Chevalier Tower. Unlike those who lived in much of the surrounding area, Virgil had never had anything to fear from ASH. As long as you stayed away from the Tower, you were fine. There was no street crime within ASH's reach, a tiny pocket in the ghetto only whispered about by those few in the know. He liked to watch the tower out of his window in the neighboring apartment block. The lights in the windows were like a hundred eyes while its stark silhouette waited in the night.

Virgil admired the men and women of ASH. They seldom spoke to outsiders, and when they did, they were cordial. They were feared, but more importantly, they were respected. They earned good livings, they never went hungry, and they did it in such a way that they could hold their heads high in the neighborhood.

Virgil didn't have a lot of options growing up where he did, and ASH represented the best of them. Sometimes he pictured himself in the black-and-gold of ASH, the eyes of the locals on him, respectfully giving him the space to go about his business. It was hard to imagine ever wanting to be anything else.

Violence was something to worry about with any gang. The men and women of ASH carried in public, but Virgil never saw one draw down, and only heard the story of one act of violence. A drunk had been screaming at the tower for a full night, throwing empty bottles at the side. His body was found the next day, throat cut by something serrated. After that, everyone knew to leave the Tower alone, and there was never any trouble with ASH after that.

Until a winter day before Virgil's sixteenth birthday. He was across the street, walking home through the light flurries of snow when he heard the report of a pistol. He whirled, and across the street they were already running. Two large men, bundled against the cold, the swatches of blood red marking them as a rival gang. On the curb, bleeding away into the gray slush on the sidewalk, the ASH man breathed his last. There was more red on the streets for two weeks after that.

On the first clear night after the snows, Virgil was watching the tower in the late evening when ASH came boiling out. There were at least twenty of them. In the next hour, gunshots popped through that five block radius. More bodies dropped in the next eight hours than most months. ASH returned to the tower in the wee hours of the morning, their dead avenged. No gang ever tried to nose into the territory again.

That was the final straw. Virgil knew he had to join ASH. On top of the money, on top of the respect, a family who always had your back. Like everyone else in his neighborhood, he heard the stories. Someone's cousin had joined, or else a friend of a friend. They said there was only one way to do it, and that was to get to the top of the tower and talk to the big boss himself. Long as you weren't caught on the trip up, they let you in.

As winter turned to spring, Virgil watched Chevalier Tower nightly. The vacant lots bloomed into green. The neighborhood nice and quiet since the failed encroachment. He turned sixteen in the late spring, and as the weather warmed, the plan crystallized in his mind. He didn't bother to tell his mother goodbye, because he'd see her soon as a junior member of a respected organization. He could tell her in the same breath that she'd never have to worry about bills ever again.

The corner of Chevalier Tower facing Virgil's room gave him a perfect view of the back door. A single door, seemingly never locked, opened out onto a short concrete staircase leading into the greenery of the two vacant lots bordering it. He would have to hop two fences, but it was a clear path.

There was almost always a guard just beyond the door. Virgil could see him through the window in the door as a dark shape that occasionally shifted in place. But right around midnight, the shape would vanish for about a minute to be replaced by another one.

Virgil waited until after eleven on a Tuesday. It was a school night, but if things went as he thought they would, he wouldn't need school for that much longer. He opened his window, and with a last glance into the quiet apartment, hoisted himself out. Below was the vegetation-choked alley running alongside the apartment. He hung by his hands from the window, and in one motion pushed off and let go. Landing lightly in the leaves, he went along the fence, heading away from the tower.

The foliage was thicker at the edge of the lot, and Virgil wanted to get as close as he could before breaking cover and heading for the door. His goal in the meantime was the rusted hulk of the red Ford Pinto now rotting twenty feet from the back door. Virgil skirted the edge of the lot, hiding amongst the large and flat leaves the size and feel of notebook paper. The shape behind the door was dim and indistinct, but the occasional shift betrayed its presence. The tag was barely visible in the diffuse street light, but Virgil could still see the simple, jagged letters. Soon, those letters would mean home to him. Virgil felt a surge of pride in his chest. Premature, he knew, but there was nothing that would keep him from that top floor and the meeting with the big boss.

Virgil crouched by the nose of the Pinto, focused on the silhouette behind the door. His legs burned from the crouch, but he ignored it. When the shape vanished, Virgil did not wait. He never considered that it might be a minor shift in posture. He knew the schedule of the man behind the door, having obsessively observed over the past several months. Virgil sprinted over the open ground, turned the knob, and slipped through the door silently.

A hallway split off to the right before leading all the way to the lobby at the front of the building, and a large man was slowly strolling away, nearly eclipsing the whole thing. This had to be the guard. Virgil moved to the corner and slunk around it, grateful that the man never turned, but also positive he wouldn't.

Virgil allowed himself a smile. He was inside Chevalier Tower. The only people who ever did that were full-fledged members, or else became so shortly thereafter. He followed the hallway. On either side were the closed doors of apartments. The floor was hexagonal tile, the kind Virgil had only ever seen in bathrooms. The light came from expensive antique fixtures high along the walls. The walls themselves were a neutral beige, or else they were a dark, stained wood.

The hallway opened up on the left. He peeked down it, seeing a short hall leading to a windowed door. Beyond was the courtyard, presently empty. The place looked well-maintained, with a clean fountain, concrete benches, and patches of manicured green. He continued down the main hall, and after only a single apartment door, it turned left as well.

He crept down the second hall, heading toward the front of the building where the lobby would have stairs leading up to the second floor. So far, so good. Chevalier Tower was eerily quiet, but it was in the middle of the night. Still, he had expected some noise. A thudding beat coming from one apartment, maybe. The boisterous chatter of a card game. But there was nothing.

Virgil peeked around the corner into the small lobby of the tenement. This is where the mailboxes were, a large alcove of little brass doors. Another large man was here, walking away from Virgil, a pit bull clicking along beside him. The dog had no leash and never looked up, but was keeping pace with his master. Virgil waited until both of them turned the corner, and then quickly ran up the stairs, hunched over so that he was not visible over the bannister.

The stairs led to another hall, switching back to go up another floor. Virgil paused at the top, and could hear the steady footfalls and clicking sounds heralding another of the gang members with his dog patrolling the hall. Virgil emerged onto the second floor, when something caught the corner of his eye, and he froze.

One of the apartment doors was open, looking into a living room. Two men, a woman, and a pit bull sat around a low coffee table, while another woman stood by them. All four had bologna sandwiches on paper plates, the standing woman holding hers like she was at a picnic. She picked it up, displayed it for them, and took a bite, carefully chewing. One of the men tentatively picked his up and took a bite. The other two followed suit, concentrating on every movement. The dog finally leaned down and slurped up the sandwich in two bites.

The three people at the table didn't look brain damaged. They looked normal, and in point of fact better than normal. Attractive, fit, they could have been models if they had wanted to be. The dog was also incredibly well-trained not to have eaten the sandwich as soon as it was in front of him.

Virgil did not stay to speculate, and instead, smoothly inched along the staircase and made the turn to the next flight up.

He smiled. Three floors up already. What had been so difficult for the others who had tried? Or was he the first one? What if the stories weren't true? He shook it off. Of course they were true, and even if they weren't yet, he could make them true.

The third story was empty. Deep in another corner of the building he heard the clicking of pit bull claws on the tiles. He had enough time. All the time in the world. And a few doors down, he saw that one of the apartment doors was slightly open.

He crept over to it, his ear hovering just over the scarred surface of the wood. He could hear nothing beyond. Slowly, he pushed on the door, which opened silently into one of the apartments.

What should have been a living room was bare, save for racks and racks of clothing. Most of it was in simple black, with the gold accents of ASH visible in scarves, bandannas, and rags. The racks looked almost like something in the Salvation Army, only the outfits were nearly identical. A table sat against one wall, covered with clean jewelry boxes. Virgil opened one and found gold. Ropes, earrings, rings. All kinds of gold jewelry in various sizes. He picked up a handful, savored the pleasing weight, and nearly pocketed it.

Robbing the gang would be wrong. They were going to be his brothers and sisters soon. Same as robbing family. With money coming from the gang, Virgil could buy his own jewelry. Virgil put the gold back, went to the door, and listened. The dog sounded far away, so Virgil came out and rushed up the next flight of stairs.

As he turned on the landing, what had once been silence turned into an industrial rumble. Somehow, the soundproofing in the floor was so good that there was not even a hint of whatever it was until he was on the floor itself. The sound was almost like a laundromat when every machine was in use. The doors up here were closed, and there was no way to hear guards patrolling the halls over the sound, but Virgil wasn't worried. The ascent into Chevalier Tower had been a joke thus far, and there was no reason to think it was any different on the fourth floor.

He ducked by the landing, hiding behind the bannister as he peered into the hall. It was open, so he went to the corner and peeked around it. Once again, clear. He thought of going up the stairs, but it had been so easy. He had a chance to learn more about ASH, and it was not a chance he could pass up.

He started trying doors until the third one opened, and he was through it. The sound was momentarily louder, although not deafening. It was deeper than that, rattling through bones and muscles. He closed the door behind him, and turned and looked into what should have been an apartment.

Four nude bodies were lined up against the wall. They each lay on something that was almost a dentist's chair, but a sleek and clear helmet enclosed each head. Tubes snaked into the inner elbows, machines hissed with loaned breath. Their limbs were all moving, as the chairs moved each limb individually as though the unconscious person were riding an elliptical.

Captured people? That was the first thought. But who and why? They didn't seem to be injured in any way, and in fact their bodies were utterly without scars. He reached out to touch one of the women on her smooth, golden skin. She was warm, and he could feel her pulse pounding. But her eyes were closed and to all indications she was fast asleep. The others were in similar shape.

The windows were covered with clean shades, like something

he would expect in a doctor's office. The walls were bare, except for a large tube coming down from the ceiling and curving at the floor, where the top was open. It was big enough for a human being to comfortably fit.

Virgil knelt by the side of the chair. The guts were clearly visible; whoever had built it hadn't bothered with a casing. Wires and tubes came from a chunk of crystal. There were similar chunks, all irregular and of different colors, in each chair. Virgil got up and looked over the group of people seemingly running in a supine position while sleeping peacefully.

He almost didn't see the door open.

Virgil slipped through the other door purely by reflex. The room should have been a kitchen, if the layout was anything like a normal tenement. Instead, it was another room with more bodies on similar contraptions, the same kind of tube snaking down from the ceiling. Virgil glanced around, seeing the dividing line that used to be in the wall, where the kitchen would have been before it had been removed and combined with the apartment next door. Moving fast, he crossed the room, listened at the next door, and was through.

Another room of bodies. And another after that. In perverse fascination, Virgil kept going through these converted apartments, surveying what had become a bizarrely familiar sight. He had no idea if whoever had nearly interrupted him in the first room was still going room to room or not. Curiosity had eclipsed the slight taste of fear.

He had gone through more rooms than he kept track of, and was expecting another clinical display of exercising corpses. But when he opened the door, he was surprised by a new sight.

It was the size of a living room. The drapes were heavy and velvet. An ornate circle was cut into the hardwood of the floor, and when Virgil knelt to trace the silvery lines, he found that metal had been poured into them. Symbols in some unknown language, similarly filigreed into the floor, decorated the circle. In one corner was an antique chest, an embroidered drop cloth over it. Curious, Virgil moved the cloth aside and opened the chest. Inside, he found a pewter goblet like something a king would drink from, a green bottle of wine partly encased in a gold lattice, a silver dagger, and several candlesticks. Virgil shut the box and put the drop cloth back over it.

Satanists? That seemed weird. Possible, maybe, but it wasn't like ASH was known for doing anything like that. Perfect neighbors. Maybe it was that Santeria shit, or voodoo. Some of the members could have been Caribbean. Virgil had a couple relatives from the islands, and until they said certain words, it was impossible to tell.

By his calculation, he was probably on the other side of the tenement, as far from the staircase as it was possible to be.

He went through the other door into another room full of unconscious people. Moving quickly, he was across the room and his hand was on the doorknob when it turned in his hand by someone on the other side. He had no time to hide. No time to get to another door. He whirled and dove into the opaque tube that ran from floor to ceiling in every room, snaking into it. Still thin with youth, Virgil wiggled up the pipe to the elbow where it went straight up into the ceiling. Light shone through the top.

Inside the pipe, it was hard to hear anyone moving around in the room he had just left, and Virgil did not want to chance it. He braced his forearms and feet on the side of the pipe and began the ten foot climb to the source of light. It was a quick climb, and even as he was half up, he began to hear different industrial sounds. The constant rumble of the chairs was replaced by a deep hum. The hole in the top of the tube was easily large enough for him to fit through, and he crawled out, freezing when he looked up.

The walls of the room were covered in silvery capsules, giving Virgil something easy to hide behind. A large vat dominated one side. A man stood on a platform on the lip, a short metal staircase leading up to it. He was stirring the vat with a long steel pole. Virgil was motionless in the alcove between capsules.

At first glance, the man looked normal enough, even though as a white man he would be a rarity in the neighborhood. He was barely more than four feet tall, his freckled skin stretched tight over his skull. He had small, piggy eyes, a button nose, pursed lips, and tiny ears. He wore a red lab coat over a turtleneck, and nice slacks. The strange man was totally focused on the task of stirring the vat.

As Virgil watched him, he began to notice odd things. The man was barefoot on the metal, his toes almost as long as fingers. His shoulders were great knotty masses of muscle, and his arms seemed just a little too long. Virgil watched the little man stir for several minutes before taking the pole from the vat. It dripped a viscous liquid the color of blood. The little man rapped it on the lip of the vat to discharge some of the drips, and hung the pole against the wall. He then loped down the metal stairs and out the door. His arms hung almost to his knees.

Virgil crept from his hiding place. He stood up on tiptoes and peered inside. The scent coming off the liquid was coppery. Too thick for blood, even if it looked like it. Unrecognizable chunks bobbed to the surface every now and then, only to be swallowed up almost as quickly. Drugs? Possible. ASH wasn't known for selling drugs, but it's possible they just didn't sell it in their own neighborhood.

The vat was being fed by several more pipes disappearing up into the ceiling. Unlike the other human-sized pipes, these were not much bigger than the kinds of pipes used for plumbing, although these appeared very well-maintained.

Virgil turned back to the capsules. Whatever was inside them had to remain a mystery. The surface seemed to be plastic. In the base, he found more unrecognizable machinery, once again plugged into a crystal. Shaking his head, he went to the hallway door. Hearing nothing, he slipped out into the hall.

It was empty, and he heard the sound of clicking off to the left, getting farther away. He followed those sounds to the elbow of the hall and peeked. A guard paced with one of the pit bulls around the far corner. Virgil followed, his steps light on the tiled floor. He made it to the corner as the guard was rounding the next. The stairs seemed to beckon him up. He took the steps two at a time until he got to the landing.

The temperature dropped at least twenty degrees. Virgil shivered, huddling into his jacket as he took the last few steps onto the sixth floor. The air was frigid up here, and his breath came out in big white gusts. He went to the nearest door and touched the handle. It was so cold it burned. He peeked into the room and found a meat locker. Sides of beef and pork hung from hooks in the ceiling. Racks of canned goods covered the walls. He stepped in, shivering even harder. The room had no borders, disappearing off into the misty ice where the tenement curved. An entire floor devoted to nothing but food storage. The gang could survive for years with what was up here.

Virgil closed the door and went up the stairs. The temperature returned to normal. As Virgil reached the seventh floor, he stopped and listened. There was no sound of pit bulls moving through the halls. Maybe security didn't go this high. Even with the weirdness of the last few floors, things were getting easy.

He went to one of the closest doors and opened it. The entire room was filled waist-high with stacks of money. There were foot-wide breaks leading through the stacks and to the doors for people to move amongst the cash. For a moment, Virgil wondered if the gang got rich through counterfeiting, because he could never have imagined this much real money in one place. But when he picked up the bills, they were varied. Some old, some new, some drawn on, some worn to cloth. If this was counterfeit, it was perfect.

Some of the piles were the wrong color, but as he inspected them, he saw that the money was foreign, with different languages and unfamiliar faces.

He crept to the next door and peeked in. Inside, more piles of cash. Across the room, men fed money into counters. Virgil sneaked back out into the hall and up the stairs. He might have taken the money and ran several floors down. But now, he was beginning to see the strange power of the gang. Only six more floors and a share of the money was his. He was already over halfway home.

Virgil paused at the top of the stairs.

The eighth floor was entirely open. The only walls were those of the building itself; every inner wall had been torn away. The seams along floor and ceiling were still barely visible. Virgil could see all the way to the other side of the tenement. Racks of weapons leaned against the walls. He would have expected Glocks, AKs, and the like, but instead he found wooden swords and spears. Virgil walked to one of the racks. The weapons were nicked with use, the handles worn shiny. The floor was scarred, with deep stains forming maps across it. The blood had sunk into the floor and permeated the giant room with a haze of promised violence.

Virgil went to one of the inner windows and peered out into the courtyard. If he pressed his face into the window and looked upward, he could see the sky peeking over the lip of Chevalier Tower. He glanced back to the old blood splattered across the room and climbed the stairs to the ninth floor.

The lights were softer. The doors of the apartments were in good repair. Virgil had the eerie feeling he had somehow stepped back in time. At any moment, a dapper ghost would round the corner and fade into nothing at the moment of contact.

A shudder fought off the cold finger in his spine. He nearly turned the corner and went up to the tenth floor, when a whisper came from the shadows at the corner of the hall. "You."

Virgil froze. The whisper was high and reedy, carrying easily through the still darkness.

"You," it repeated. "Follow."

"I need to make it to the top."

"Will not stop you. Not here." It tittered after *here*.

"Who are you?"

"Come and see."

Virgil could barely hear the retreating scratching sounds, like rats in the walls. Virgil followed the little scrapes to the corner. The hall leading to the back of the tenement was empty, pregnant shadows hanging from the walls to pool across the floor.

"Come and see," the whisper repeated.

Virgil squinted into the dark, trying to track the scratches that now echoed through the hallway. Dimly, he thought he saw something at the far corner of the tenement, a slip of movement, bone white against the deep browns and blacks of the hall.

"Who am I seeing?"

"Sadhvi Deva," came the whisper, and the white thing slipped around the corner.

Virgil glanced back at the stairs. He could move on, take his chances on the upper floors. But the way the whisperer laughed, it sounded like following it was the best way to prepare for whatever was above. So Virgil went down the hall, the shadows folding around his body and welcoming him in.

As he turned on the far side, the door in the center of the hall swung partly open. He opened it into the first normal living room he had seen since the second floor of the Tower. The windows were open, light flooding in from the courtyard. The room was sparingly furnished, but what was there was nice. Virgil swept the area with his gaze, jumping back when he got to the darkest corner.

What looked like a giant wasp hive was stuck to the walls, ceiling, and floor. Paper white nodules, each with a black hole like a mouth, about six inches across, formed the bulk. Inside, he could hear more of the scratching sounds, like a hundred rats moving around inside, although each one sounded huge. He recoiled.

From behind him, he heard the whisper again. "Come and see."

Virgil turned, and a door leading into one of the inner rooms opened a little. Behind, he saw a slash of white movement. He opened it the rest of the way.

The woman sitting at the other end of the room smiled. Candles burned along a mantel behind her, wax stalactites dripping down. A low table sat in front of her, a tea service on it, a wisp of steam threading upward.

"Sit down. Please," she said, gesturing across from her. Her voice did not sound young, nor did it sound old. She had an accent, almost English, but with something else beneath it. Her hair was long and black, her eyes liquid brown. Her face was elaborately painted ash white, accented with oranges and reds. She wore the same colors in silken layers and sat ramrod straight.

Virgil sat, pretty certain he could not refuse this woman even if he tried.

"Tea?" she asked.

He nodded.

A tiny man, one foot high, nude and skeletal, scampered from the darkness. His head looked like the skull of a cat Virgil had once seen rotting away in a vacant lot two streets over. The other boys had teased Virgil when he shied away from the animal's body.

The little man blinked yellow eyes, reflecting the dim lights of the candle.

Virgil screamed, scrambling backward.

"Calm yourself," Sadhvi Deva said sternly. "He is merely a gnome. You are in no danger from him."

The gnome cocked his head at Virgil, then hefted the teapot, poured two cups, and scampered away on all fours, behind Virgil and out of the room.

"What is that thing?" he asked.

"As I said, a gnome." She smiled, picking up the cup. "I realize that doesn't quite answer your question. Think of him as a servant from somewhere else. Somewhere very far away."

"Where?"

"Beyond the veil between this world and the next. Why are you here?"

"I want to join the gang. I want to join ASH."

"And you will, once you finish climbing the tower."

Virgil picked up the tea. It warmed his hands, and the scent was reassuringly normal. "Who are you?"

"I offer guidance to those who want it."

"Like me?" He sipped the tea. It calmed him, flooding his limbs with sweet energy.

Sadhvi Deva nodded. "Tell me, why do you want to join?"

"ASH runs the neighborhood and does it well. Nobody has to be afraid. Nobody gets robbed, nobody gets killed."

She smiled. "The way is open for you, but remember. Nothing is free. You do not have to join to support us."

"I know."

"Thank you for coming to see me," Sadhvi Deva said.

He finished his tea and got up, heading for the door. Remembering something the gnome had done, he paused and turned back to the woman. "The gnome laughed earlier. He said nothing would stop me here, and then he laughed. Like something would stop me somewhere else."

Sadhvi Deva sipped her tea. "He was referring to the vree-ka-vree."

"What are those?"

"Death. You will find them upstairs. Good luck."

Virgil left the way he came. On the way out, he saw the gnome climbing up the hive. It turned, its head swiveling all the way around like an owl, and regarded Virgil for a moment before crawling into one of the holes. Virgil shuddered and went back out into the hall. Now the sounds of scratching had a horrible source, and he jogged back to the stairs and up the next flight.

The tenth floor was mirrored. Walls, ceiling, floor, every inch reflective. A few non-mirrored sconces provided light. In places, Virgil could see the reflection had been fractured. He could barely make out the faint outlines of doors, still there, but reflective. Looking across the landing, he saw himself reflected into infinity and was surprised at the amount of fear he saw staring back at him. The words of the painted lady were still fresh in his mind: the vree-ka-vree were death.

The Virgil who had broken in on the first floor would have laughed. But by now he had seen enough. The bodies on the fourth floor, the stunted man on the fifth, and of course the gnomes in their hive. Even now, thinking of the odd sight of the people and the dog eating the sandwiches had taken on an eerier quality. He thought back to the men in the counting rooms. Was it memory that gave them spidery fingers and bulging eyes, or was it fear?

He turned to find the staircase up, and like everything on the floor, this was mirrored as well. His gaze seemed to slide right off it, and his head hurt trying to see reflected outlines. Virgil stepped up and onto the mirrored floor, and he heard a low moan, like distant traffic racing through the silvery halls.

Virgil froze on the stairs. There was an answering moan. He tensed to run up the stairs two at a time when something in the mirrored wall moved.

He turned to it, seeing the hall behind him, his back, his face, the wall in front, and so on, until he was tiny and far away. It started as a shimmer, loping along the hallway. Unlike the reflection, it never flipped back and forth between the two mirrors. It steadily grew, moving inexorably forward through the looped hallway. At first it was only the sensation of movement without context, the same silvery color as everything in this endless hall of mirrors. Then it passed in front of one of Virgil's reflections, and a piece of it momentarily became the same dark brown of Virgil's skin.

Virgil stepped backward. The shape moved up to the reflection. Virgil's face, staring into the mirror, distended like a soap bubble before shifting back into place. Whatever it was had passed through the membrane of the glass, and had come, sounding its odd traffic moan into the hallway. It padded down the stairs and into the hall in front of him.

The flesh shimmered, and a ripple passed over it, revealing a moving strip of pink skin amongst the reflection. Virgil got a sense of the creature, and immediately wished he had not. The silhouette was almost like a bear, although far thinner and strangely boneless in the way it moved. It had six legs ending in human hands, and it walked on its fingertips. Its head came forward like a dog, but was featureless. The momentary shift in its skin tone seemed to be accidental, as it quickly returned to its nearly perfect camouflage, mimicking the endless reflections on all sides. Most horribly, Virgil saw his own face on the monster, again and again, the same expression of abject terror.

It advanced, while Virgil backpedaled until his back hit the smooth mirror behind him. The thing had a raised hump behind its neck, just above the first pair of legs. That shimmered, and suddenly Virgil's face was on it, though it as not the reflection of the fear he knew he was displaying. Instead, the expression was gleeful.

Virgil ran.

The thing was close on his heels, the tapping of thirty fingertips on the floor growing faster and closer. Ahead, in the mirrors at the end of the hall, Virgil could see himself growing larger. He saw the glimmer of the creature behind him. On every wall, in the floor and ceiling, the heat-shimmer of the monster.

He might have missed it had the reflection not broke. In the shape of his body, running toward him, he saw his chest split open on six lobes, revealing a bluish and fleshy opening. Blooming from that, a six-petaled claw, unfolding and moaning.

Another one of the monsters, leaping from the wall in front of him, its featureless face splitting open to reveal the horrible thing within. Virgil slid like he was stealing home. He felt the whoosh of air as the leaping beast soared inches over his face, heard the angry moan as both monsters collided. He saw them in the mirror, their camouflage momentarily going haywire, showing flashes of pink skin, of graffiti-covered asphalt, of brick-and-mortar. Virgil knew then that these things, the vree-ka-vree, left Chevalier Tower. They used their camouflage and boneless bodies like an octopus, hiding around the city in plain sight, their calls indistinguishable from the sounds of the city.

He leaned into the slide, and in a smooth motion was on his feet again, sprinting down the hall. He heard the creatures right themselves and pursue. Too close. Virgil dug in, trying to keep his feet from slipping on the treacherous glass. The *tap-tap-tap* of the monsters pulled in closer, and he could see more shimmers playing over the skin of the mirrors. They were closing in on their prey.

He slammed into the mirror at the other end of the hall, rolled off it and sprinted for the stairs up. He felt a hand close on the back of his jacket: one of the things with their perversely human limbs. Virgil shed the jacket and took the stairs two at a time.

The mirrors stopped at the landing. Virgil no longer heard the tapping of fingers on glass and turned.

There were seven of them, shifting restlessly at the base of the stairs, featureless heads pointed up at him. His jacket was pinned under the hand-foot of the foremost one. Their faces opened up periodically, the claw-mouth extending, opening, closing, and retracting. One by one, Virgil's face appeared in the humps, smiling serenely.

He shuddered and climbed the stairs. There was no turning back now. He would never go through the tenth floor without the blessing of ASH. Their power became more understandable, even as he understood it less.

The eleventh floor hummed with electricity. Virgil was grateful for something that felt so normal. The inner walls had windows, transforming what should have been another tenement floor of apartments into an office from the 1930s. Inside, he could see human shapes silhouetted against banks of monitors.

The closest one was just across the way. Virgil crept closer, staying behind the low wall. The monitors looked like surveillance feeds. He watched them flicker through images, and slowly began to recognize parts of New York, some clear on the other side of the city. The images kept moving, and he saw images he recognized from movies. Other cities. Los Angeles. Chicago. Washington, D.C.

The man sitting in front of the bank was small, much like the man stirring the vat down where the world still made a little bit of sense. Earbuds poked from his ears, and his fingers played over a bank of controls. Suddenly, he turned around in his swivel chair.

Virgil dropped behind the wall, but not before getting an image of the man's face. He had innumerable eyes, all over the top half of his face. Virgil didn't wait for the man to check for him, and ran for the staircase. After the vree-ka-vree, Virgil would take no chances.

He heard the click of nice shoes on the tile floor behind him, but Virgil was already up the stairs to the twelfth floor.

It looked much like the last one, with the glass windows and low walls dividing what had once been residential space into offices. Only there were no shapes up here, the lights dimmed, and the screens dark. There was only one more floor left, the thirteenth, where the leader of the gang waited to welcome his newest member. Virgil had the time to look around a little.

The silence of the twelfth floor was strange. It was peaceful up here. A series of meeting rooms, even a few kitchens, and the first bathrooms Virgil had seen in the Tower. The inner circle of apartments were given over to four rooms, each with a table as long as the inner wall. The windows looking out were still only small, but they let in a generous amount of moonlight.

In the few offices at the corners of the tenement, Virgil found desks and workstations. There were file cabinets of paperwork, and strangely, on the desks, pictures of smiling families and little knickknacks. He opened up the file cabinet marked PERSONNEL. There were strange headings in here: "Priestess," "Serpent," and "Lion" among others. He paged through "Lion" and found one marked "Edunara."

The pictures were of a horribly burned man, leaning heavily on a cane. Then there were other shots, this time of a man wreathed in electricity. In one, he stood on a hilltop, hands skyward as lightning speared through him. His body seemed to be atomizing. In another, lightning leapt from his hands to another man in paramilitary garb. The man was smoking, the electricity cooking him.

Virgil looked through the information, though it barely made sense. This man was in Nairobi, and the file questioned if he might be from there. It listed him as extremely dangerous, and linked him with someone named Zara Iblisa, though it didn't bother to explain what that might mean. As though the file expected the reader to understand who and what all of these people were. Virgil replaced the files where they were, momentarily marveling at the names within: La Dame Dorée, Tōriki Satoru, Coldheart. The contents of the files would be his to peruse, like the jewelry, like the money, like the secrets of all the strange creatures he had encountered on the ascent. They would be his.

He replaced everything as he had found it and returned to the stairs. As he turned on the landing, he saw that instead of the entry to the final hall, a door blocked the way. On the dark brown wood in shining gold numbers: 13.

The penthouse apartment, where the leader of the gang would be waiting, ready to accept Virgil into the gang. He knocked.

"Enter." The voice was deep and booming, coming from beyond the door, but seemingly everywhere. Virgil took a deep breath, and for a moment regretted that he hadn't dressed up. He smiled. No guarantee that the clothes would have stayed intact on the way up. The big boss would understand. This was his castle; he knew what it took to make it to the top.

Virgil took the gold doorknob, and it felt warm in his grip. He opened the door.

The top floor was a single apartment. The floor was hardwood, the walls paneled wood. The light fixtures were ornate and gold, giving the entire room a burnished appearance. Windows, both those lining the inner courtyard and those facing the street were open. Outside was the corner of Avalon and 142nd, the corner Virgil had seen so many times he barely saw it anymore. It was just home. He had never seen it from the angle he was presently at, and had to resist the urge to run to the window and peer out. He had someone to impress.

Although who that was wasn't apparent. The penthouse looked empty. There was furniture here, a casual living room with lots of open space between stylishly modern sofas and chairs. The walls were covered in pictures, mostly black and white photos of structures being built. In the center of the far wall, the first thing that a visitor would see, was a stuffed buffalo head.

Virgil stood at the threshold for several minutes.

"Come closer." The voice came from all around him, sonorous and smooth. "Virgil Alves."

Virgil jumped. "How did you know my name?"

"You climbed the tower and you still have to ask that question?"

"Yeah… I guess you see a lot."

"I have to."

"You're the boss?"

"In a manner of speaking."

"The King of New York?"

The voice laughed. "Oh, no. New York has no king. Think of me as a Prince, and the Queens own so much more than just one city."

"The Avalon Street Homeboys are in other cities?"

"That name… I suppose it was inevitable. But that's not what we are."

"What does ASH mean then?"

"It's what I choose to call myself. Please, Virgil, come closer."

"Where are you?"

"Come inside. You'll know when you've come far enough."

Virgil made his way into the apartment. There were more couches, more chairs, many places to sit, but nowhere that looked like a home. He walked to the end and turned. In the center of the room, Virgil found his destination.

The pool was circular, and twenty feet across. Candles burned at even points, melted onto the lip. The liquid was the same he had seen in the vats downstairs, and he had no doubt that the pipes he had seen from time to time running down the walls and feeding the vats had their origins here. Gnomes capered about in the candlelight, scratching along, sometimes on two legs, often on all fours. They turned to peer at Virgil, their eyes glowing and amber.

As Virgil stepped toward the pool, the gnomes loped forward, one by one. Soon, they were surrounding it, a gnome at every gap in the candles. Virgil was forgotten. They hunched forward and back, moving rhythmically, their whispers at the edge of understanding. It grew louder, faster, louder, faster. The words never resolved into meaning. Finally, they dove in, their ash white bodies stained crimson with the bloody muck.

They continued the frenzied whispers, moving around through the liquid. Their splayed, skeletal hands danced over the viscous surface, rubbing, stirring, moving.

A shape began to form in the center of the pool. This seemed to encourage the creatures. The whispers continued at an even greater pitch, and they gathered liquid and laved it onto the hemisphere now emerging. More and more, grabbing the thicker pieces in the pool, working them into the shape, slathering more of the red onto it. And the shape rose higher. Soon, it was recognizable.

The face of a handsome man, eyes closed, mouth shut, rising from the pool. They kept up the task, creating neck and shoulders, chest and abdomen. The man the gnomes sculpted from the bloody pool looked like the statue of a god. When the feet were done, seemingly walking on the liquid, the man's brown eyes opened.

The blood sloughed off him, dripping into the pool, leaving behind smooth, chocolate skin. Where the candlelight touched him, runes blazed in his skin like molten gold. The man stepped from the pool.

"I am Ash Wednesday," the man said in the same booming voice Virgil had heard emanate from everywhere and nowhere.

"You're ASH."

Ash nodded. "Myself and those who serve me."

"I want to join you," Virgil said.

"You made it this far. There was no other choice for you."

Ash's arm, which had until recently been nothing but blood and viscera, grabbed Virgil's shoulder. With unnatural strength, Ash hefted the boy and flung him into the crimson pool. Virgil felt the splash, the liquid warm like a body enfolding him. He looked up at Ash, standing on the lip, the candlelight revealing runes along his heavily muscled legs.

"You are part of Ash now," the man whispered.

The liquid closed over Virgil's head, and all he could see was red. He felt no fear. He felt no pain. Only the warm sense of peace as his consciousness stretched and finally disappeared.

Wait

THE NOD WAS A CASUAL ONE, the kind traded between friends who have developed a familiar shorthand. Respect was there, but any wariness was entirely imagined, perhaps because of the FN-FAL 50.63 assault rifle cradled in his arms. He wore a simple khaki desert uniform with a wide-brimmed hat protecting him from the bright day. The only insignia was a badge sewn on the shoulder, the Death's Head Spider, marking his allegiance to the few thousand people on earth who would recognize it.

He was in his forties, the black stubble on his face fading to gray in spots on either side of his chin. His skin was a deep olive, burnished by the sun. He wore mirrored sunglasses, hiding golden brown eyes that were keen and narrow. His body was lean and powerful, pounded into shape by a lifetime of service to a paramilitary organization. He dabbed at his cheeks with the *shemagh* scarf around his neck. Years ago, he had said his name was Daoud, but that had been a pleasant lie between friends.

Michael Barnes nodded back, reaching into one of the buttoned pouches on his ammo belt and removing a 5th Avenue bar. He tossed it to the other man, who snatched it out of the air like a snake striking, and grinned thanks.

Rose Cross, shrouded in red, a red parasol shading her sensitive skin, went through the door in the tower, and moments later the sounds of her heels on the stone floor echoed outward into the courtyard. Barnes took up his position on the other side of the door from Daoud, who was already making crinkling sounds as he attacked the candy bar.

"I keep telling myself, I'll save this one," Daoud said in Egyptian-accented English.

"I don't know what the big deal is. You can get them in Khem," Barnes said, using the League word for Africa without even thinking about it.

"I know, but they never taste quite right."

Barnes laughed. "It's your imagination."

"Probably. Thank you for indulging me."

Barnes waved it off. "If you brought tea, we're even."

"As though I would forget."

Daoud removed a thermos from a pocket on his belt, then grabbed a pair of tin cups from where they hung on his shoulder strap. He poured the fragrant tea into the cups and handed one to Barnes. Barnes raised his cup to the other man. "Here's to fifteen years."

"Has it been so long?" Daoud shook his head.

They leaned back against the cool stone of the tower, listening to the waves crashing fifty feet below. They were on Darius Island, a spit of rock rising out of the middle of the Atlantic Ocean. The men had been calling it Pride Rock, after Ramirez, one of the younger guys in the squad, nicknamed it that. It was on no maps, but travel far enough east-southeast from Bermuda and it might be possible to find. From what Barnes had heard, it had been raised up from the depths a hundred years ago by Zara Iblisa, Apprentice to the Lion, and Grandmother Coyote, Apprentice to the Twins, as a place where emissaries of the Twins and the Lion could meet in relative safety. For many years, that meant Iblisa and Coyote, until Grandmother Coyote's body had been found, torn to pieces by an unknown assailant. These days, the emissaries were Anansi and Rose Cross.

Darius Island was a rocky plateau jutting fifty feet from the surface of the gray-blue ocean. Two floating docks were on the eastern and western ends of the island, each with several small fishing boats, and today, would have the two yachts used by the Apprentices for these meetings. At first, Barnes wondered why they would even need face-to-face meetings in the days of telephones and email. Rose had given him her indulgent schoolteacher smile when he had voiced that concern.

"Spies, Michael. Assume every telephone conversation has a third party listening. Computers? I know the Machinist says they are safe, but the Artisan taught her everything she knows. Anything she makes, he can break."

So truly important business was conducted in person, and there were places like this for each combination of the nine organizations to meet with one another.

From the dock, a winding path climbed the fifty feet to the top of the plateau. A stone wall protected the inner house from the ocean, and because this was stone raised by two Physurgists, it was latticed with veins of iron and thus harder than any normal rock. Inside the walls, two stone houses stood at opposite ends of the compound. They were deceptively luxurious, as they were made of the same hard stone as the outer ramparts. Barnes had been in the one on the west, the Mueller home, and it had been very pleasant. Every amenity they could want, all running off a generator provided by the Machinist. The only things they didn't have were guns. None of the island's staff were allowed weapons.

Inside the compound, in the areas where they would get the most sun, small vegetable gardens bloomed. Fertile soil had been raised up along with the rocks, and when it was depleted, more was brought from the mainland. The island received shipments of food and other goods once a month from each side, more than enough to live on. They supplemented that with fishing and a little farming.

In the center of the courtyard, a stone tower went another thirty feet into the air. Barnes had never been to the top of it, and had only seen into the south-facing door he now waited outside of. From a distance, the crown of the tower appeared to be an outdoor patio. He guessed there was a table and chairs up there, probably sculpted from the living stone, and the view was the entirety of the endless Atlantic. Rose and Anansi were up there now, discussing whatever Apprentices discussed.

Two families had run the island for its hundred-year existence. The Muellers, taken from Nova Scotia, were on the west. On the east, the family was Ghanaian. Apparently, the custom for surnames in Ghana had more to do with the day of the week the babies were born than anything to do with lineage. It seemed silly, but when it came to names, Barnes had lost the high ground.

In theory, the two families were supposed to keep to their side of the island and never interact with one another. They were never to go into the central courtyard between the two houses where Barnes and Daoud now stood. The number of obviously-mixed children in both households said that rule had been ignored. No one commented on it, but Barnes was fairly certain that at this point the two families had far more loyalty to one another than they had to either the Lion or the Twins. That was probably for the best.

From what he understood, the families were unclear as to the nature of their employers. Sometimes he wondered what they thought these strange, well-armed people were. Drug-runners maybe. Pirates probably. Anything but what they actually were. The people lived there for that very reason. They were, in theory, another line of defense against the Apprentices present actually using their magic. In practice, the people were the nice folks who occasionally brought Barnes and his men tall glasses of fruit juice.

The locals referred to Rose Cross as "the Red Lady," as she only wore black and red with the occasional accent of silver or gold. In the sun, she covered every inch of flesh with fluttering red, looking like an uptown Bedouin, a parasol in one gloved hand. They called Anansi "the Dark Man" in whispers, referring to his long black coat and the hood pulled up over his head. His skin was an unhealthy pale gray, and whenever he passed Barnes, the soldier felt his skin tighten with instinctive revulsion.

Barnes had been the second man off the boat an hour earlier, following Ramirez onto the floating dock. Barnes didn't have to issue a command, his men fanning out into a protective zone around the Apprentice. They swept the landing zone with their weapons, short and brutal H&K MP-5s. No one was expecting trouble, but that didn't mean they would let anything slide. Not with the safety of Rose Cross in their hands.

There were ten men, seven of them former Navy SEALS like Barnes, Bennett, an ex-Army Ranger, Tomko, an ex-Marine, and MacDonald, ex-Joint Task Force 2 from Canada. Though all were cross-trained, they had their specialties, from Corso the medic to Righetti the driver. The final member of the squad could not be seen, as she was being carried in the mirror in Barnes's breast pocket. She was Zeryss, a thraxian eta-female, perfect for evening the odds and a nasty surprise for anyone who tried to catch them unaware. Barnes had once found thraxians creepy, and it was a normal rite of passage for anyone working for the Twins to slowly soften their stance toward the inhuman members of the organization. For his part, Barnes found them to be useful tools, and he considered Zeryss to be a full member of the team, as important as any other.

Barnes thought the men working directly for Rose were the finest in the organization. Like their mistress, they were the intellectuals amongst the soldiers. They weren't meatheads like the Machinist's grease-parade or the bums who sat on their asses claiming to work for Ghostwalker. Rose Cross was the right hand of the Twins, their spymaster, their diplomat, the one they loved even more than their heir. And Michael Barnes was the leader of the team whose only job was to keep her safe.

He loved Rose, of course. Everyone on her team did. In his younger days, he had nurtured romantic fantasies about the woman whose life he valued more than his own. In his mind, he saved her and she confessed her undying love a hundred times. The danger with fantasies around a Theurgist like Rose was that his mind was an open book to her. Hell, it was possible she planted those fantasies in there herself to create loyalty. It would have been less than a trifle.

She was beautiful, and in the beginning, that had been the source of what he thought was romantic love. With her ghost-white skin, her pale red eyes, the fall of white hair, she was unique and exquisite. Then there was her power. She was one of the most dangerous people in the world, who worked in thoughts the way sculptors worked in clay. And then he had actually gotten to know her. Unlike many of the other immortals in the League, Rose stayed close to her humanity through the minds of others. It created a contradiction, someone both of and above mankind. As he had aged farther and farther past Rose's apparent youth, the love started feeling more and more like a schoolboy crush, and he left it behind.

The tattoo on the inside of his right forearm was a memory of that crush. He kept it covered now, a little ashamed of his earlier romanticism. A lot of the men got them for either the reasons Barnes did, or out of a sense of *esprit d'corps*. It was her sigil, a rose winding around a cross. He thought Daoud and the rest of Anansi's men had the right idea with their spider patch, although sometimes he felt that a mere patch didn't convey the depths of loyalty a soldier had to his mistress.

The men had waited on the dock as Rose stepped out onto the wooden planks. Her red robes snapped and rippled in the stiff salt wind, the silver earwig brooch on her chest flashing in the sun. The two largest of the men, Tomko and Washington, stood on either side of her, big bodies ready to intercept any bullets no one thought were coming. The path, partly shielded by rocks on the seaward side, wound the fifty feet to the top of the plateau. The two switchbacks made it an easy walk, but it also made it a nightmare to secure.

Barnes ordered Ramirez and Bennett ahead. They sprinted up the path to secure the top. A moment later, he waved again, and MacDonald and Righetti sprinted up to secure the second switchback. And a moment later, he gestured and Sakai and Gardea took the first. The final group was Barnes, the medic Corso, and the two big men, Tomko and Washington, around the Apprentice. They went through the stone arch to the western house. The structure was in two parts, a second story connecting them. A path led beneath this out into the courtyard.

As they stepped back into the sun, Daoud nodded to Barnes, and the American nodded back.

It had been the same routine for fifteen years. The first time he had gone with Rose up this path, he had known her in much the same way as the inhabitants of Darius Island. She was Rose Cross, but Barnes didn't really know what that meant. She might as well have been the Red Lady.

He had been terrified. His commanding officer had been vague about the purpose of the meeting. Barnes knew now that was because the old man didn't have a clear idea what it was for either. Another of the unguessable things immortals did with their time.

Barnes had been jittery on the ride out, barely managing to sleep on the boat. He thought it would go away when the meeting finally happened, with sick anticipation turning into relief. Instead it got worse. He fought the persistent feeling of needing a toilet, telling himself it was all in his head. It wasn't so much the fear of being shot, but the terror of disappointing his new employers. There was no telling what they did to soldiers who failed at their tasks.

When they emerged into the courtyard, he saw the Lion's men for the first time, arrayed around the east side. No one was leveling their weapons, but they were there, assault rifles cradled in their arms, an unspoken threat. At the time, he didn't know what to make of the spider with the skull on its abdomen, but it was ominous. Most of the men, Barnes knew, were recruited from various militaries, gangs, and criminal enterprises. They weren't up to the Twins' men in terms of training, but this made them unpredictable. Barnes went into that meeting not knowing what to expect.

He made eye contact with another man in his early twenties, who was regarding Barnes's group with barely-hidden fear. The other man nodded to Barnes reflexively. He nodded back. He saw it in the other man's face, and knew it was in his own: the silent greeting calmed them both. That was how he met Daoud, though it would be several years before he would actually get the name.

Though the soldiers sometimes vanished, most often killed but rarely retired, Barnes and Daoud remained constants. Eight years ago, Daoud was the head of Anansi's detail. The year after that, Barnes was the head of Rose's. At his first meeting as squad leader, he found himself fidgeting while they stood outside the door to the tower.

He looked down to find Daoud holding out cigarettes, one dark brown smoke extending from the pack. Barnes took it with a thankful nod, and both men smoked in silence. The tobacco was sweet and spicy, the exotic taste adding to the surreal feeling of finally being in charge.

At the next meeting, Barnes held out a hand. "Barnes," he said.

"Daoud," he said, and took it. Barnes knew Daoud was not the other man's real name, not the one his parents had given him, but it was real enough.

"Thanks for the cigarette."

"It was nothing."

That was the limit of their talk. Occasionally they would share a smoke. Later, Daoud started bringing tea in a thermos, and Barnes ended up craving the stuff. It was always in the back of his mind to try to get some for his home, but that felt wrong. The tea was a way for two soldiers on opposite sides to bond while waiting for their masters, and to have it somewhere else felt like he was trivializing it.

As they were drinking it, listening to the Atlantic roar angrily against the rocks down below, Daoud cleared his throat. "Barnes, I was wondering."

"What were you wondering?"

"Do you know this? The 5th Avenue bar? It's candy."

Barnes chuckled. "Yeah, sure, I know it."

"It is very good candy. But it only tastes right when you get American ones."

"Oh? When were you in Pemhakamik?"

Daoud blanched, but he forced a grin Barnes could almost believe. "I *hear*."

"I'm sure you do."

After that, Barnes started bringing a candy bar for his friend. The other man ate slowly, savoring each bite. Barnes was positive even if Daoud could get them, he wouldn't, for the same reason Barnes avoided the tea in his normal life.

It was another several meetings before they traded origins. Daoud had pegged Barnes's accent as American, but nothing more than that. Barnes explained that he was from a small town in New Jersey called Penns Grove. Daoud nodded politely.

"How about you?"

"Ever hear of Al-Uqsor?" Daoud asked, and it was impossible to miss the pride in the man's voice.

Barnes knew damn well what Daoud was talking about, but couldn't resist messing with him a little. "Luxor? You mean like the casino in Vegas?"

"Vegas? No! It's the... oh, I see. You think you're funny." Daoud smiled. Apparently he thought Barnes was funny too.

"There are houses and stuff?"

"Oh, yes. It's a modern city! We have the ruins of Thebes, of course. Incredible things from the dawn of man. Egypt is the cradle of civilization, you know."

"Don't tell the Artisan's men that. They're always going on about Baghdad."

Daoud made a disgusted sound. "Clay farmers. Luxor is home to the Valley of the Kings. That's what we have. Kings."

"Had."

"Well, yes, had. Although I suppose you and I know differently," he said, nodding up to the tower where the Apprentices spoke.

"I suppose we do. To the true kings and queens of this world."

"That, I will drink to."

They clinked their tin cups together in front of the yawning door into the tower.

That had been the final barrier to conversation. After that, during the meetings, Barnes and Daoud would spend the time talking, each leaning up against the cool stone of the tower, tasting the salt on the wind and the spice in the tea. The conversations were casual, and Barnes could almost forget both of them were soldiers on opposite sides, carrying loaded weapons.

Sports talk was inevitable. It started when Barnes must have been looking preoccupied, although he hadn't realized it.

"What's wrong?"

"Oh, nothing. The Giants lost on a field goal." He paused, then clarified. "Football."

"I love football!"

"No, you love soccer."

"I love what you call soccer."

They couldn't agree on anything with a ball, but both men enjoyed mixed martial arts. They had undergone some of the same training, and could follow the action with an expert's eye. It became a tradition between them to dissect the previous fight nights, or if the other had missed it, update him on the particulars. They debated endlessly over effective techniques, Barnes siding with wrestlers who smothered their opponents, while Daoud preferred crafty jiu-jitsu artists. "They don't win as much, but when they do, they finish."

"Winning is the whole point," Barnes said many times.

Daoud would dismiss that with a wave.

At one meeting, Daoud took a deep drink of his tea, and said, "You know, the first time I came here, I was frightened of you."

"Of me?"

"Of the Twins' men. Oh, yes. American Special Forces all? They say you're all seven feet high, that you train to kill a man with your bare hands, all sorts of things."

"We're not all American."

"I did not know that then."

"Actually, you should be scared of the Canucks we have." Barnes smiled, putting the other man at ease, but it was true. Almost every Canadian soldier in the Twins' organization came from Joint Task Force 2, cold-weather specialists who were exclusively trained to go into enemy territory and kill high-value targets. "We hear horror stories about you too."

"Oh?"

"Sure. We hear how many of you are just butchers who used to work for some warlord, or ex-pirates who would kill and eat you without thinking twice."

"Well, we're not cannibals." He glanced at Barnes out of the corner of his eye, and the American laughed. Daoud broke into a smile as he saw his joke landing.

"That's comforting at least."

"Sadly, it is not far from the truth. The Lion makes do with what he has. In the old days, if he wanted real, professional soldiers, he comes to Egypt. But sometimes he wants those bloodthirsty killers you were talking about. At least now we have men from the African Union joining the organization. They are good men."

"Sometimes you have to wonder what they're thinking."

"Soldiers?"

"No, the Magi. You said the Lion wants bloodthirsty killers. How do you know? Have you asked him?"

Daoud looked scandalized. "We've never spoken."

"Of course you haven't. I've never spoken to my mistresses either, and you and I are fairly highly-placed soldiers. Sure, we're not guarding the heirs, but both Rose Cross and Anansi are vital to our respective organizations."

Daoud nodded, hiding the swell of pride. Barnes felt it too. Even just saying the words reminded him of the importance of his task.

"What are you trying to say?" Daoud asked.

"We're trying to give human motivations to the Lion and the Twins when it's possible they don't have them. They're something greater than human now. Sure, they're young by the standards of the League, but they have a couple hundred years under their belts."

"You're saying that there is another reason why my master might want these men?"

"Sure. And we have no way of really guessing. What if he's preparing for something a hundred, or two hundred, or a thousand years down the line?"

"With mortal men?"

"Okay, maybe not. But you never know."

"I suppose not."

"When I first joined, I thought that just because the Twins look like girls, they were girls. Once you see the things they do, that goes right out the window."

Daoud nodded, obviously seeing a memory in his mind of the Lion wielding his power. They were quiet for the rest of their time, trying to understand the nature of their immortal masters, but knowing they never truly would.

At another meeting, Daoud finally asked Barnes a question he had been waiting for. "So, tell me. Are you married?"

"Oh, no," Barnes said, maybe a little too quickly.

"Is that policy in your organization?"

"Not really. It's frowned upon, I guess. Anyone you marry would have to be read into the secrets, and it's seen as an extravagance. It still happens every now and then. Most guys wait until they retire."

"Is that what you're waiting for?"

"Hell, no. I don't even know if I'm going to make it that far. Odds are, I won't."

Daoud offered a rueful nod. "So you're not waiting. Why then?"

"It's a cliché, but I haven't met the right woman."

"Every woman can be the right woman if you meet her on the right day."

"That what happened to you?"

"Oh, yes. It happens to everyone eventually, I think. It will happen to you."

Barnes didn't ask for Daoud's wife's name. It would have been rude, forcing the other man to give a false name. A man should never have to lie about the person he loves.

And now, the friendship had lasted long enough for the two of them to discuss things they probably should not have. So a little more than an hour after Rose Cross disappeared into the tower, and Daoud had eaten his candy bar and they had hashed over the most recent fights, they started really talking.

Daoud looked over Barnes's men. "A lot of new faces," he said.

"Lost a couple men recently. There was a little dust up this last winter with some of the Priestess's people." The Twins had gotten what they wanted out of the situation, but six of Barnes's men were dead. The new guys had yet to see a fight and were probably as nervous as he had been during his first meeting here.

"During the creation of the new Familiar."

Barnes nodded, raising an eyebrow.

"Sorry," Daoud said. "When the Twins create a new Familiar, it is news. No other Familiars have that kind of raw power."

"Or need such elaborate rituals to make."

"You have my sympathies for the loss of your men. Jihaz claimed two of mine not long ago," Daoud said, naming the Artisan's finest engine of war.

"Only two? That's a minor miracle."

"Fortunately, my master was kept in reserve, just observing if Edunara could do anything special against Jihaz. You know, lightning against machinery?"

Barnes nodded. "And?"

Daoud shook his head. "We succeeded in angering him, I believe."

Barnes chuckled. "We didn't know that could be done either."

"Then I call it a victory. None of yours create lightning, do they?"

"No. I was just curious. Sometimes I thank God we don't have to deal with the Artisan that much."

"I do the same thing, except about the Priestess."

"At least we don't work for the Artisan. Ki is totally surrounded."

"True," Daoud allowed. "But at least then you wouldn't have to be worried about Jihaz."

"Yeah, there are four others just as bad."

Both men laughed. Barnes realized something as they joked about the supernatural enforcers of the secret masters of the world: he used to think of himself primarily as an ex-SEAL, but that was no longer accurate. He had much more in common with Daoud—a man from the other side of the world, whose real name he would never know and who used to serve an entirely different military—than anyone still in the United States Navy. Barnes had taken an oath to the USA, but when he started working for the Twins, that oath was gone, replaced by one far more powerful to someone far older. The particulars would have been different, but Daoud probably had much the same experience. The loyalty Barnes had for Rose Cross and the Twins, Daoud had for Anansi and the Lion. Barnes had more in common with Daoud than he had with almost anyone in the world. This epiphany came in the midst of the subdued laughter, and he was positive Daoud had come to the same conclusion.

"It's a strange life we've found, no?" Daoud said.

Barnes opened his mouth to respond when he heard a keening wail. It was nothing of this earth, and it was coming from the top of the tower. A second later, the unmistakable sounds of Rose's heels quickly descending the stone staircase echoed from the open door.

He knew it even before his conscious mind had made the connection: the reason he was there, the thing that had never happened in fifteen years was happening. Daoud gaped up at the tower, mind putting things together a fraction of a second slower than Barnes.

No matter what had happened before, each man had one responsibility: make certain his master made it out alive.

Daoud turned to Barnes, fear bleeding into his eyes. Barnes never had time to consider a decision. It was already made, nerves already firing, muscles already tensing. In reflex, we learn what is truly valuable. Conscious thought and feelings are nothing.

Daoud put a hand up. "Wait!"

But Barnes had already shot his friend three times at point blank range.

Daoud crumpled to the ground and was still.

A half-second later, the automatic weapons fire chattered through the courtyard. Barnes felt Zeryss, the thraxian, tapping inside his breast pocket, ready to come into this world. He tapped twice, a signal to hold for the time being. He dove into the tower, Tomko and Washington right behind. Rose was already down the stairs, her parasol gone. She clutched her chest as though her heart were giving out, and when she saw her men, relief exploded across her face.

Barnes looked up, seeing the interior of the tower for the first time. A stone staircase spiraled up the inside of the walls. Anansi was near the top. Barnes sprayed the stairs with bullets, forcing Anansi back while the other two men hustled Rose out into the courtyard. Barnes fired once more, and was back out into the sun.

The courtyard was littered with bodies. The last of Daoud's men fell with a bullet in his head from Sakai as Barnes's men retreated down the rocky path toward the dock. They cast off, and the yacht was heading back for Pemhakamik. There were several wounded, but only one man, Righetti, had been killed.

Corso went to Rose first, but she said, "I'm fine. A few scrapes. See to the men."

No one else would die that day. Barnes tried to find some comfort in that.

Several months later, they returned to Darius Island. Barnes never got the specifics, but Rose and Anansi had worked everything out. Apologies had been exchanged, and the relationship had been repaired to the point where they could once again meet. Rose never elaborated, and he never asked. He had received a new man, Berg, and had been satisfied with the kid's performance while putting him through the paces.

They tied up at the docks and Barnes sent his men up the same way as he had before. They emerged into the courtyard to find they had arrived before the Lion's men. Rose Cross went into the tower to await Anansi while Barnes took up his position outside the tower. The other men he arrayed on the west side of the courtyard.

The blood from the previous firefight had been cleaned up. The only evidence anything had happened were a few chips in some of the stone walls. The people were a little more nervous, staying inside and away from the windows this time. He wondered if any of them had been hit with a stray round. That was another question he'd probably never get an answer to.

Anansi came into the courtyard, shrouded in black. His group of bodyguards were all new faces, and Barnes felt a little pride at the efficiency of his men. Anansi passed Barnes and went up into the tower. The commander of Anansi's detail took up position on the other side of the doorway.

He was tall and lean, maybe in his late thirties. His skin was a deep black, and a scar spanned one cheek. He looked over at Barnes, and the American saw nervousness in the other man's keen eyes.

Barnes gave the man a nod.

The man nodded back.

The
Menagerie

THE DINER STOOD AT THE INTERSECTION of two roads. Light spilled from the picture windows onto the gray gravel spread unevenly over the dirt parking lot. There were only a few cars there at that time of night, cold and lonely under an endless sky. The two roads were at right angles, a pair of simple stop signs marking the intersection. Each road disappeared into the distance, two-lane ribbons of gray cutting through green fields all the way to the horizon. Look far enough, and there were individual buildings to be found, mostly farmhouses sitting at the end of dusty access roads, but the diner was as remote as it was possible to be.

A blind man worked the grill, though at the time it was empty. He got his instructions from the tired-eyed waitress in a raspy warble, a rapid-fire burst of jargon that the cook never forgot. The waitress leaned against the counter, gazing off into the dark beyond the windows. Occasionally, she would come out to freshen the coffee of the two people in the diner, sitting in one of the booths lining the picture window.

One of these people was Brian Lopez. He was in his late-twenties and handsome, clothes stretched tight over a gym-hardened body. His olive skin was smooth, his dark hair short. He looked like a man who spent time on his appearance, but the cracks were beginning to show. There was the beginning of a sweat-stain on the armpits of his v-neck shirt, and his blue jeans were covered in road dust almost to the knee. Lack of sleep bruised his eyes, patchy stubble growing on his cheeks and chin.

The coffee had made him jittery, but he spent more of his time stirring and staring at it than he did drinking. He was barely coming around to a point. "It's around here somewhere. I know that much. I can't find it, but when I went looking, I found you. Thank you for meeting me here."

"Think nothing of it."

"I heard you can help."

"Perhaps."

"I need to tell you the whole story. Then you'll know if you can help me."

"Yes."

* * *

I don't remember which one of us actually suggested the road trip. I had just gotten my sommelier certification and Paul had a whole week of PTO saved up. It was just the right time for some kind of vacation together, and we had been a couple for a year at that point, and it was beginning to look like we were in it for the long haul. A nice long trip would be the last first for us as a couple.

Paul has a thing about Americana. Some of our friends mistook it for a hipsterish appreciation of irony, but that was only one small part of it. Truth be told, Paul legitimately enjoyed silly things like the world's largest ball of twine. He loved greasy spoons in small towns. He was fascinated by local legends. It was in the back of his mind to write a book, and I wanted to encourage him so maybe he could quit the office job he barely tolerated for something he was passionate about. After all, he had supported me while going after my dream.

The idea was to go from our home in Portland all the way to visit Paul's cousin in Charleston. Paul's whole family knew he was gay, and his cousin was the one most cool with the idea. She wanted to meet me, which was terrifying.

"She'll love you," Paul said.

"How do you know?"

"There's the obvious, that you're you."

It was a big step for anyone, and the stakes were higher for us than they would be for a straight couple. Paul looked so hopeful, his round face set in a hopeful smile. I kissed him. "Stop being cute."

"So that's a yes."

We left a week later. Paul seemed to want to hit every single landmark on the way across the country. I drove for most of it, while he flipped through one of several guidebooks, each one covered in his scrawl. "Oh, take this exit," Paul would say. "Down this road here. There should be a turnoff."

And I would ask what we were doing winding through some back road through the Rockies or down a dirt access road in the middle of fields of green.

"Carhenge!" he would say. Or "Matchbook Museum!" Or "Bugsy Siegel's favorite pancakes!" His happy exclamations were all the elaboration I was going to get. Knowing that something so simple would bring him that much joy, I couldn't very well say no. So I was subjected to every last curiosity the country had to offer.

Subjected. No, that's not right. I mean, I complained. Who wouldn't? It started to grow on me, even though I knew every ridiculous knickknack he bought was going to have to go somewhere in our apartment. It was more about the little smile he had on his face after one of these stops, when he would add a little check mark next to the entry in his guidebook.

We were in Kansas, I think, but I can't be sure. We had gone up and down so many roads, I was all turned around. "Pull over here," Paul said.

"Why, is there a reptile zoo nearby?"

"No, I have to take a leak," he said with a laugh.

I pulled off the road and got out. All around us were rolling fields. A soft wind ruffled the grass, and it was just one of the most peaceful moments I had ever experienced. There was no one else within sight, and I could see for miles up and down the road. On the other side of the little gravel turn off, Paul had climbed down into a little wash for some privacy, but it wasn't like there was anyone to see. For all I knew, we were the only people in the world.

I closed my eyes and felt the wind and smelled the fields. It was clean and quiet in the way nothing ever is in the city. I wanted Paul up there with me so he could feel it too. Nothing is really real until you share it with the person you love.

"Brian?"

I opened my eyes. The world was blue. My head buzzed. Paul called me again, and I went around the far side of the car. Paul was about three feet below, standing in the depression by the side of the road.

"What?" I asked him.

"Come down here."

"So I can stand in your piss? No, thanks."

"Just come down here."

I picked my way down the little hill to stand with him. A little vegetation grew in the stony dirt at the bottom of the wash. "Okay, I'm down here."

"I was thinking of taking a walk. Stretch my legs a little. I don't think we have another stop until Kentucky."

"We're stopping in Kentucky?"

"Don't worry, you'll love it. It's a hotel haunted by some country singer."

He was right, a walk would do the both of us some good. The

day was warm, but not unpleasantly so, and at that moment the thought of being cooped up in the car for another second was a bit more than I could take. "All right," I said.

He and I followed the furrow in the field, moving out perpendicular to the car. It would make finding our way back that much easier. We could see over the top of the little gully, to the endless fields of whispering grass. A trickle of water ran down the middle of the wash, tracing our path. A few dragonflies hummed in the still air, stalking their prey.

We walked in silence. I don't really know why. The air closed around me even though the wind was obviously blowing. I felt as though I were backstage somewhere, and as I looked, the prairie, the wash, all of it started feeling two-dimensional. If I went to it and peeked around the side, I would see that it was unpainted wood. I didn't, though. I couldn't do anything but follow the wash because no matter what I thought I saw, I didn't want to do anything else.

We kept walking, and I felt like the car was miles behind. I never looked at that either. Out in the field about a hundred yards away, there was a farmhouse. I didn't remember seeing it before. It seemed to have folded up from the prairie, yet it looked like it had stood in the same spot for a hundred years. Outside, I could see people moving around, a woman with a cotton dress flapping over her thin frame shading her eyes to peer back at me. Her laundry fluttered in the wind. Even she looked like a flat cut-out, and when she moved it was in the stuttered cadence of animation.

I don't know if Paul saw them too. We kept walking, and the wash deepened. Soon the house was out of sight, and all I could hear was the steady whirring of the dragonflies. The sides rose up around us, and I could see rocks buried in the dirt. Some had the whorls of fossils, others little crystals in clumps. These details alone had no sense of the unreality of the world above, existing in three dimensions while everything else was only two. The walls of the furrow had become concave, the lip overhanging. Living vines totally different from the grass dripped from them, hiding the dirt walls in a green curtain.

That's how we almost missed it. Sometimes I wonder what would have happened if we had kept walking. We were both in such a state, I think we would have had I not said anything. Like that day would have gone on forever and we would still be walking.

At least we would be together.

I saw it out of the corner of my eye. For whatever reason, I had to point it out. I don't know why. The long silence had turned my voice into a rusty croak, but it was enough. "What's that?"

Paul stopped as though on a tether. He was silent, consciousness rolling back into place. He turned and looked at me, and for a moment, it was as though I was a stranger. Then recognition flooded back into his eyes. "What's what?"

I pushed aside the hanging vines while a dragonfly hummed past.

It was a door. Circular and made of banded wood, it looked like a hobbit hole. An honest-to-god hobbit hole, somewhere out in the middle of the prairie. It was larger than you would have thought. Even at six feet tall, Paul would have more than enough clearance to go in without stooping.

"A door?" he said.

We both stared at it, the sun's rays leeching the will from us.

Finally, Paul moved to it and put his hand on the brass handle. "Let's check it out."

I don't know why I was afraid at those words. But it came on me suddenly in a wave. I wanted to turn around and head back for the car, and I knew that for the first time I would be able to do that. I opened my mouth to say something.

But Paul opened the door.

The door looked like it should have sounded a sepulchral creak. It was almost completely silent, save for the deep inhale of a cavern being exposed to the day. It was a tunnel, sloping gently downward into the earth. Evenly spaced antique wall lanterns lit the way.

"What is this place?" The kind of wonder I heard in Paul's voice has usually been burned out of us by adulthood to make room for cynicism.

"I don't know." Though I was still scared, the same wonder was in my voice.

Paul took a step into the tunnel. I didn't stop him and couldn't if I tried. The lure of the place was too strong. I took a step into the cool darkness. The air smelled of jasmine. The walls were mortared stone, and the floor was marble. It looked like a tunnel that might lead into a castle. I couldn't tell how long it was. Though there was light, the exact dimensions were baffled with shadows and perspective.

The door closed behind us. With the soft thunk, the fear returned. "Are you sure we should be doing this?"

"Don't worry. Whoever lives here, we can tell them we got lost. It's all innocent."

"What if it's some crazy militia of homophobes?"

"What self-respecting homophobe builds with real marble?" he asked, pointing at the flagstones under our feet.

"Paul..."

"Don't worry," he said, putting an arm around my waist. "We'll be fine. Trust me."

I knew I wasn't going to win the argument, especially not since I wanted to see what was in this place almost as much as he did. So I nodded, he took my hand, and we started down the tunnel.

The lanterns were not a uniform color. Some were the soft amber of open flames, but others were electric blue, or glowstick green. We passed the first one, and found that between every lantern, tapestries hung from the walls. I was no expert, but they looked medieval at first. We paused at the first, splashed with gold light from one lantern and purple from another. The tapestry was in rich, subtle, and deep hues of gold, red, and a little bit of green and blue. It depicted a cityscape, and I thought it might represent New York, but could not be certain. Where the knights should be, and in the same repeating style, were men in suits and fedoras, carrying tommy guns in the place of swords and shields. They were being led by a large black man whose skin was marked with symbols.

"What the hell is this?" Paul asked me.

"I was going to ask you."

"Come on, there's another one."

The next tapestry was in a similar style, this one showing a giant snake fighting with a huge stone man. All around them were more of these odd knights, although these were dressed in more modern representations of army fatigues. The other tapestries were like this, with some more self-consciously modern than others, though all in the same style. Some had various monsters doing battle with one another, others had what looked like wizards, or armies of bizarre creatures. From the weaving, it was clear that someone had spent a great deal of time making these things, yet from the subject matter they were obviously not antiques.

We were far into the tunnel before it dawned on one of us to look at the lanterns. Something had moved out of the corner of my eye, and I went to the closest lantern shedding amber through the tunnel. A small swarm of fireflies whirled in a little tornado. "Paul, come here. These are full of fireflies."

"No, they're not. You're not going to believe this."

He was at another lantern, this one lighting his face in a clean, underwater blue. I went over to him and looked in. The light was coming from these impossibly delicate fish, like nothing I had ever seen. They were slender, with huge gossamer fins lined in sparkling luminescence. Other glowing patches adorned their heads, flanks, and back. They swam through the lantern, casting their gentle light into the hall.

Paul and I went from lantern to lantern, fascinated by what we found. In another container, a verdant fern sprouted from black soil. The light came from little worms we first thought to be caterpillars. As Paul put his face close to the glass of the lantern, one of the caterpillars reared up on the back third of its body. The bottom unzipped, revealing bladed grasping limbs. Paul jerked his head back, then smiled at me self-consciously. "Guess he doesn't like me."

At another, the lantern was half full of water, with a muddy bank leading up to some flat rocks. The light came from minute salamanders, swimming through the clear water, or basking on the rocks. Their sinuous bodies glowed all over in a pleasant blue-green.

Tiny birds, each one no bigger than a fingernail, fluttered through another. They were close to hummingbirds, the light coming from little diamond-like dewy drops on the tips of their iridescent feathers. They fed from fiery jungle flowers that I was pretty certain were not from this planet.

In the next, furry creatures the size of pennies cavorted on bonsai trees. The light came from their luminous eyes, shining like red-gold flashlights. They played with one another, totally unaware of the giants peering through the glass at them.

Paul gasped at one of the lanterns, and I couldn't imagine what had surprised him. Not after seeing creatures that obviously had no earthly analogue. I looked into the lantern he was gazing into. A tiny city looked back, the lights coming from the windows of skyscrapers, of streetlamps lining the minute streets, or the neon signs on the various buildings. I thought it had to be a model until Paul pointed to something moving. "People," he breathed.

They were like ants, but I could see that they were human. Going about their business in the city in the lantern. "It can't be," I said.

But it was, and we both knew it.

"We have to see more," Paul said. He was right. Whatever this was, the first of the wonders were just being used as simple lights. Made me wonder what could possibly be ahead.

The tunnel opened up twenty feet ahead and below. There were no more lanterns, but there was plenty of light falling in from whatever was there. The floor evened out. It was difficult to know how far underground we were, but it felt like miles. The door into the tunnel had been swallowed up in the gloom, although I wondered how much of it was the odd feeling that had descended as soon as we began our walk.

We stepped out onto the level floor and found ourselves in something that was almost an antechamber. The stone floor stretched in a rough semi-circle for thirty feet around the mouth of the tunnel. After that, the floor seemed to just stop, except for three looping paths in different directions.

As I looked up, there were neither walls nor ceiling. It was impossible to conceive of. We were underground, yet where there should have been stone or dirt was a starry sky. It was not an earthly sky; everything seemed too large, too close. Ribbons of luminescent gas wound through the cosmos. Planets, like nothing in the solar system, loomed large. Stars shone of every color, glittering like fist-sized jewels. I was stunned, taking in the beauty of what was around me. I thought that I should be dead, but the temperature was comfortable, the air tasting softly of flowers. For the hundredth time since we found this place, I wondered where we could possibly be.

I reached out, taking Paul's hand. His fingers twined through mine. I felt the wonder flowing through him. Neither of us could believe what we had found.

I don't know how long we stood there gaping at the sky. Paul snapped out of it first. "What's that?" he asked.

I followed his attention down to a machine sitting at the edge of the flagstone floor. I walked over and looked down past the lip of the stones. There was more of the big sky spinning into infinity below me. Vertigo pushed me back.

The machine was a box about as tall as I was, with pipes and tubes running over and through it. It was almost self-consciously retro, like some hot-rodder's conception of what something would look like in the future. A menu was on one side, and there were six lighted panels on the front, each one cycling through several different still images of the food described on the menu. Lastly, in the middle, right at about the level of a kitchen counter, was a larger, unlighted panel.

The top items were all fairly normal, the kinds of things you'd see at some hipster food truck. There were golfball-sized cinnamon donuts, a lobster taco, and watermelon with jalapeños and pickled tomatoes. After that, the selections became at best unappetizing, and at worst poisonous. There was a raw beef heart with wasabi mayo, a blood sausage with chipotle ketchup and dijon, and a live rat with blood oranges and scallions. It offered a cone of Northern California topsoil finished with fresh moss and ginger, a deer bladder filled with sage smoke and rosemary, and a gold bar topped with flakes of copper and platinum.

Paul and I exchanged a look. He hit the button and made his selection. The machine gave an authoritative thump, and a plate appeared in the unlighted panel. The lights kicked on, illuminating a silver plate slowly rotating, the gold bar, covered in metal shavings, all of it glittering. The panel opened, and Paul pulled the plate out.

"Is it real?" I asked.

"I don't know. It looks real."

The question was, who would put gold as an option in a vending machine, especially one that didn't charge? The answer was whoever had built this place, and it was abundantly clear that there were many more wonders to be had.

I touched another panel, and with a thump, my selection appeared in the central panel. It was a serving of the lobster tacos. I tasted one. Piping hot, it was the freshest lobster I'd ever had, and I have family in Baja who pull them right out of the water. The seasonings were a perfect blend of sweet and spicy, bringing out and balancing the fluffy lobster meat. Had I gotten that taco from the fanciest restaurant I had ever been to, I would have called it great, and it had been spat out of a vending machine.

As I finished, a previously-hidden panel opened in the front, and I placed the silver tray in. Satisfied, the panel closed. Paul was still standing there, holding his gold bar, the shavings fallen to the floor as precious excelsior. Finally, he put the bar in his pocket, where it bulged and made his pants sag.

"We're dreaming, aren't we?" I asked him.

"Then we're having the same dream."

"Or one of us is dreaming the other."

"Wouldn't be the first time," Paul said.

We picked one of the stone pathways arcing through the night sky. Though there were shining stars and glowing planets all around, the light in this place was constant and pleasant. It felt like the path should go crumbling into space, since it was much too big and delicate to be supported, but underneath the ground felt solid.

The path split, and we turned to the right, and there it was. Since there were no walls, we should have seen it coming from far away, but for whatever reason we didn't. It simply appeared as we were making our way along the path.

What it was, I have no idea. The first thing I noticed was a shimmer in the air, where it would go opaque in a roughly circular section and then become transparent again. Or maybe it was the sheer size of everything: look close enough at anything and it ceases to have meaning. It's only a vast plane of color and light.

When I was finally able to understand what I was looking at, my breath caught in my throat.

I would say it was almost a jellyfish, or at least that's the closest thing I had ever seen to the impossibly huge creatures floating there. There were three, and they seemed to be enclosed by the shimmer, though the wall was invisible until something brushed against it. Inside, they were not floating in water, but rather amongst clouds. A waterfall roared behind them, dumping frothing whitecaps into the abyss. The jellyfish moved their tentacles restlessly, intertwining with all three of the behemoths floating in the sky. Their bells were translucent, organs flickering and flashing in every color I could imagine. I couldn't escape the thought that they were communicating.

There was nothing Paul and I could say to one another. We stayed, enraptured by the massive creatures. When I finally moved, my back and knees were stiff. We had been standing for a long time, though I had no clear memory of it, and I didn't really mind. My hand closed around Paul's and he jumped a little, coming back to reality. We continued along the path, rounding another corner.

This enclosure had the same transparent shield. It shimmered once when a dragonfly the size of a small dog alighted on it. Beyond was a thick jungle, though all the plants looked like ferns of different sizes. It looked like it stretched back a long way and from the sheer size of everything around me, I had no doubt that it did just that. As we stared into the green, I thought maybe this was just some kind of garden. Then there was a rustling.

The dragonfly took flight, but a mass of feathers streaked bright green and black, pounced from the undergrowth and tore the dragonfly from the air. It pinned the insect down with one foot while it ate. I thought it was a bird at first, especially when a frill of blue-and-orange feathers extended from its back. When it looked up, there was no beak, just a mouth of teeth. It cocked its head and darted off into the undergrowth.

At that moment two more almost-birds stalked silently out of the ferns. One dipped a feathered head to sniff at the dragonfly while the other hissed softly. Sickle-claws gleamed from their feet as they peered after their prey. I've seen *Jurassic Park*. I knew what I was looking at. Dinosaurs. Real ones, living and hunting in that cage.

Paul's face was lit up. I had never seen him so happy, a pure sense of joy radiating from him. He only spoke when I nudged him, hard, after a soft poke failed to do the trick. "Dinosaurs, Brian! Here!"

"I know. What do you think? Rich geneticists or something?"

"Who cares? Do you know how much I've always wanted to see real dinosaurs? And there they are! How many do you think they have?"

"I don't know."

Paul moved from his spot only reluctantly and only after I pointed out that there might be more dinosaurs somewhere ahead.

The shimmering bubble enclosed water this time, a deep azure. The creatures lumbering through it were almost whales, but they dwarfed anything on earth. They lacked eyes, but I could feel a humming as they focused their ancient attention on us. The hums became audible a second later, turning into a series of rumbling groans and lingering whistles. The long ribbons streaming from the animal's head and sides were almost like fins, the webbing a diaphanous sheen. The creature's glabrous flesh was unmarred by scars or barnacles.

The pair of leviathans swam down to point their snouts in our direction, and the hums moved in and out of hearing. It was like being stared at by gods. They were trying to talk to us, but there was no way to respond. Eventually, the creatures gave up, flipping over and with a twitch of their massive flukes, soared up and away. I stepped back reflexively; even the idea of their power was enough to move me.

We continued on the path through the stars. It swept over to the right, the night sky growing darker. The nebulae, like shining silk scarves, disappeared. The planets were smaller, darker. Though the amount of ambient light didn't change, this section felt gloomier. The path swooped around, and the next enclosure came into view.

It was a Chinese farming village set against a muddy cliffside. Dilapidated and filthy houses slouched on shelves of ground with emerald green grass sprouting liberally wherever it could. The sky was misty, trees disappearing into the thick fog. At first, I thought the people shuffling through the village were merely beaten down by their imprisonment. I kept looking. Most of them were Asian, though there were a couple white men sprinkled throughout. Their skin was stark white, all of them, and their milky eyes looked at nothing. They went about the business of a village in pantomime. Their muscles remembered what they did, but their conscious minds, if they had those, had forgotten the purpose. It was a village of zombies.

The next enclosure was an open plain, red rocks sprouting from orange soil. Scrubby plants dotted the landscape, along with a few trees. It took me a moment to recognize it as a reasonable facsimile of Australia. The figure standing in the shade of one of the trees might have been human. At first, he looked nude, but his head, hands, and feet were covered in what almost looked like a space suit. There was no demarcation between flesh and suit, so when my eyes traced the thick white lines that ran along the figure's limbs, I had an eerie feeling along my spine. I felt the person's unseen eyes on me, but it neither moved nor spoke.

We moved on. The next enclosure was a step pyramid in the middle of a field in a Central American jungle. A single woman sat on the side of the pyramid. As Paul and I came into view, she waved at us, hopping up and running toward the screen. Her skin was olive, lustrous, and entirely smooth. She had no belly button, no vulva, no nipples. She ran to the edge of the field, right before the shimmering barrier.

"Hey! Hey! Who are you?" She addressed me in Guatemalan-accented Spanish.

"I'm Brian," I said, still trying to figure out what was going on with her.

"Who do you work for?"

"Dominic's. I'm a waiter."

"God damn it."

"What's she saying?" Paul asked. He doesn't speak a word of Spanish. I translated for him. "Ask her why she doesn't have lady parts."

"I speak English," she said, throwing a dirty look at Paul. "And if you prefer..." Her body resculpted itself, first the flesh taking the proper shape, then sprouting hair. As it did so, it took the appearance of polished wood before the olive skin tone reasserted itself. Still, her flesh shone like freshly-buffed furniture. "Better?" she asked, hand saucily on her hip.

"What are you?" Paul said.

"Trapped. The *putas* have me in a fucking zoo!"

"Who?" I asked.

"You have to get me out of here. Find the Keeper. It has the keys. Steal them and come back here. I promise you will be rewarded."

"We don't even know where the locks are."

"I'll help you. Please. You can't leave me here."

We did, Paul dragging me away from the wooden woman's enclosure while she hurled curses after us. First, they were in English, then slipping into enraged Spanish, before becoming something altogether more primal.

The path arced around back toward what I loosely thought of as the center of this zoo. I don't know why I had this feeling exactly, but the enclosure we found here seemed to be in a place of honor. It was a cave in the middle of a peat bog. Distantly, I could hear crashing waves, implying the enclosure was huge.

The creatures inside were humanoid, though each was eight feet tall. Their skin was gray and rubbery, looking like the flesh of a dolphin. They were hunched over, and their noseless faces had only a single vertically-slitted red eye. Their mouths were distended, their teeth almost, but not quite, human. All were male and nude, even in what looked like a chilly environment. There were four of them, and they were sitting around a small fire at the mouth of the cave, cooking a side of beef on a spit. As Paul and I arrived in front of them, they looked up and quickly dismissed us, turning back to the meat crackling and splitting over the fire.

Paul and I moved on. The stars grew bright in the sky, and a nebula fluttered out overhead like a flag. We passed a gas giant looming large just to our right. The gloom had been banished. The pathway split, and Paul and I chose the left one. As the next enclosure came into view, we stopped dead.

The shimmering bubble enclosed a blasted wasteland. Black trees were like gnarled fingers against an ashy sky. A pile of elephant-gray stones rose up in the center, and on the top, a brown serpentine shape brooded. It took my brain a second to register what I was seeing, but it was a dragon. A real dragon. It stretched leathery wings and huffed smoke, its reptilian attention focused on the front of the enclosure.

It was looking at the people there. A woman was kneeling in front of the bubble, looking like she was taking a reading with a machine that had the same retro-future design of the vending machine. She was Hispanic and almost every bit of skin I could see had a tattoo on it, and in her halter top and pedal-pushers, there was a bit on display. She was the hot-rodder whose ideas about future aesthetic created those machines.

Another woman stood nearby in a cotton sundress, eating from a paper cone. She barely seemed to be concentrating on what was happening, granting a little bored interest to the dragon.

"I don't know what you're seeing, but the field is just fine," the kneeling woman said with annoyance.

"The beast keeps testing the boundaries. It's waiting now, because it knows you're here, but as soon as you're gone, it will be back to trying to escape. And what if it does! This is the mistresses' favorite! They would be heartbroken if it got out!" The voice had an odd echo, and sounded masculine. The woman eating didn't seem to be talking, and it wasn't until the speaker moved across the path that I identified it.

A sun, around the size of a beach ball, and glowing yellow, swept over to the kneeling woman. Small planets, ranging from the size of basketballs to golfballs orbited it. Some were gaseous, roiling with many colors. Others were monochrome rocks or chunks of ice. Some had rings, others had tiny moons. It spoke again, huffing prissily, "I'll not be the one to explain that to them."

It was a miniature living solar system.

"Calm down, Keeper," the woman said. "I'll make sure the field is at full strength and keyed to the dragon." She lowered her voice to an irritated mutter that nonetheless carried. "Like it already is."

The woman with the cone turned around, and she fixed me with the greenest eyes I have ever seen. "Come on," I said to Paul.

We quickly backtracked down the path and took the other fork. The enclosure here held a plain of ice, with carved stone stelae poking up through. The creatures lumbering over the ice seemed to be cleaning and maintaining the stelae, occasionally etching a new symbol into the side of one. They were roughly insect, although they were the size of compact cars. Their carapaces changed color in hexagonal patterns. Each creature had a pair of hooked arms coming from the front of it, and a face that almost looked human, though it looked to be formed of iridescent plates.

I was so fascinated by the insects that I almost didn't notice the man lying on the path. He was plainly starving, his skin stark white, his belly bulging, and his limbs under his clothes were like twigs. He had a wispy beard that was mostly brown with a little white. He lay next to a woman's body. She was rotting, but there was no stench from it. His rheumy eyes were focused on the beetles.

I knelt next to him. "Sir? Sir, can you hear me?" I wished I had that taco to give him, but in his state, he'd probably just throw it up.

He whispered something.

"I can't hear you." I leaned closer.

"They're beautiful," he said.

"He's dying," said a female voice behind me.

I stood up and turned. It was the little woman in the sundress. Her bare feet were completely silent on the flagstones. Her black hair was in a tousled pixie cut, and she wore no makeup. She reached into the cone and popped something in her mouth. I remembered the vending machine: a cone of Northern California topsoil with moss and ginger.

"Who are you?"

"You can call me Blackthorn," she said, offering a hand.

I took it. Her skin was soft and cool, like moss. "My name is Brian."

"He's lost," she said, nodding to the dying man.

"What do you mean? Can you help me get him out of here? Maybe to a hospital?" I tried to think. We were in the middle of nowhere. A hospital was a tall order.

"No, I mean, don't waste your time." She sighed. "I'm sorry, that sounded horrible. People who find this place can be fascinated. They don't eat, they don't sleep, not really. They just watch whichever of the creatures caught their fancy until they die." I wanted to argue with her, but there was no lie in what she said.

"What is this place?"

"It's called the Menagerie. It's very hard to find. You have to be in the right state."

"Kansas?"

"Of mind. State of mind. What were you doing in Kansas?"

"I don't really know."

She popped some moss and ginger in her mouth. "You two are in love," she said. "I'm glad for you. But listen, you have to get out of here before that," she nodded to the dying man, "happens to you. I think it's already happening to your friend."

I turned to find Paul enraptured by the beetles. It was similar to how he had stood, frozen, in front of the dinosaurs. I had been the same way when I first saw those magnificent jellyfish creatures. And now we knew what would happen to us if we let that take over.

"Thank you," I said to her.

"Go back the way you came," she said, "and at the first split, go right, then left, then right. Alternate like that until you find the entrance, all right?

"Why are you helping me?"

She shrugged. "I'm a soft touch I guess. Good luck, Brian." Blackthorn turned and walked away. Right as she was about to move out of sight, she called over her shoulder, "Avoid the Keeper if you can."

I grabbed Paul, shaking him. It took him several long moments to drag his eyes off the beetles, and even then he kept glancing in that direction. "What? What is it?"

"Paul, we have to go. Now."

"Go? Why?"

I pointed at the dying man. "This place is dangerous. People can get fascinated. They stay forever, until they die."

"That's ridiculous," he said, though the sight of the dying man had shaken him. "Is he okay? Can we help him?"

"We can't. But we can help us. We can keep from becoming just like him."

I had to drag Paul back down the pathway, and he kept looking back, not at the dying man, but at the beetles and their flashing carapaces.

"Brian, there's more here. You saw the other paths. This place goes on for miles and miles. We've barely seen any of it."

"Are you not listening to me?"

"This is the most amazing place I've ever been, and you want to go! What's wrong with you?"

"Did you forget what I just said to you?"

"You're being silly," Paul said. And now he was fighting me, digging in his heels, trying to shake me off of him. I dragged him past wonders that I could have never imagined, and every one of them pulled at Paul's attention, trying to keep him in the Menagerie forever. He fought without meaning or trying to. It was a battle for every inch of ground, as demons and angels watched from their prisons. Finally, we were close. I knew it was only a single turn to the entryway.

The dinosaurs were out in front of their jungle. Each one ruffling gorgeous multicolored feathers in patterns that hadn't been seen on earth for millions of years. Paul came to a stop. This time he would not budge, leaning away from me, standing stock still, his attention consumed by the creatures he had loved since he was little. A beatific smile spread over his face.

"Paul! We have to go!"

He didn't respond. I was screaming at him, crying the whole time, but it was like he couldn't hear me. He was gone, his attention utterly dominated.

At that moment, the Keeper floated around the corner. The planets orbiting its sun moved a little faster at the sight of us. "You! Stop right there!"

I knew I had a choice, and even though it saved my life, I hate myself for it. I ran.

I don't know if the Keeper followed me. All I could hear was my footsteps on the flagstones and blood in my ears. I ran past the vending machine, to the door, and past all the lanterns.

And then I was outside. It was early morning, the air wet and chilly. Everything was still. I ran along the wash to the car and drove, and kept driving until I couldn't.

* * *

Brian was silent as he finished his story, staring at the cup of coffee in his hand. He never took a single sip and it had gone cold.

When he spoke again, his voice had turned ragged. The memory of crying had shredded his throat as sure as the actual act. "I did the wrong thing. I knew that pretty much immediately. But when I looked for the wash and the door, I couldn't find it. I've been all over the area, and it's just not there. I've heard you can help, and I thought maybe you could show me the way."

"What are you going to do?"

"Get Paul back. Or if he won't come, I'll go in there and die with him. I just know that I don't want to live without him. Can you help me?"

The woman at the other side of the table laced her snow-white fingers together. She looked up at Brian, her red eyes meeting his. "You should try to forget," she said, and then she spoke a few words in no language Brian had ever heard, but the syllables reached into him and plucked the strings of his mind.

She placed a twenty dollar bill on the table, paying for their coffee and giving the waitress the most generous tip she had ever seen.

The woman said to Brian, "Good luck, young man." And she was gone.

Brian sat in the diner, staring at the cold coffee. He thought about the odd albino woman, and wondered what she wanted.

For the life of him, he couldn't remember.

Dead Drop

THE MOTEL ROOM STANK OF SMOKE. Stale smoke, baked into the beige comforter on the bed, into the chair by the window, into the drawn and threadbare curtains, and into the shag carpeting. Fresh smoke too, twining into the room from a burning cigarette clutched between long and shapely fingers. An ashtray on the table held more butts, ground out into dead stubs with more force than was necessary. The smoke hung in the air like a blanket, hardly stirred by the overworked air conditioner stuttering in the corner.

Cecelia Ho paced a worn path through the carpet, occasionally going to the window and peeking through the curtains. The motel was V-shaped, one side running along the side of the main drag, the other poking out toward the water. She looked down at the two-lane thoroughfare of Clementville, and across the street at the combination liquor store and bait shop. The inhabitants went about their business, completely unaware or unconcerned with the woman in Room 15 of the Motel Clement.

She tried to block out Hirrust's face, but it kept returning. The bafflement was strange on the non-human contours of the demon's face and as she followed them in her mind, the guilt reached up to strangle her. She tamped it down with another cigarette, continuing to pace in the cramped and hot room.

She had arrived the previous day around noon. Clementville wasn't even a speck on the map. The car's GPS hadn't known where it was, and if not for Faisal's detailed directions, Cecelia would have missed the turnoff entirely, hidden as it was by magnolia trees, and driven aimlessly through the deep bayou. The sign was old and rusted, though the sultry air had a habit of chewing almost anything apart given enough time.

She had been pleasantly surprised to find an actual town. Certainly not a wealthy one, though nice enough to stay in for the six or so hours she had planned. Perched at the edge of a lake, shores enshrouded by cypress trees, Clementville was a place largely forgotten.

The main street was asphalt, while most of the side roads were dirt or gravel. It wound around once, first approaching, and then following the coastline. The Motel Clement was almost at the end, next to a wooden honky-tonk. Cecelia drove around to the lakeshore side of the motel, parking her rental car in the back of the dirt lot where the cypress trees would shade it from two sides.

She got out of the air conditioned interior, and her clothes immediately stuck to her skin with a fresh layer of sweat. The swamp hummed with insects. She glanced over her shoulder, positive she had already been found. The lake was calm out into the distance, where it disappeared into more cypress trees. Some men waded in the shallows, noodling catfish the size of terriers from underneath rocks or trapping angry crawdads in fine nets.

She hurried into the small lobby, where there wasn't much respite from the oppressive humidity and enervating heat. The desk was chipped, and a single clock ticked beyond. The man behind the desk was fat, and was staring at a football game on a small television that looked older than he was. He barely looked up at Cecelia when she entered. She gave a fake name and paid with a credit card matching that name, the first and probably last charge that card would ever see. She showed him the fake ID and he nodded, checking Anne Chen into the Motel Clement.

Faisal was supposed to be there within the day. In the breathless conversation on the burner, a burner since hurled into Puget Sound, he had calmed her down. In an even voice, he asked what she was doing calling him, and she explained the whole thing. Told him where it went wrong, and why she was using the things in the bag she wasn't ever supposed to have to touch.

The motel room had become a tiny prison. Evidence of her enforced stay was clear. A couple of empty styrofoam containers that had contained greasy catfish po' boys from the honky-tonk next door sat by the ashtray. The bed was unmade from a sleepless night. Her previous day's clothes spilled out of her go bag. Any other change would have to be bought from town, since she was already here longer than intended.

Faisal had not given specifics. Merely to meet him in Clementville, at the only motel in town. He said they would get out from there. She could guess at the broad strokes of the plan. Probably take one of the swamp boats at the little harbor at the end of the street, and from there make it to the edge of the bayou to rendezvous with a seagoing vessel. Sail from the soft Caribbean borders of Pemhakamik to Cuba or the Dominican Republic, and then a flight to somewhere in Ki.

But Faisal was a day late. She tried to avoid speculating on the reasons, but it was impossible not to. Every moment he did not knock on the door was another moment to spin these tales, see another hunter on Faisal's trail, another death for him, another confession tortured from him. She could not concentrate on anything else, so there was no way to kill the time with a book or the antique television that got mostly static. So she was left with her cigarettes, parceling them out, with no idea how long they had to last.

The air conditioner continued to rattle in the corner, doing little to dispel the blanket of heat over the room. Cecelia wasn't used to the heat, and it made the waiting, already interminable, into hell. Seattle had never gotten this bad, even in the grips of a summer storm. The Pacific was there to whisk the heat away, while Louisiana festered beneath it.

Odds were, she would never set eyes on Seattle again. It had been her home for almost twenty years, and now it would exist for her only in memory. The job offer had seemed too good to be true. Fresh out of school on the GI Bill and looking for a job, she had gotten a call. The appointment was at a local office that looked too new—she learned later that these offices were set up as needed and abandoned just as quickly—and Rose Cross had interviewed her. Cecelia had administrative experience, gained in the Air Force. She was CPR certified. She had glowing letters of recommendation. Rose had whispered a few words, and Cecelia had felt a brief ripple through her mind, and then the albino had smiled, shook her hand, and offered the kind of money she wouldn't have seen in years.

Cecelia had to relocate across the country, but she was fresh out of the service and never had much in the way of family, so it wasn't a difficult choice. Orientation followed, and at first, she did not believe what they were saying. Magic was real, and those who used it were locked in a war that stretched back before Christ. Ash Wednesday had come in to talk to her, showing the power of Diablerie, gating in creatures from other dimensions and sending them away just as quickly. They taught her to recognize the major allied races of the Twins: the thraxians, the vree-ka-vree, the gnomes, and the orrerites. And they had explained that there was no going back to her other life. She had nodded, numb from the revelations, some part of her positive she was in the middle of the most elaborate practical joke ever conceived.

She had arrived at the large house on Puget Sound on a clear day. It was located in a nice suburb, at the winding end of a forested road, every other house at least a mile distant and invisible through the trees. Her escort was a large and taciturn former Marine who called her ma'am and dropped her off to get acquainted with her new home. The job was as way station operator. She had to keep the place stocked with emergency supplies, see to the needs of the people passing through, and make sure it remained secure. Representatives, mostly mundane soldiers, in the Twins' organization would be using it as temporary housing for business throughout the Pacific Northwest.

The place was huge. She took a walking tour through it, finding seemingly endless guest rooms, a huge kitchen, half a dozen bathrooms, and a vaulted safe room in the basement. She barely noticed the shadow in the mirrors she passed until it stuck its head through in the process of pulling the rest of the body into this reality. She screamed and retreated to the nearest bathroom.

She had recognized it, of course. Thraxian. Wednesday had shown her one and had mentioned that every installation in the organization had at least one as security. She hadn't been prepared for actually seeing one in the flesh. The predatory form had a horny exoskeleton covering only parts of its oil-black flesh, human features on a distended skull, and a tail that never seemed to stop twitching. It was a nightmare.

For the first several weeks on the job, things had been quiet. She avoided the demon, as she thought of it. It seemed to understand, and could only be glimpsed in flashes in mirrors out of the corner of her eye. She went about her duties, but keeping the house in order left her with free time. She spent it reading, or watching videos she rented from a store nearby. The accommodations were more than comfortable, and her salary paid for everything she could want.

Maybe if she had been placed fifteen years later, when the internet could have given her some contact, things would have turned out differently.

In the beginning, she dreaded having her way station used for its intended purpose. It happened for the first time two months into her tenure. Blackthorn arrived with a full squad of her soldiers. Actually meeting the dryad was intimidating, and her bubbly demeanor only exacerbated the initial fear. Cecelia had seen to it that all the men were comfortably quartered, that food was ready for them before they had to ask, and that all of Blackthorn's special requirements were met. When the group left the following morning, Cecelia breathed a sigh of relief.

Over the next year, she averaged a visitor once every three months. Sometimes it was a lone agent returning from an operation overseas. Other times it was an Apprentice and their extended entourage. Most of the time Cecelia would know in advance who was coming and when. Sadhvi Deva, Ash Wednesday's right hand, would call Cecelia at irregular hours to inform her of the impending arrival of guests. She grew to envy the Familiars and Apprentices who passed through. Their lives seemed so much more exciting than hers, to say nothing of the remarkable powers at their fingertips. While they moved on doing important work for the organization, they left Cecelia at the way station. A lonely cog in a secret machine.

Between those visits, there were long days and longer nights. She soon grew to look forward to the visits. Some of the visitors were pleasant, others brusque, and others terrifying. Eventually, she needed someone to talk to beyond the brief contact she got while running errands.

One night, after finishing the movie she rented, *When Harry Met Sally*, she turned around in the dark living room. The thraxian was there, clinging in the corner of the ceiling in that strange way of theirs, openly defying gravity. It bowed its head in contrition and turned to skitter out.

"Were you watching the movie with me?" she asked in the silent house.

It paused. After thinking, it nodded.

"Did you like it?"

The thraxian whipped its tail about. It hung on the ceiling, though its claws weren't sunk into the wood or plaster. Finally, it nodded again. "Didn't understand," it whispered.

The demon was vulnerable, honestly confused by the film. It didn't seem as frightening, and Cecelia could concentrate on the parts of it that looked human. "What didn't you understand?"

The thraxian hesitated, and cautiously crept forward along the ceiling. Cecelia stifled a yelp as it dropped to land on the couch, where it curled up like a cat. "What did they want?"

It took some time, but eventually Cecelia was able to tease out that the creature had no understanding of romance. Thraxians had two genders (and sixteen subgenders to complicate matters), but no concept of love. Mating was done as was convenient. He—and he was one of the various kinds of male—did not understand the dance going on between the leads, although he found it fascinating. His name was Hirrust, and that night became Cecelia's friend.

Movie nights were their tradition. Popcorn for her, ammonia-based cleaning products for him, they would settle in on the couch for whatever tape she had rented. His favorites were the romantic comedies. No matter how clichéd the plot, Hirrust found them endlessly surprising simply because he had no idea how they were supposed to end. It was an exciting day for both of them when she brought home the first DVD player either had ever seen.

He began accompanying her on the various sweeps of the property, reporting in detail on the pocket dimension on the other side of the mirrors. Occasionally, he would mutter something about a threat and disappear for a few hours, only to return later with fresh scratches, informing her that the trouble had been taken care of.

Eventually she taught him games like chess and backgammon, but he preferred puzzles, especially ones with man-made landmarks. His favorite was one of the St. Louis arch, which he would happily assemble over and over, with no hint that it was ever getting old.

Hirrust was her only friend for the first eight years on the job. He was the one thing standing between her and crippling loneliness. The one thing blocking her from the reality that this was her life until she retired. She had been forced to a revelation: she would never move to something bigger and better. She had only one friend in that gilded purgatory.

At least, until she met Faisal.

It was on one of her many errands to restock the way station. Rose and Shahmeran had come through with a full complement of soldiers and even a couple thraxians. The cupboards were partly emptied out, cleaning supplies were running low, and even little things like toothbrushes and soap needed to be replaced. She loaded up the minivan—replaced every two years, and each one modified by the Machinist to outperform most sportscars—and pulled into the parking lot of her favorite coffee shop before heading home. She hadn't even noticed the handsome man until he approached her, and realized later she had stopped noticing anyone who wasn't a guest in her station. She hadn't been celibate those eight years, but she had limited herself to one night affairs with the soldiers passing through.

This man, though, was different. She bumped right into him on the way in, spilling his coffee across the floor. While she apologized, he merely smiled, and in a soft musical accent graciously deflected. She offered to buy him another cup, and he accepted only on the condition that she would drink it with him.

She returned to the way station bubbling over. She found Hirrust in the bathroom mirror, prowling through the reflection. He came to the surface, and in an act she would never quite get used to, stuck his head through. It almost looked like someone surfacing in a pond, except it was vertical, and the water had an unnatural silvery sheen as it clung to the crevices of his exoskeleton. Hirrust sensed something in her manner, and seemed just as excited. She explained she met someone, and after a couple tries, Hirrust managed, "Marry him! Marry him now!"

She laughed and shook her head. "Just a date, Hirrust."

He happily nodded the bizarrely distended skull. "And then marriage. I understand. So happy, Cece. So happy." He wrapped a claw around her shoulder in a way that once would have terrified her. Instead, she laid a hand over his.

"Thanks."

The relationship with Faisal started with dinner, but soon grew serious. It seemed like he knew everything about her, said everything right. He loved Stephen King, just like her. He hated tomatoes, just like her. He brought her orchids on their first date, bought her a sapphire necklace on the fifth.

He told her all about himself. Faisal Al-Jarallah was a Saudi-born lawyer who had been living in the States for fifteen years. He had recently moved from Boston because of the perfect job offer. His mother had died when he was thirteen and was estranged from his father. His five brothers and sisters were still in Saudi Arabia, though he talked to all of them frequently on the phone. He liked kids and dogs, but was allergic to cats. And he was completely fascinated by her.

She tried to tell him who she was a hundred times. In the afterglow of sex, in quiet moments before they kissed, in the clear summer air or in the dark of night. She had to be evasive. She couldn't say what she actually did for a living, who actually paid her, or that her closest friend was an extradimensional entity who lived on the other side of mirrors and could comfortably guzzle bleach. She tried not to lie, but it was killing her.

Finally, one night, she could take it no more. "Faisal," she had started, stroking the dark line of stubble down his jaw, "I'm not quite who I said I am. I work for an organization you wouldn't believe exists."

The air in his apartment seemed to hum for a moment as the silence stretched between them. Finally, he said, "I know."

She leapt out of bed, pulling the sheets with her to cover nudity she was suddenly ashamed of. There was a gun in her purse. One step and she could get it and put a bullet in the man. A call to Rose would clean everything up. Witnesses would forget, the body would be disposed of.

No, he was not "the body." He was Faisal.

"Please, Cecelia. Don't."

"You were lying this whole time? You knew?"

"I knew. But I wasn't lying." He sighed. "Please. Sit down. I'll explain everything."

In later years, Cecelia sometimes wondered what would have happened had she run out that door. In the motel room in Clementville, under the suffocating haze of heat and smoke, the thought came to her again. She chuckled bitterly and stabbed the cigarette out.

"I work for the Artisan," he said. Another of the League, the Artisan ruled the Middle East, known to the immortals as Ki. Faisal told her that it had been his assignment to recruit her as an asset, but—and as he said this last, he placed a hand on her thigh, a hand she did not brush away—he had developed real feelings for her. He proposed a simple trade. She would feed information to his master and the affair could continue. He reassured her that the information could be vague, and it would not be used for direct action. The Artisan just needed to know about the ebb and flow of the Twins' men through the Pacific Northwest. Cecelia was in the unique place of providing that.

"No one gets hurt?" she asked.

He smiled. "Except me if you say no."

And so she had said yes.

She had returned to the way station and Hirrust peppered her with questions he had gleaned from their favorite romantic comedies. He wanted to know if Faisal had covered a room in rose petals, or had a string quartet, or bought her a puppy. She snapped at the thraxian, saying they'd broken up. After that, when she saw Faisal, the guilt twisted her up. She couldn't tell her friend about the other most important person in her life.

When Sadhvi Deva would call and give Cecelia a copy of the upcoming schedule of visitors, Cecelia would find a pretext to tell Hirrust that she was going out. In her car, she would hastily write out a note, including names, numbers, dates. All the information Faisal had asked for and nothing more. She drove downtown. The dead drop was a garbage can that looked like any other on the corner of 2nd and Pike. She dropped the note in, and she knew it vanished and would find itself in the hands of whoever the Artisan used for his spymaster.

Because that is what she was. A spy.

It was difficult to come to terms with that. She was giving information to an enemy. It flew in the face of who she thought she was when she said her oaths, first to the United States, and then to Pemhakamik. She was a different person. A stranger only Faisal really knew.

The dead drop had another function. If she needed to speak to Faisal, she had only to draw an X in lipstick on the side of the can. She had done it for the first time only three weeks after making the devil's deal, after going over to Faisal's apartment and finding it empty, the man she had thought of as her boyfriend gone. As soon as the X was finished, the lipstick vanished as though it had never been there.

Faisal made contact the next day when Cecelia was at the market. He came up behind her, pushing a cart of his own, and without looking asked, "Is something wrong?"

"You moved! You weren't going to tell me?"

"I had to. If you want to meet, we can get a hotel room, but we can't be seen in public. If Rose Cross suspects anything, or worse, gets her hands on either one of us, we're finished."

She breathed, staring at the shelf of cereal in front of her, feeling small and stupid. "What about us?"

"Draw a circle on the dead drop, I'll find you, and we can see each other somewhere private."

But "see each other" just meant sex and room service. It was enough for a time, but eventually she had to stop fooling herself. If there was going to be a reward, it had to be something more than this. At one of their meetings, after the furtive and increasingly unsatisfying sex, Cecelia sat in the dark room, contemplating the smoke of her cigarette.

Finally, she spoke. "I need more."

"More what?" Faisal asked, the tenderness in his voice still there but grown hollow.

"More from you."

"I wish we could," he said, caressing her thigh.

"No. I mean, I need more from your master."

Faisal sat up, suddenly interested. "Such as?"

"A way out when I'm done. A place to go and spend the rest of my life."

"Already done."

"I'm not finished. I want one of his devices."

The silence that followed was thick. "You want to be a Familiar?" Faisal said.

"Nothing so powerful. I know he can't promise me that. Something minor. Something to make my life easier."

"Never get sick again? Live longer? That kind of thing?"

"Exactly."

"I believe I can get him to agree to that. But only if you become more of an asset to us."

She had already made the decision. "Talk to him."

Faisal met with her in two weeks. The Artisan had agreed. She had something to work toward, and with the extended life the Artisan's device would provide, she could find new ways to move up in the organization. Things to do beyond rotting away in some way station waiting for excitement that would never come.

The information grew more damning. She began to talk to the men who were at the way station. Some of them would occasionally let slip details of their missions. In most cases, nothing would happen.

And sometimes, she would hear through the grapevine that one of the soldiers, nearly always the team leader, had been assassinated. She kept a tally in her head of the men she had gotten killed, but knew the real number was higher. For every one she heard of, there were others that had never gotten back to her. The humans bothered her most, even though there was the occasional Servitor thrown in, a vree-ka-vree used on scouting duty, an orrerite administrator, or worse, a thraxian sentinel.

It was difficult talking to Hirrust. He was still the same creature, terrifying and childlike at turns, but his face reminded her of her betrayal. She told herself she would never get him hurt. It never worked, and so instead she would concentrate on her reward. A long life, a rich home, a possibility of something more than what she had found with the Twins.

So it went for almost nine years.

The dead drop was normal. She was giving information on a small three-man team of operatives who was looking into a possible cell of the Butterfly's Servitors in the area. It was not the kind of intelligence the Artisan would normally care about. As she dropped the paper into the trash, she saw a lipstick X on the side of the can. As soon as she registered it, the red faded and disappeared.

Cecelia immediately came up with several errands to be out in public and easily findable. Faisal located her at the coffee shop where he had initially approached her. They did not acknowledge one another, each buying a drink, and apparently going their separate ways. In fact, Faisal tailed her to an out-of-the-way motel. In the room, they finally spoke.

Sex was no longer on the menu, and had petered out over the past decade. It stopped without either of them saying a word. Neither bothered to initiate anything and so it didn't happen.

Faisal was as animated as he ever got, which is to say his meticulous cool was layered over a seething excitement sparking in his brown eyes. "We have a request."

"Oh?"

"The Machinist," he said. "We need to know when she will be at the way station."

Cecelia knew better than to ask why. It was a question Faisal would never answer, even if he knew. "It might be a while."

"Fine. As soon as you know, contact us."

"If there's going to be a hit at the way station, you're going to need to extract me."

"We will. This is almost the end." With that, he left.

Though it was pointless to speculate, she did anyway. That an Apprentice should be the target was no great surprise. Of the empowered members of an organization, Apprentices had the highest rates of attrition. Lacking the resilience of Familiars and the power of Magi, and yet responsible for large swaths of the organization, they made attractive targets. Most feuds between Magi were fueled by proximity or history, pointing to the long-running battles the Twins had fought against the Priestess and the Serpent. Yet the murder of an Apprentice, if traced, would be an act of total war. Additionally, that it would specifically be the Machinist and not Ash Wednesday or Rose Cross was interesting. The Machinist was an Enchanter, trained by the Artisan. It was possible he thought of her as a threat to his rule as the Enchanter in the League. But who knew how he thought? With genius came other baggage.

It was almost a year before Cecelia got the news that the Machinist would be coming to the way station. It was for a retrofit, the Machinist installing a few devices to assist with security. Cecelia asked Sadhvi Deva if there would be others, under the guise of needing to know relative numbers of supplies and whether she had to provide anything special, such as raw cow hearts for that new Familiar Coldheart. Sadhvi said the Machinist would be bringing her standard complement of bodyguards, but other than that, there would be nothing.

Cecelia thanked Deva, and immediately grabbed her purse to go out. Hirrust poked his head through the mirror in the foyer. "Getting a movie?" he asked hopefully.

She flashed a brittle smile. "Yeah. Requests?"

"I like Meg Ryan," Hirrust said, his barbed tail flicking back and forth. "Meg Ryan and Tom Hanks."

He had broken his last copy of *Sleepless in Seattle*, so it was probably time to get him a new one. "I'll pick it up. Be back soon."

She drove to the dead drop and deposited the folded piece of paper into the trash can. She didn't forget Hirrust's movie, but that night when they watched it together, she could barely concentrate. She kept thinking of the impending arrival of the Machinist, and beyond that, the hit. The important thing would be keeping Hirrust out of the line of fire. He would attack the hit squad, whether it was another Apprentice, Familiar, or group of Servitors, heedless of his own safety. She had to make certain he would be safe. Afterwards, she could vanish and pray he would never know she had caused it all.

The Machinist arrived just before noon, and Cecelia was out front to meet her. The Machinist's convoy was always more impressive than those of the other immortals. She drove her modified 1955 Ford Skyliner at the head, followed by pair of '70s muscle cars, with a 1948 Packard bringing up the rear. They pulled into a loose ring at the front of the house.

The Machinist got out of the driver's seat of her Skyliner— she was the only Apprentice who insisted on driving—and nodded at Cecelia. Though the Apprentice looked barely out of her teens, she was at least as old as her car. Her skin was light brown, the tattoos covering her from shoulder to wrist, crawling up neck and temple. She wore a pair of vintage sunglasses, enchanted, like everything else, and her black hair was done up in a simple red bandanna. She affected a '50s style of dress, from the cherry lipstick to the pedal pushers, but it was a mistake to think of her as soft.

And in a few hours, she would be dead.

Her men got out of their cars. Their style reflected their mistress, looking more like greasers and less like what they were: former SEALs, Army Rangers, and the like. Some of them probably affected the style to curry favor. Others probably liked being what passed for the cool kids in the Twins' organization. They were on guard, peering into the foliage and at the house, their pistols and shotguns not currently leveled at anything.

The next sight stopped Cecelia's heart.

Blackthorn climbed out of the passenger side of the Skyliner. The fire-engine-red top had been up, and had hidden her. As was her custom, she wore a simple cotton sundress and was barefoot. She smiled and waved at Cecelia, and for an absurd moment it felt like a taunt. *Here I am. All your plans have gone to shit.*

The hit squad, whoever they were, were not expecting a Familiar. Cecelia had to call it off. Now.

But she couldn't run off. She had to stand, stoically greeting the woman she had, until that moment, been planning to kill. Blackthorn scampered up the steps first, ostensibly carefree, although Cecelia knew the Familiar would always lead the way for an Apprentice she was protecting.

"Cecelia, right?" Blackthorn asked. She had a spritely face, her mixed Caucasian and Asian heritage evident in her freckles, gold complexion, and short black hair. Her eyes were a deep, unnatural emerald, evidence of the dryad sharing her body.

"That's right. Welcome to Seattle. How was the drive?"

Blackthorn threw the Machinist a friendly glare. "Fast. Extremely, dangerously fast."

"We're all pretty hungry," the Machinist said, her heels clopping on the steps.

"Of course. If you'd like to follow me to one of the dining rooms, I can have some sandwiches in a few minutes. I'm sorry, Blackthorn, I wasn't informed you'd be coming, so we're low on fresh soil."

She waved it off with one small hand. A hand, Cecelia knew, could kill her with no effort at all. "As long as it's vegetarian and I can soak in some sun, I should be fine."

"Now is when I mention the city's notorious cloud cover."

Blackthorn made a face before breaking into a broad smile. Despite herself, Cecelia wanted to drop her guard. But she couldn't. Not with the hit squad out there.

She led them into the dining room. The soldiers fanned out, checking the building room by room. They didn't expect to find anything. It was a standard precaution whenever one of the truly important members of an organization was present. Still, Cecelia was tense as they moved through the house, as though they would see evidence of her betrayal in every room. And then, it would likely be Blackthorn tasked with killing her. The fey girl who even now was in front of the house, pulling her dress over her head, and stretching in a shaft of sunlight, eyes closed in bliss.

Cecelia quickly made sandwiches for all of them, with larger portions for the soldiers, who tended to eat like horses. Pitchers of iced tea and lemonade, a plate of vegetables, and even cookies and chips to make them all feel like they were back at home rather than some paramilitary outpost for a supernatural being. They converged on the dining room, although the soldiers would eat in shifts. Blackthorn came back inside, straightening her dress as she did so.

The Machinist was talking to the head of her security, a beefy Asian man with graying hair. She called him Brad, and the way they spoke it was clear there was a lot of affection between them. It was common for Apprentices to grow close to their security, as they had far more need for protection than Familiars did.

As Cecelia brought the trays in and put them on the table, the soldiers dove right in. Every one of them was like this; they learned never to miss a chance to eat, even if it seemed like there was nothing wrong.

"Can I get anything else for anyone?"

The Machinist looked over the table. "Nothing for now," she said. "Thank you. Later on, I'd like to speak to you about the layout here, where you tend to spend most of your time. I want to optimize the security for you personally."

"We can do that as soon as I get back." Every moment Cecelia spent at the way station, the hit squad got closer. She had to call them off, or her cover was blown and for nothing.

"Get back?"

"I want to get a few things to make Blackthorn's stay a little more comfortable," Cecelia said.

"Oh, I'm fine," Blackthorn said, eating an avocado like an apple, rind and all.

"Still. I take pride in what I do here. I'd really like to get you a few things. It would make me feel better."

"You're much too nice," Blackthorn said. "But thank you."

Cecelia faked a smile and tried not to look like she was rushing out the door. She had to get to the dead drop immediately. She'd write the note on the way while she sped through traffic. Hopefully the Artisan was waiting for magic hour to do the hit. She had some time, but not so much she could dawdle.

She was on the pathway leading to the road when the gunfire started. It was a very distinctive sound. Unlike the sustained chattering of automatic weaponsfire, it was a quick rattle, directly on the heels of a rapid clicking. A human shout, a scream of pain, and more gunfire followed.

They must have come in through the water. The flashes were concentrated around the general area of the dining room, the sounds of clicks and shouts converging as the Machinist's security detail ran to her side. The *chatter-tick-tick-tick* was getting closer together, and came from a number of sources. A window shattered, one of the Machinist's men flying through it to splatter on the front drive. His neck was bent, his body covered in hideous lacerations.

Cecelia was frozen. She felt like she had to help, but there was not much she could do for either side. As though to confirm that, the side of the house rumbled and exploded into splinters of wood. A thorny tendril, throbbing and alive, pushed through the wreckage of the house. On top of it, a figure clung with one hand. She was green and brown, her body equal parts plant and human. Blackthorn.

The tendril split off into several smaller tentacles. Some reached into the house, others pulled their prizes out through the hole. The figures were humanoid, but Cecelia could see flesh had been torn away like paper. Where the thorns ripped in, gears and scrolls of parchment spilled from the wounds. Their right hands were odd winding guns, making the distinct *chatter-tick-tick-tick* as they fired dry and rewound themselves for another volley. These were the Rajol Hadidi, the Artisan's Clockwork Men.

The massive tendril undulated once, cracking through the front facade of the house. As remote as it was, the neighbors had to hear that. The curious would be converging, along with police and fire departments. A colossal mess Rose Cross would have to spend days cleaning up.

Her view into the carnage now unobstructed, Cecelia could only look inward in horror. The bodies of the Machinist's men lay all around the house, cut to pieces by the clockwork guns. The remaining Rajol Hadidi fought with Blackthorn, though the result of that was almost a foregone conclusion. Against a Familiar of the Twins, a team of Servitors had no chance. Most importantly, the Machinist, bleeding from her shoulder and side, was being partially carried by Brad, the head of her security, toward the cars with two of the clockwork soldiers in pursuit.

The Machinist partially turned, leveling an ornate pistol and firing. Ozone scorched the air as blue-white energy lanced out into one of the Rajol Hadidi. He hissed, his innards melting into a gold pool across the floor.

Cecelia felt a cold hand on her shoulder. She turned. The face would have been that of a handsome Middle Eastern man, but his papery skin was ripped away in patches, revealing the gears and parchment within. "Ms. Ho. It is time to leave."

She looked back in time to see the other clockwork man fire a volley from his gun, ripping Brad to pieces and hitting the Machinist in the arm, making her drop the weapon. The Apprentice cried out in pain, but scarcely seemed to notice the grievous wounds all over her body. Instead, she threw herself over the dead man, trying to shield his body from further desecration.

"Cece?" The voice was unmistakable. And it was too late to say anything.

Hirrust came from the shadows to pounce on the clockwork man. Claws tore through the paper flesh, exposing the golden gears. The artificial man shoved Cecelia away, his clockwork muscles clicking. She sprawled onto the driveway.

"No, stop!" she shouted, but whether to demon or machine she wasn't sure. Neither one had to die.

The clockwork man pushed up his machine gun and fired a volley right as Hirrust tore the master engine from the clockwork's chest cavity. Both beings fell to the ground in a tangled mass of alien flesh and machine-tooled parts.

Cecelia ran to Hirrust anyway. He was already gone. His chest was shredded, but his face was perfectly intact, locked in a mask of puzzlement. The thraxian had probably heard her shout. Maybe it had made him hesitate that fraction of a second. Maybe that's why he was dead. Maybe. Maybe.

Cecelia looked up in time to see the last clockwork man level his wind-up weapon to finish the job on the sobbing Machinist. There was a thump and a shudder and his weapon chattered, but the bullets went wide. He was in the sky, carried aloft by another tendril bursting through the floor of the house, the thorns tearing him into little pieces. The Machinist was on the floor, bleeding, but alive. And there was no one left for Blackthorn to kill.

The hit was a failure, the cost all around. It wouldn't take long. If Blackthorn suspected anything, she had every authority to kill Cecelia on the spot, no questions asked. Cecelia got into her car and hit the gas for the main road, passing the first of the curiosity seekers coming up the road. In the distance, sirens wailed. She obtained her bag from the airport locker where she had stashed it and flew out of the city shortly thereafter.

And now all she could think of was the puzzled look on Hirrust's face. She wished she had seen something else. Sadness. Battle-rage. Anything would have been better than confusion.

The cigarette crinkled and hissed into the filter. She stabbed it out and reflexively reached for another. The pack squashed in her hand. Empty.

She wasn't supposed to be in this motel for that long. The smokes should have lasted her easily. She should already be on her way to Dubai or someplace. She went to the window and looked out over the main street of Clementville for the millionth time. The chances that someone would find her were as remote as this tiny town. She could go out, grab some cigarettes, and maybe even get something to eat that wasn't delivered by the honky-tonk next door. She wouldn't be out for more than twenty minutes, and it might do her nerves some good. The thought of fresh air when the goal was cigarettes was a little funny, but she ignored the irony.

She quickly grabbed her purse, pulling on a hat and sunglasses just in case, and headed out into the sweltering heat of the afternoon. She barely looked the clerk at the minimart in the eye, merely handing him the money, accepting the change and two packs of cigarettes without a word, and walking back out onto the raised wooden sidewalks of Clementville.

The dirty white walls of a diner shone in the sun. Cecelia glanced around. A few of Clementville's inhabitants were out and about, and no one looked as though they didn't belong. She didn't feel safe exactly, and had not since the first rattle of the clockwork guns, but this was as close as she had gotten. She stepped off the wooden sidewalk and crossed the street toward the diner. Chances were, it would have roughly the same menu as the honky-tonk, but maybe they used less mayonnaise or better catfish. The idea of different food put a spring in her step.

Cecelia stepped onto the gravel sidewalk on that side of the street, and was able to see into the smudged picture windows at the front of the diner.

She threw herself against the stucco wall.

Ghostwalker was in the diner.

Her breath came in panicked gasps. Her heart thundered in her chest. She was certain Ghostwalker would hear it, even as she knew intellectually he did not navigate using his human senses. He ignored sight and sound in favor of the more sublime perception of the creature bound to his soul. True or not, having Ghostwalker on your trail was an execution.

He was unique amongst the Familiars of the Twins. The other four maintained some connection to humanity with their human staff: their servants, cooks, drivers, and soldiers. Ghostwalker technically had men and women earmarked for his service, but he used none of them. The other Familiars were employed for a variety of purposes, often as bodyguards. Not so Ghostwalker. He was the hound of the Twins, the creature they released when they needed someone dead. Though not quite the eldest of their creatures, Ghostwalker had refined himself into the most inhuman. He was murder incarnate, and he was coming for Cecelia.

She didn't dare look into the diner to see if he was still in there. Her mind saw him at the window, sniffing the air, her fear forming a clean road back to her. She stayed low, creeping down the gravel alleyway between the diner and a series of shops, heading for the water. She winced as her shoes crunched on the gravel, knowing the sound trumpeted her position.

That explained what happened to Faisal. She wondered how much he had given up before they killed him. He was in an unmarked grave while she had wasted her time waiting. She had to find another way out of Pemhakamik. But first, she needed to evade Ghostwalker for enough time to make that relevant.

At the other end of the alley, the clean slope dipped right into the brackish water of the lake. Back toward the motel, there were a series of short piers, a few boats tied to the pilings. That might have seemed like a method of escape, but there was no cover on the lake until the trees more than five hundred feet distant. And there was the simple fact that her hunter could literally walk on water.

The little wharf dead-ended in a stand of trees. Right on the other side was her car, and beyond, the motel. The car. Get back inland, track back to Texas, and try to cross into Mexico. Keep going south until there was no more south to be had, and spend the rest of her days in hiding.

She glanced back toward the street. Ghostwalker was nowhere to be seen. Cecelia ran over the wooden planks and dove into the stand of trees. She slipped in the mud on the way down to her car. Her nerveless fingers fumbled for the keys in her purse. They popped out, and fell into the gravel. She scooped them up, let herself in, and turned the key in the ignition.

The car was silent. She was muttering now, begging the damn thing to start. Another turn, and nothing happened. A third. The car was completely dead. Ghostwalker had found it first and had trapped her in Clementville, allowing him to hunt her at his leisure.

If he knew about her car, he knew she was staying at the motel. Hopefully he had come and gone. She thought she could try to make it overland, to a main road, and hitch a ride. She cursed inwardly: her bag was back in the room. Money, fake IDs, everything she'd need for a few days on the run. It was already somewhat depleted from her enforced stay in Clementville, but still enough to help her if she was smart about it. She prayed it was still there.

She ran back into the motel, past the man listlessly watching his television, back up to her room. She opened up the door and sighed in relief as she found her bag right where she'd left it. Nothing was missing. She shoved her things back in and zipped it up, scarcely breathing.

Cecelia went to the window, parting the curtains with one finger to look down onto the street. Ghostwalker was coming up the sidewalk, focused on the motel. He was not much to look at: a rangy Native American man, dressed in faded plaid and denim, eyes hidden behind mirrored aviators. The Familiars of the Twins always betrayed their humanity in their eyes, and Ghostwalker's were pure white.

As he entered the motel, she wondered, had he intended this? Was everything else just a ruse to get her someplace relatively quiet to kill her? She tried to get her breathing under control. Panicking wouldn't help her. Her eyes flicked around onto the perversely silent street below when something caught her attention on the roof of the bait shop across the street. Where the building's fan was located, an X was drawn in lipstick.

The symbol she would draw on the dead drop when she wanted a meeting. Faisal. He was alive, and somewhere in Clementville trying to contact her. Had the sign been there before? She tried to remember, but could not be certain. She knew she could not stay put. Ghostwalker would be coming down the hall in seconds.

Cecelia tore the window open and dropped her bag onto the soft ground between the sidewalk and the wall of the motel. She followed it without hesitation, landing nimbly. Picking up the bag, she glanced back at the open window and walked as fast as she could down the street toward the town's main wharf. The crowd was thicker here, composed mostly of fisherman coming back in from the day. She kept her head down, not even certain where she was going.

"Come on," said a voice next to her.

She looked up. Faisal, sporting rings under his eyes and a day's growth of beard, was walking next to her, focused on the road ahead.

"Faisal!" She winced as soon as she said it, hating how it made her sound like a child. She was still in danger, but at least there was someone to share the fear with. "What is the plan?"

"I had a boat already hired, but Ghostwalker has sabotaged it."

"He got my car as well."

Faisal glanced at his watch and offered a curt nod. "Come on. If we move quickly, we can make it to the next town before he knows we're gone."

As he led her to a small service road near the wharf, she fought the urge to look over her shoulder. Whether or not the rumors of his inhuman senses were true, giving Ghostwalker a look at her face was the wrong thing to do.

"Your contact in the Gulf," she said, her voice coming in staccato bursts, "will he still be there?"

He checked his watch again, although the information had not changed overmuch. "Again, if we move fast."

A car was waiting for them, something old and beat-up, fitting in perfectly with the rustic surroundings. Faisal let her in and soon they were both leaving Clementville behind. Only then did she look backward. She imagined she saw Ghostwalker's lean silhouette in the middle of the street, but it was likely fear that put him there. She turned back. Faisal looked at his watch as he merged onto the main road and hit the accelerator.

"What's wrong? You keep checking the time."

His chuckle was brittle. "Meeting my contact is not assured. I'll have to drive quickly."

Her whole body was tense as they drove. It didn't help that Faisal kept getting himself boxed in, stuck behind big rigs going ten to fifteen miles below the speed limit. He checked that watch every twenty minutes or so, and Cecelia imagined he saw their lives ticking away with every second.

Faisal turned down the first side road, toward another town deep in the bayou. Slightly larger than Clementville, the streets were alive with people. Faisal drove to the end by the wharf, pulled the car to the side of the road and turned off the engine. He mustered a weary smile. "Let's go," he said.

Cecelia followed onto the piers. It was late, and most of the fisherman had gone in. Very few would want to go out this late, especially on so light a boat. She hoped Faisal had enough money to make it worth someone's while. He scanned the docks, settling on a man whose boat seemed the most seaworthy of those present. The captain, an old and portly man, was swabbing the deck when Faisal approached.

Cecelia waited on the edge of the wharf, superstitiously watching the gathering dark in the trees. She checked her watch, but not knowing when Faisal's contact would leave, learned nothing. She laughed a bit at that, some pitch black humor to match her mood.

She turned around the second time she heard it, realizing she was being called. "Anne," Faisal said. "Come. We have a boat."

She walked past the fisherman, who was counting the money with greedy glee. "You bought the boat?"

Faisal shrugged. "Bought and traded. He owns the car now as well. I think he thinks I'm some oil sheik's son."

The wonder in his voice would have summoned a girlish giggle from her once. Now all it gained was a wan smile. Faisal was already starting the engine when she gingerly stepped into it. She was certain that this would be the moment Ghostwalker would choose to catch up with them, but the town, whose lights now buzzed with insects, was quiet. Even as the boat churned away into the surf, she imagined Ghostwalker coming from the dark, assuming his true form, loping over the water, and killing them both.

It wasn't until the cypress trees faded behind her that she exhaled a breath that seemed to come from the depths of her soul. The Gulf of Mexico was wide open in front of them, black water underneath a bright and starry sky. She looked up at the open bridge, where Faisal was steering. He checked his watch.

"How are we doing for time?"

"Well!" he called back, not taking his eyes off the sea. "Get some sleep."

She drifted off on some curtains that smelled of fish and diesel, slipping into dark dreams. Hirrust was there, asking her why, but she couldn't answer, because Ghostwalker was just out of sight, ready to kill her. She woke with a gasp, the sunlight blinding. She blinked.

The Atlantic was all around her, the boat moving slowly through the water as the sun peeked over the horizon. She was covered in an old and ratty blanket. She smiled. Faisal still cared on some level. Cecelia sat up, lighting a cigarette. She shivered in the stiff wind, and her back was sore, but she felt hope. Ghostwalker had not found them. She might survive after all. She climbed the little ladder up to the bridge.

Faisal was exhausted, but he kept driving. "How are we doing?"

"Good, I think," he said, checking his watch.

"Where is your contact?"

"Around here somewhere. Don't worry, Cecelia. The worst is over."

She nodded, taking a steadying drag on her cigarette.

"How did you sleep?" Faisal asked.

"Better than last night."

"Good," he said.

He seemed about to turn to her when the boat lurched to a halt. Cecelia caught herself, nearly tumbling off the bridge. The engines groaned, churning water, but doing no good. The vessel seemed to be caught on something.

Cecelia climbed down. "What is that?"

Faisal didn't answer. Wrapped around one of the sides of the boat was a strand of sargasso. As she was watching, two more tentacles of seaweed surfaced, dripping from the blue water. They wrapped around the boat like the arms of a kraken. Her fear choked a scream from her as she turned to Faisal.

He cut the boat's engines.

She turned. More sargasso came from the deep to wrap around the boat.

On the port side, bubbles frothed the water. In the center, a machine surfaced. Long and torpedo-shaped, it was almost recognizable as a submarine, but it looked like no submarine any military on the planet had ever made. Its skin was decorated with runes like tattoos forged into the metal itself. It crackled and hummed with no earthly energy, and wide portholes made it almost appear as a great steel fish.

A hatch opened in the top, and two figures rose into view on an unseen lift. One was a woman whose flesh looked like the sargasso now covering the ship. Cecelia recognized the face, even beneath the wrinkled leaves and buoyant bulbs. Pixyish and pretty, that face had once smiled at her happily. Now it was grim. Blackthorn.

The other was bandaged, and when she walked, it was stiffly, wounds tugging at her. She carried a pistol of elegant design by her side. Her face was a mask of cold rage. The Machinist.

Faisal was coming down the ladder. When he reached the deck, he took a step away, his face carefully blank.

"You," Cecelia said. "You sabotaged my car. You were checking your watch, because you had to kill enough time for them to meet us here. Weren't you? *Weren't you?!*" The last was a shriek as she hurled herself at him.

He grabbed her wrists and threw her to the deck. There was no malice in the action beyond the harsh desire to get her away. "I'm sorry," he said in a careful monotone. "They wanted you more than we needed you."

The Machinist reached into the pocket of her jumpsuit and handed a thumb drive to Faisal. Like everything else she built it was a strange and beautiful design. "The information you requested," she said.

"Thank you." He never looked at Cecelia, pocketing the drive and moving to the bow of the boat.

"You," the Machinist said, contempt curdling her voice.

"Please," Cecelia begged. "You can't. You can't just kill me!"

"No?" the Machinist asked. "Let's test that theory."

Cecelia smelled ozone and heard a great sizzle and her world went black.

Stillwater

THE SMALL YELLOW CAR WOUND its way through the baking Arizona desert. From far enough away, in the aching blue of the sky, the little Toyota might have looked like a beetle marching past the red sands. The road was not a highway, but one of the many almost forgotten thoroughfares spreading through the desert like capillaries. Cracks and potholes, baked there by the punishing sun, were so common it was almost more treacherous than the rocky terrain rising up all around. The sands had partially consumed the little roads, only to be pushed back by the wind of the occasional and hopelessly lost car.

But the yellow car did not seem lost. It did not slow around the cacti that looked a little like road signs, nor did it pull over at the wide tracks of windblown sand by the sides of the roads, right before giving way to the asparagus green of desert plants. Unlike every other car that found this road, the little yellow Toyota with the California license plates seemed to be there on purpose.

The backseat was dirty. The floor covered in wrappers, mostly trail mix and protein bars, empty water bottles and the odd soda cup from some fast food place. Blankets were wadded up behind the passenger seat, the only hint that the car had been used as a motel room more than once. The dusty seats had maps, large state ones, smaller local ones, scattered all about. As they flapped and crackled and fluttered in the hot desert wind blowing in from the open driver's side window, handwritten markings could be seen on every one. Circles drawn in pen, each one round and round until the borders looked like bird nests, arrows indicating tiny towns at the edges of remote roads, points in some lost area of the wilderness, scrawled lines connecting each one. Right at the top on a map recently folded and unfolded, was a point near the road on which the little yellow car stuttered and bumped.

The radio hissed and crackled. An hour ago it had dimly received a country western station, though every third verse was swallowed by the rocky hills on every side, some near, some far. In the old days, they had been packed with silver and copper. Now they had mostly been sucked dry, the scars in their sides bolstered by crumbling wooden beams.

A half-empty water bottle rolled around on the passenger's seat over a rip in the upholstery where the amber padding billowed outward and turned hard and dark in the sun. A dreamcatcher dangled from the rearview mirror, bouncing and shaking with every pothole. The gas tank needle sagged toward the bottom, and every now and then a light would appear on the dash, only to wink out in a few hundred feet.

The woman behind the wheel was exhausted. Even behind her thick-framed glasses, her brown eyes could be seen, tired and red from desert sand and lack of sleep. She was dressed for the heat, in cut-offs and a light t-shirt with a large dragonfly off center, its thorax over her heart. Her dark hair was pulled up into a ponytail, sweat collecting at her temples and the back of her neck. Her name was Ellen Mestrovich and she was making a big mistake.

At least that was the thought going through her head, her dark eyebrows wadding into a glower that her girlfriend—ex, now—called the Serious Look. She got it whenever she was doing something she objectively knew was stupid, and yet was doing it anyway. How else do you describe driving off into the middle of the desert at the height of summer looking for, of all things, ley lines?

It even sounded stupid to her, but she couldn't stay out in Claremont. Not after catching Kari in bed with someone else. Hurt worse that it was a guy, but that shouldn't have mattered. Betrayal was betrayal. Still, this made the previous two years feel like a lie. Ellen left the week of finals knowing that best case scenario was she had to repeat her junior year. Worst case was she would lose her scholarship. It seemed even more meaningless, after three years, she was no closer to understanding how to live in the world.

Housing for the following year had already been done, meaning that was another year living with Kari. After the break up. After the cheating. They said not to date your roommate, and though Ellen had rolled her eyes at the advice, she understood it now. At least next year, they only shared a living room and that was only if Ellen was still a student in good standing. Might not have to see Kari too much. Might not hear her with whatever new girl or guy she was dragging home.

Ellen didn't want to think about it. Couldn't deal with all the big, messy feelings trying to drown her. So instead this. Take a lingering idea in the back of her head and turn it into the most ill-advised road trip imaginable. Clear her head and flush out the relationship. Going off into the desert to see if there was anything to it.

"It" being a book. A silly little book with pictures of fairies rendered in loving detail. Said they lived by standing stones, places that occurred where ley lines intersected. The idea burrowed into her young mind and lingered. As she went off to Scripps College as an art history major, she often compared what she saw, even unconsciously, to the drawings of standing stones. In places where mystical energy gathered, these monuments sprang up. Whether built by human hands or spontaneously created, they were older than any recorded history.

And now she was in the middle of the Arizona desert in the grips of a sweltering summer, looking for something that probably didn't exist, all to forget a girl who was done with the Ellen phase of her life.

It was right around then that she noticed the car smoking. Little threads of white smoke drifting from under the hood like ink dropped into a glass of water. She cursed, pulling the car over onto the sandy road. She got out into the blistering heat, almost immediately wilting. The sun was high overhead, moving inexorably over her right shoulder where it would eventually fall behind a red rock mountain several miles distant. Ellen looked up and down the road, not even knowing what she expected to find. No cars approached through the heat shimmer, and the only sound she heard was the hot wind scraping through the leathery plants dotting the desert.

She popped the hood, releasing a puff of white smoke. Coughing and waving it away, she peered at the engine and nearly laughed at herself. Wasn't like there was anything she could do. She was no mechanic. It was hopeless enough that it was nearly funny. She remembered a dirt track about half a mile back up the road, going in the direction of that almost-mountain. Where there was a road, there might be a phone. Hers wasn't an option because there wasn't a cell tower within miles.

Ellen pulled her backpack out of the trunk. She had some warm clothes in case night fell, some trail mix, and a plastic water bottle. She threw in a couple more bottles of water, zipped it up and buckled the belt around her waist. With a last look at her car, a few wisps of smoke still rising from the engine, she walked up the road. She moved quickly, wanting to arrive in the shadow of the mountain, to find relief from the punishing sun. She reached the track winding off from the main road and up into the shade, took a deep breath, and began the ascent. The road was paved, though it was buried under a layer of sand, completely unmarred by tire tracks.

The slope started gradually, switching back and forth as it climbed. Ellen turned, and the sun winked at the top of the mountain, proximity turning it red. With the mountain, sunset had come hours early. Two more steps and she was in the shadow entirely. The temperature dropped like a stone. She shivered, the coating of sweat now turning on her. She thought she saw a twinkle near the crest of the mountain. A few weak lights glittering up there, throwing a fitful glow over dim shapes of buildings clinging to the slope. She smiled. First good news since the car blew up.

She turned around to look at the car, but the slope of the mountain now hid the road. She almost went back to walking up the hill, but something caught her eye. She turned. Tucked into a small dell, shielded from almost all sides, was exactly what she had been looking for.

Standing stones. The five largest, arranged in the center and at what Ellen was pretty sure were the cardinal directions, were around ten feet tall. Smaller ones, maybe six feet high, formed a ring around the large center stone, and four spokes to connect to the other four big stones. Finally, more of the six foot high stones completed an outer ring by connecting the spokes. The rocks were of the same red sandstone of the mountain, and were it not for the lengthening shadows—and the breakdown—she would have rushed down the slope, grabbed her digital camera, and filled up the thing's memory card. The trip had gone from an abject failure to success in the time it took for the car to give up the ghost.

They would still be there in the morning, and odds are she would be too. Find a mechanic, get him to tow her car, and hope there was something that passed for a motel up there. Bright and early, head down, get as many pictures as she liked, and return. Hopefully whatever was wrong with the car was something cheap and fixable.

As the sun glittered crimson at the crest of the hill, Ellen came to a single sign whose post was sunk into the earth at the side of the road. The post was wood, partly rotten through. The sign itself was metal, rusted, with black letters on what was once a white background. It said, simply, STILLWATER.

Ellen fought the judgmental fear. Just because the sign was a little rusted and the town remote didn't mean the place was full of crazy rednecks. She tried to swallow what years of city living and movies had put in her mind. Be polite, be friendly, and be safe.

The town was a few more switchbacks above, the road forming little terraces for the buildings to cling to, the first stories looking to be much smaller, while the second stories spread back against the darkening face of the hill. Something about the town looked wrong, even from a couple hundred feet below, and it took Ellen a few moments to understand what that was.

There were no electric lights.

There was illumination glowing above, a few flickering golden lights. Some were obviously outdoor fires. Ellen identified a fire set in an old oil drum. A torch blazed in a makeshift sconce. Far more common were things that she couldn't make out at first, little diffuse smears of molten amber. As she came up another switchback, the first of these things, swinging against the side of a house, became clear: it was an oil lamp. They winked along the town like fireflies.

The first house she saw, situated on a bend in the switchback, looked deserted. It was old, the wood weather-beaten. Boards crisscrossed the windows, though some of these had fallen away and others looked partially broken. The scrubby trees grew close to the house, a root breaking through the concrete foundation. The roof sagged, the walls were filthy. Paint had been chipped in large flakes the size of oak leaves. The oil lamp swinging from a hook was dark.

Ellen slowed as she turned the corner, leading out in to the first real street of the town. The road was cut into the side of the hill, houses and businesses on both sides. Every single building was in the same shape as the first house: dirty, battered, falling apart. There were a few cars parked along the sides of the road, but the dirt and spiderwebs on the wheelwells said they hadn't moved in a while. The windows were opaque with grime.

The town had seen better days, though in the deepening gloom of sunset, Ellen could not imagine when those might have been. The architecture had a distinct western flare to it, with certain buildings looking like they could have been clinging to the hillside for over a hundred years. Others had taken the style and updated it: a future generation interpreting rustic grandeur. Only now, age and wear had battered the entire town to a dying, broken thing.

Ellen fought the feeling in her guts, the twisting, queasy fear trying to get her to turn and run. It was a town, like any other. Poorer than most, sure. But it wasn't a reason to run. She had to fight the middle-class college student snobbery. Find a mechanic, pay the man, and maybe sleep in the car that night. Poverty did not automatically mean ignorance and intolerance.

She went up the street. Every building looked empty. The darkness looming beyond the broken windows was black and depthless. The left side of the road had been swallowed by falling dirt, the right side had been laid bare so that the edges of the old asphalt could be seen eroding into the desert. Piles of desiccated leaves swirled in lazy eddies. Were it not for the lamps glimmering higher up on the hill, Ellen would have assumed the place to be one of the many ghost towns dotting the Arizona desert. Just another place starved out when the last bit of precious metal was dug from the mountain.

She turned on the next switchback, the hill turning steep for the fifteen or so feet that the road doubled back on itself, cutting deeply into the soil. Some of the buildings from the lower street had floors that opened up onto this side as well, a first and second story that were both technically ground floors. Others were on stilts, and one of these had collapsed, the house at a crazy angle on the road, the walls cracked, spilling its rotting innards.

The lanterns increased in number on this level of the town, though not enough to fight the encroaching gloom. Fifty feet up the road, Ellen saw the first positive signs of life in the town. Four people were gathered in a small circle. Two of them, both men, wore old canvas knapsacks that, judging by the way they sagged, were mostly empty. The young one, who couldn't have been much older than Ellen, carried an old baseball bat, chipped and worn, a dark stain across one side. The older one held a pickaxe, the prong crusty. The young man was embracing a woman about his age as she cried softly against his shoulder. An old man spoke with them. All four people wore old clothes, ripped, repaired, and dirty. Their clothes were that kind of western ranch wear that was never precisely in or out of style. The house they were in front of was in better shape than most, though the windows were boarded up.

The man with the pickaxe looked over, his face lighting up as he saw Ellen trudging up the road. "Hey! Hey, you!"

He jogged over. Ellen tensed. The man's face was scarred and craggy, bruised eyes said he hadn't slept in a lifetime. There was muscle on his frame, but he looked half-starved. Despite the potential weapon in his hand, he didn't seem like he was going to attack. On the contrary, seeing Ellen had filled him with hope.

"I don't want any trouble," Ellen said. "Is there a mechanic here?"

"Do you have a car?"

"Yeah. It broke down by the turnoff. Do you have a mechanic?"

"Jared!" the man called over his shoulder. "We have to go!"

The younger man nodded and kissed the girl. She finally let him go, her sobs growing louder in the thin dusk. Jared jogged over to join the older man. "Miss," said the man, "you should come with us. Maybe there's still time. We can get to your car, maybe me and Jared can fix it, maybe not. Or we can find another town."

"There are no other towns," Ellen said.

"Miss, please. You have to come with us."

The man was desperate, and Ellen fought the urge to take a fearful step back. She wasn't going anywhere with two armed men, let alone ones that were so insistent about it. "Is there a mechanic in town?"

The man sighed. "Yeah. Up the road, look for Lester. Don't say we didn't warn you." He exchanged a nod with Jared and the two men jogged downhill.

"Warn me? Warn me about what?"

They were gone. Ellen turned to the old man and the young woman, but they were already hustling inside their house, the closing door followed by a heavy thud like something had been thrown across the barrier.

Her guts were twisting up and the shivers she fought were no longer due to the deepening chill. She had no other choice: her car was dead in the middle of the desert. There was no one else to help her, and if the man was telling the truth, there was a mechanic in town. She continued on, up another switchback. Over her right shoulder, she could see out into the Arizona desert. The shadow of the mountain swallowed up the reddened sands until it would darken the world. She reached into her pack and pulled on a sweatshirt, though that didn't fight much of the cold.

The third street was much like the first two. There were a few more people, and in every case, they were heading back inside their battered homes. All of them were in a similar state to the group she had seen earlier. Some carried axes, knives, clubs, and other seemingly repurposed tools, none brandished them at her. If she was acknowledged at all, it was with a sad shake of the head before the person disappeared into their house.

Finally, right off of the third switchback, Ellen found the gas station and garage. It was one of the older looking ones, and she could imagine gas station attendants who used to work there. Crisp white uniforms and paper hats, rushing out to fill and detail every car. It was an image she had from movies, and one that might have been true at one time. Now the gas station was in the same shape as the rest of the town. The windows on the garage were broken. The little minimart in the front was missing a door, and the wood that had been nailed there had been torn away and was scattered on the asphalt, partially buried by leaves and dirt. A rusted pickup sat by the pumps, its tires flat and windows broken.

A door opened behind her. Ellen turned. A woman in her fifties, in the same filthy clothes as the others, held a hatchet in one hand. "Miss! Miss!"

"Um... I'm looking for Lester?" She tried not to stare at the hatchet, even though the blade was dull with a dark stain.

"Quick! Come inside!"

"No thanks. I just need a tow. If I can just get a tow, I'll be out of your hair."

"It's too late for that! It's almost dark!"

Ellen put her hands up and backed away. "It's... it's okay. I'll find something else."

"Miss, please!" The woman glanced toward the top of the hill where the sun was steadily vanishing.

Ellen was moving back the way she came. The town was full of crazies. Armed crazies. And she had no intention of being raped or murdered. Walking briskly, she resolved to spend the night in her car, hope no one came down the hill, and figure out what to do in the morning.

The air was turning blue. The cold of the shadow deepened, burrowing past her skin and settling in muscle and bone. She looked forward to bundling up in the backseat of the car and waiting the night out. She had gotten used to it and could almost sleep a full night back there.

A state trooper would be by at some point, and this could be a funny story to tell everyone when she got back to school. She had almost forgotten the people when she reached the second switchback.

The sun winked out. Ellen turned to the desert and saw that beyond the town was completely black. Strange trick the day pulled, dying slowly and then, all at once, vanishing. The little light she had was from the few glowing lanterns, the fire in the oil drum, and the one torch. She had thought Stillwater was a ghost town, but now it actually looked ghostly. The night sky was filled with stars, more than she could ever have imaged. More even than the skies she had seen other nights, sleeping out in the desert. A ribbon of pinkish purple wound through all of it, and a star far larger than any should have been blazed in the center.

There was something very wrong about the sky.

As she made this connection, standing in the middle of the street, shivering in the cold, a shriek reverberated through the air. High pitched and reedy, it carried an undercurrent of music, almost a chime sounded at the same moment as the discordant scream.

It was not human, and it was not animal. Ellen had never heard anything like it.

Until it sounded again, and closer this time.

She began to run, her long legs eating up the road, but not quick enough for her liking. She sped up, even if the cracked road threatened to throw her to the ground with a bad raspberry over both knees. She didn't care. Any knowable injury was preferable to whatever it was that made that sound.

The shriek was closer this time, and Ellen could pinpoint it. Above and behind, closing fast. She threw herself to the asphalt, biting off a yelp as her chest and knees slammed into the road. She felt something pass overhead, a rush of wind, and the stench of sulfur with it. She heard the click of claws hitting the asphalt, and the thing wheeled around, just a black silhouette in the gloom. Ellen was only partly up, not sure if she should freeze or run.

And then a line of blue globes blazed to life along the thing's sinuous body. Teeth spilled out of a tremendous jaw. Huge, lidless eyes stared out from beyond the translucent teeth, emotionless and alien. A ridge of spines stretched down its back, a glittering membrane already retracting into its back. Though it had flown, there were no wings. Little nodules, almost like the tentacles of an anemone, waved along its side, and it had so many clawed legs Ellen didn't even bother counting.

It opened its horrible, carnivorous mouth, and shrieked again, its purple eyes focused on Ellen. Though it was hideous, there was something about it, the bioluminescent organs, the bizarre grace, that rendered it beautiful. It was a perfect killing machine, a predator sitting at the top of an unknowable food chain.

Ellen scrambled to her feet. The monster tracked her, writhing forward, its claws clacking on the asphalt. She had nowhere to run other than back up the hill. At that moment, she longed for the old woman and her hatchet, if only for something to put in the beast's way. Ellen was trying not to turn her back, but that was inevitable, if she wanted to get away from this thing. She turned, stumbled, and the creature struck like a snake, whipping out the first third of its eel-like body to bite.

Ellen screamed, falling back onto the street, the monster's teeth snapping closed inches from her ankle.

A woodaxe slammed into the thing's side. One of the bio-lights exploded, a gout of glowing blue liquid splashing outward and going dark, even as black, sulfur-stinking blood spurted from the creature. It shrieked again, this time muddied. The axe came free and slammed into the abomination again and again. It never had a chance to defend itself from its attacker and soon it was nothing but a ruined mass of meat and stench.

"Come on," said a voice.

Ellen turned to see her rescuer for the first time. The woman was a little shorter than she, her hard and angular face covered in scars. She wore a gun belt with a pistol on one hip. A sheriff's star rode on the dirty red flannel shirt. She held out a hand to help Ellen up. "Come on. We have to move our asses. Everything out here knows right where we are."

"What's going on?" Ellen asked, allowing herself to be led as the other woman jogged back up through the town.

"Those particular things ain't pack hunters, but they ain't alone neither."

The street was almost black, only splashes of gold swaying madly in the night wind. The sounds of the creatures echoed off the mountainside, chasing the gusts. They seemed to be all around, the screeches of predators, the metallic rustling that sounded inorganic but was clearly alive, the mushy writhing of a thousand tongues. Ellen's instincts wanted her to hide, curl into a fetal ball, pray for daylight. She knew that was useless.

These were night hunters.

The woman pulled Ellen toward a darkened house. It was on the downslope, the second story effectively at ground level. There were no lanterns hanging in the eaves, the windows were boarded up. A porch sagged under the weight of years, but there were no visible holes in wall or roof, making it better than many of the houses of the town. It looked as dead as anything could ever be.

The woman knocked quietly, hissing in a voice that barely carried. "Jean! Open up! It's me!"

A loud *clunk*, and the door opened to a woman with graying hair and tired eyes. She clutched a baseball bat with a large spike driven through the business end. "Hurry, get in!"

Ellen and her savior stumbled through the door while Jean shut it quickly and almost silently. She grabbed a heavy block of wood from next to the door and fit it through two rungs bolted to the wall. It looked like the last line of defense of a medieval castle.

A light flared, and with a squeaking, it dimmed until it was a soft amber. Jean held a lantern up, the little candle-sized flame burning. "Jesus, Carmen, what were you doing out there?"

"Hank said he saw a newcomer. She was trapped out there."

"What... what the hell is going on?" Ellen asked, her voice shaking in the thin darkness.

Carmen and Jean exchanged a look, the deep shadows on their faces making them look even more tired. "Come on," Carmen said. "We'll explain what we can."

There was no lie in Carmen's hard-edged face. The woman's hair was cut short, little strands of gray picked up in the flickering light.

Ellen nodded and got to her feet. The hallway was bare. No rug covered the worn planks of the floor. No pictures were on the wall, though holes in the dirty wallpaper said there once had been. Jean led the way, turning Carmen into a silhouette, sometimes eclipsing the struggling flame of the lantern. Ahead, there was another light, this one brighter. Jean led them through a doorway into a small dining room. Another lantern sat in the middle of the table. There were four people waiting, an old man and woman, and two young kids.

"This is Bob and Ginny," Jean said, indicating the old people. "And Jack and Meg." The old people smiled at Ellen; the kids barely looked up from the light, staring deep into the heart of the flame as though it was the only thing that could keep them safe. "I'm Jean, and the lady with the gun is Carmen."

"Ellen."

"Welcome to Stillwater." Jean made a face, acknowledging the ridiculousness of the statement but not knowing what else to say. Her voice and cadence seemed somehow old-fashioned to Ellen. Everyone was dressed as the others had been, in dirty and worn clothing.

"Are we safe in here?"

"Safe as we are anywhere else," Carmen said, glancing at the walls and ceiling. "Long as we keep quiet and they don't find a way in."

"What are they?"

"Don't know, really. Animals of some kind. They're not very smart, so they mostly look for ways in that are already there. But they can get riled up pretty good if you get too noisy."

Jean nodded. "In the old days, when there were more of us, they used to attack when we were fortifying. It was tough. Eventually, we learned to do it in shifts, or create big distractions elsewhere while we worked."

"What's going on?"

"Please, sit down," Jean said.

Ellen collapsed into one of the chairs. Neither one of the kids seemed to notice. Carmen sat down on the other side of the table, putting her hands palm down on the scratched wood. Scars crossed over the backs of her hands, disappearing into the repaired sleeves of her flannel shirt. She leaned the axe against the table, never farther than an arm's length away, Ellen noticed.

"Stillwater was a mining town," Carmen began. "A vein of copper through the mountain brought people to settle here. The mine went dry at around the turn of the century, but some people stayed on. It became an artist colony in the '60s. Mostly it was just ignored."

Jean took up the narrative. "One day... we're not sure how long ago anymore... a group came to town. They passed through quickly, but I remember them well. I was standing in front of my shop when they came past. A small, red-haired woman was leading the way even though she couldn't have been older than nineteen. She didn't seem to be looking at anything in particular, but... I don't know how to say it, but she seemed to hum with power. I glanced into a mirror, and I saw something looking back at me, some glowing monster. I thought it was some kind of hallucination until I saw that same monster eat John Greengrass in front of his pizza parlor the very next night.

"The woman had several people with her. A woman with purple-and-orange hair and a couple of large men. They seemed to be looking after the redhead while she searched for something, though they never spoke to anyone. Said who or what they were looking for. They walked through town and disappeared.

"And that night, things came from the sky."

Jean fell silent, contemplating her hands, made hard and ropy by living in this nightmare.

Carmen spoke up. "Nothing electrical worked after that night. People would try to find a way out, but the roads only extended to the edge of town and then just stopped. And that's when people came back at all. Mostly whenever someone left to find a way out that was the last we saw of them."

Ellen thought of that sad and frightened group who had greeted her on the way in. "Why don't you know how long ago this happened?"

"It's almost always night here now," Jean said. "Sometimes, we get a glimmer of daylight, just the moments right before the sun goes down, and a stranger will find us, and it's been days or years since we last saw the sun. I mean really saw it."

"Doesn't feel that long," Carmen said.

"Feels like forever," Jean said.

"When day dawns, some group decides to try to make it down the mountain. They always promise to send help. No one has ever came back."

"How do you live?" Ellen asked.

"Not well," Carmen said. "We lose people constantly, even now that we know what the dangers are. We're all just marking time. We ration food, and since there were a couple survivalist types who used to live here, we have enough canned goods to last us till doomsday."

"We're alive because of Carmen," Jean said.

Carmen looked at the table, uncomfortable in the praise. "I don't know about that."

"She saves the newcomers. She looks after everyone in town."

"I'm just too dumb to know any different."

Ellen saw the truth of it both in the reverence behind the words and the blush in Carmen's cheeks. If it weren't true, it wouldn't be so embarrassing. "Thank you," Ellen said. "I'm lucky you were there."

"I'd say you were unlucky it happened at all."

"Have you ever seen the red-haired woman again?"

Carmen nodded. "Occasionally we see her in the desert to the east. Heading around the side of the mountain, but never coming up to the town."

"And there's no way out?"

"You're trapped here, Ellen. I'm sorry."

Ellen was silent, trying to digest the impossibility she had been given. She pictured the woman in her head, out in the endless desert where the setting sun turned the sand into an infinite field of blood. Humming with power, and heading in the right direction, and then this, something clearly unnatural. It fit the available evidence, no matter how crazy. "Has anyone ever spoken to her?"

They shook their heads.

"What about waiting for her at the standing stones?"

"I'm sorry, the what?" Carmen asked.

"You know, on the far side of the mountain, there's a collection of stones like a Native American Stonehenge."

Carmen exchanged a look with Jean. "You know anything about that?"

Jean shook her head. "There's nothing like that."

"Well, they're there now."

"Why do you ask?" Carmen said.

"You're very close to a nexus point of intersecting ley lines. It's like a collection of spiritual energy. The stones looked like a ritual site to me, and it sounds like that's where the redhead was going. If that's the case, and if she is behind this, that would be where to find a way to stop it."

Carmen watched Ellen across the light of the lantern. With the scrape of her chair, she stood, grabbing the axe. "It's worth a shot."

Jean stopped her. "Are you crazy? If you go out there, you'll be killed!"

"If I stay in here I'll be killed too, it'll just take a little longer. This is a shot to stop this. Maybe it's crazy, but I don't see a lot of options." Carmen turned to Ellen. "You're sure about what you saw?"

Ellen nodded. It was the only thing she was certain of since coming to this town.

"I have to do it, Jean."

"I'm going too," Ellen said. "I need to show you where it is."

Carmen nodded. "Someone get this lady a weapon."

Bob handed over a mining pick. It was two-handed and the prong was crusted with some kind of sulfur-smelling stain. Everyone in the room, even the children, were staring at Ellen now, and there was something in their eyes: the faintest glimmer of hope. A bruised and beaten hope, certainly, and their faces were unused to it. Ellen felt not just wanted, but needed. Her promise had bound her to them in iron, and she welcomed it.

"You ready, Ellen?"

Ellen nodded. "Let's go."

"You're crazy. Both of you," Jean said. "Thank you."

Carmen led the way to a staircase whose steps creaked loudly. Ellen and Jean followed, Ellen's stomach tying up in knots. The staircase let to a back door, closed and barred like the front.

"Will we need a lantern?" Ellen asked.

"There should be enough light out there," Carmen said, not elaborating. "And one of those just makes you a beacon. Remember, you only fight as a last resort. If something attacks, you run till you can't, understand?"

The bar came off and the door opened into the chill air of the desert. Stars glittered all around as Ellen and Carmen stepped out onto the porch. The door closed softly behind them. They were one switchback farther down the hill, in an overgrown backyard leading to a chainlink fence and beyond that, the road.

Ellen blinked. The stars were moving rapidly across the sky in individual constellations. Shimmering points of blue and purple, green and orange slithered to and fro. And she saw that the stars were amongst the shattered buildings of Stillwater, lighting up the shadows, drifting over the ground. They were not stars, but the creatures.

"Beautiful, aren't they?" Carmen whispered.

"Like the sky fell."

The lights revealed outlines of beasts with no earthly analogues. Ellen saw distended mouths, writhing masses of tentacles, glowing eyes, pulsing organs, and other things she had no names for. They crept and crawled and slid with otherworldly grace, making the ghost town alive with an ecosystem beyond alien.

"Move quickly and quietly. We might get lucky and not be noticed."

The backyard was choked with plants that had grown wild and then died and turned to paper. The slope from the back porch to the fence was gentle. There had once been a stone path that led to a little gate, but the path had been swallowed by loose dirt and dead plants.

Carmen was first, holding the axe loosely in one hand. Ellen followed, focusing across the street, where a glowing strip of green undulated through the eaves of a fallen house. She could not see the full outline of the creature, but had the vague impression of a mouth at either end and long arms continually reaching for something out of sight.

They made it to the fence, and the gate had long since rusted shut. It was only three feet high, and Carmen hopped it with ease. Ellen followed, terrified of making it ring. The thing on the other roof had moved off, but there were more on either side of the street and in the sky above.

A swirling amorphous mass dotted with pinkish purple spots moved across the road. It took Ellen a moment to recognize it not as a surging blob but as a swarm of smaller, terrier-sized creatures. Carmen put a hand out to bar Ellen from going forward. It was unnecessary. They both waited, perfectly still, until the swarm had crossed the street and slithered down over the lip of the hill.

Then both women continued, moving quickly and lightly over the broken road, the only sound the quick and light breaths they sucked in between their steps. The creatures did not seem to notice them, though Ellen had no idea how they would perceive the world, nor what they really wanted. Did they kill to eat or just for fun?

They slowly left the eerie beauty of the alien things behind. The town thinned out to that first abandoned house Ellen had seen. Something was inside, judging by the diffuse orange lights that seemed to shimmer and shift almost like a fire. Shortly distant, the road did in fact end. It was an odd feeling for Ellen, when they arrived at the asphalt now curled up and dropping off into a sheer cliff that vanished into night. Trying to make sense of what her memory told her with what her eyes insisted, both utterly certain, she felt dizzy.

"Where is it?" Carmen whispered.

Ellen gestured helplessly down the vanished road.

"No, at the bottom of the hill, where is it?"

Ellen turned away, trying to get her bearings under the light of the stars. The road ended right before the switchbacks began, meaning if things still obeyed natural laws, there would have been the steadily steepening slope up through the foothills. She conjured the image in her mind's eye, complete with the standing stones at the base of the mountain. Finally, she pointed back the way they came, just past the edge of the first switchback. "That way."

Carmen jogged back up the hill a short way, peering into the rocks that bordered that side. "Here," she whispered.

Ellen followed, finding a narrow game path snaking its way down the mountain in the general direction of the standing stones. At the crest, the trail was barely wide enough to put a single foot down, treacherous enough so that a false step would mean tumbling down a steep and rocky slope into whatever the desert had in store. By the starlight, Ellen could see that the trail widened up ahead, though there were large rock formations that obscured her line of sight.

"Are you sure?"

"If you're sure about where those stones are. This looks like the best way down."

Ellen glanced back up the slope at the town. The multicolored stars of the creatures were woven through the fabric of the town itself. She nodded.

"Let's go then," Carmen said, taking the first step onto the path. Ellen followed, trying not to focus on the yawning black to the left. She concentrated on one foot in front of the other. Soon, the path widened enough so that she no longer felt like she was under constant threat of death.

"Bet you never saw this coming," Ellen whispered.

"Come again?"

"When they elected you sheriff. Bet you never thought you'd be fighting monsters."

"I wasn't elected," Carmen said. "I used to run the motel up at the top of the hill. The sheriff got killed right after this started. I was there, so I picked up the gun and the shield and then I was sheriff."

"You took on all this?"

"Someone had to."

"Why you, though?"

"Why not me?"

Ellen found herself nodding, the words repeating over and over in her head. *Why not me?* That was purpose. A need to be when and where she was. A desire to improve, of course, but it was the kind of direction Ellen had never seen before. She understood why the entire town admired Carmen.

The rocks loomed ahead as the path led steadily down into the darkness of the desert. The starlight illuminated them, but not as much as it had. Ellen realized that the night had been so bright in town because of those things. They had been everywhere, giving the town light even as they were invisible. Ellen passed by a boulder in a curve in the path and found that Carmen had stopped, her head cocked.

"Hold still," she whispered.

Ice seized Ellen's heart as she fought the urge to whip her head around. "What?"

"Don't move a muscle."

"I don't see anything."

The lights winked into existence all around. One at a time, tracing alien bodies, creating outlines that could not possibly exist in nature, and yet they did. They painted the rocks with the fluorescent colors of their bodies, casting shadows that confused more than revealed their silhouettes.

"Oh god," Ellen whispered, gripping her miner's pick.

"Run!" Carmen shouted.

Ellen barely hesitated before digging into the soil and running. Carmen lagged for a moment, starting to move only once Ellen was past.

The monsters made horrible sounds, some were shrieks, others gurgles, others snarls, and still others were noises that had never been named by human prey. They leapt off the rocks, some to slither through the air, others to run lightly along the ground.

Carmen grunted. Ellen turned to find the other woman throwing one of the creatures off her, through a gap in the rocks to tumble down the rocky slope. In the same movement, Carmen whirled to bury her axe in an eyeless monster's head. The thing twitched. "Run, goddamnit!"

Ellen did, concentrating not on the monsters behind, but on the road ahead. She was almost ready to celebrate when the darkness was replaced by lights. Blue ones, running down a sleek, eel-like body. The thing paused five feet off the ground, hovering effortlessly in the night. It was the same kind of creature that had greeted her in Stillwater, and absurdly she thought it was the same one, before reminding herself that Carmen had killed the first horror. Ellen opened her mouth to shout a warning when the monster struck. It darted through the air like a fish, its distended mouth gaping wide.

Ellen swung the pick. The impact chased shivers up and down her arms as her hands went numb. The pick's prong didn't hit perfectly, scraping across the slimy skin, bursting one of the bioluminescent globes. The monster flopped and hit the soil. Carmen raised her axe to finish the thing, but two more creatures, each of a different kind, tackled her to the earth.

Ellen swung the pick into one of the creatures. It was radial, like a sea urchin, lit up all around with blinking eyes and reaching claws. She heard a loud crack and there was a gout of stinking black fluid. The creature made a humming sound. Ellen hit it again, then the other one. Carmen crawled from underneath, covered in the ichor of the two abominations.

Ellen helped Carmen to her feet. All three monsters were close, and there were more sweeping in down the path. They knew prey was close, and now wounded and easy to kill.

Ellen focused on the three creatures, trying to prepare herself for the inevitable.

Then the first eel-thing lunged at one of the heavily wounded others and began to eat. With Carmen's arm over her shoulder, Ellen lurched down the path. Behind them, she could hear the cracking of the creature's exoskeleton and the wet sounds of chewing. The humming grew deeper and deeper until it stopped.

Ellen was ready to collapse, but she would not do that. Not while supporting the wounded woman. She forced herself to move, put as much distance as she could between them and the alien feast happening up the path.

And then, Carmen's legs gave out.

Ellen yelped Carmen's name, immediately cursing herself for making that kind of noise here. She helped the sheriff onto the ground, leaning against a rock. It was difficult to see where she was wounded, covered as she was by the black fluids of the monsters. Everything was raw and glistening.

"It's okay. Just let me take a little breather," Carmen said.

"I know," Ellen said, feeling the tears in her throat first. Even in the dim light, she could see how pale Carmen was. Ellen needed something to say, to fill the last bit of empty air at the end of Carmen's life. "Why didn't you just shoot them?"

Carmen smiled. "There haven't been bullets in this gun for years."

"Why do you carry it?"

Carmen answered, each word getting progressively softer until what began as a whisper had faded into nothing but a ghost. "Same reason we came out here tonight. Same reason I took the shield in the first place. People need hope. Without it, they might as well be dead."

Carmen breathed three more times, but she was already gone, her skin pale, eyes glassy.

Ellen wiped her eyes and closed Carmen's. Then she set back on the path, alone now. Not frightened. The rest of her existence had taken on the veneer of inevitability. Either she would survive or she would not.

The path switched back and dumped Ellen just beyond a rise. There were no more attacks. The standing stones were close. Ozone filled the air, and a powerful white-blue light flashed from the ground. Far too strong to be a gathering of monsters, it had to be something else. Ellen jogged over the last remaining bit of ground, taking cover behind a rock, peering down the slope at the standing stones. The light was coming from them.

Lightning wreathed every stone, scorching the air, dancing from each point, one by one. It collected in the center where, on the table rock, stood the red-haired woman. Her arms were flung upward to the sky, the lightning rebounding and collecting in them, disappearing into her tiny frame, as though she were a battery. She wore a blue gown of an archaic style, and though it should have been burned, it was not. The sand inside the ring of standing stones seemed to have turned to a mirror, reflecting the scene, although the reflected woman's movements were subtly different.

Waiting just outside the ring of stones was a thin man dressed in a white suit, watching the ecstatic figure within. The flashes lit an angular and hungry face. There were ten others, standing in a wider perimeter, these dressed casually and carrying submachine guns and watching the desert.

Ellen had no idea what she was going to do. She didn't know what she was expecting, though it was not, could not have been, precisely this. She was formulating a plan, when a weight slammed into her and carried her to the ground.

A monster was on top of her, its claws pinning her shoulders to the ground. Its toothy maw opened, strings of saliva dripping downward. It stank of fish. Ellen knew she was dead. The pick had been knocked from her hand. There was no way to take this thing. Gotten all the way here and that was the end. It leaned in to bite.

She felt intense cold through the monster's feet. A crunching sound emanated from within the creature, racing from its chest into its limbs, flesh turning hard and cold. Ellen's breath came out in a fog. The beast was lifted off of her. The man in the white suit casually tossed the monster, now frozen solid, down the hill where some of its limbs broke off. He held out a hand to help her up.

She took it. His skin felt like he had been out in the cold for days. He regarded her with lambent yellow eyes, and his frigid breath smelled like blood. "It's okay," he said, helping Ellen down the slope to the edge of the standing stones. "You're safe now." The lightning was warm, though the man in the white suit was still frozen.

Ellen opened her mouth and everything came tumbling out. "You have to help me! There's a town up there. There are monsters everywhere! Killing people!"

The red-haired woman walked toward Ellen, the lightning arcing off her body to the stones. Beneath her feet, her reflection's stride was just slightly out of sync. The power radiating from the woman was beyond palpable. It was real. It was terrifying. She gave the sense of being everywhere at once, visible both in front and at the corners of Ellen's eyes.

The woman stopped at the border, the energy burying itself in her head and hands. She looked at Ellen the way she might look at a fly who wouldn't stop buzzing around her lunch. Finally, she spoke, her voice lit with an odd echo. "Kill her."

The command was directed at the man in the white suit, the man with the yellow eyes and bloody breath. He glanced at Ellen in horror, then turned back to the red-haired woman. "No," he said.

A few of the armed men were paying attention. The man in white placed himself between Ellen and them, though he couldn't block any gunfire for long, they couldn't hit her without getting him as well. The red-haired woman turned, an indulgent smile quirking her perfect lips. "No?"

"You heard me."

"You dislike this order?"

"You're goddamn right I do. You think this woman walked through the desert for her health? Look at her! She's covered in blood. I can smell it. There's other stuff too, stuff I've never smelled before. No, whatever happened to her, she risked her life, and now you're going to listen to every fucking word she has to say!"

The woman thought it over. Finally, to Ellen: "You have melted our Coldheart."

"Speak and be heard." At first, Ellen had no idea where the sound came from, but then realized the reflection was speaking.

Ellen said, "There's a town on top of this mountain. Stillwater. Whatever you're doing, you've brought monsters. They're up there killing people. You have to help them!"

"Why should that trouble us?"

"Because they're innocent people! And they're dying!"

"They did not brave the night."

"You did," said the reflection.

"We will help you, and you alone," they both said.

"You may follow us back. In our presence, you will cross over," said the woman.

"You may return home," the reflection said.

Ellen glanced backward, as though she could see the town. They were up there, waiting for her and Carmen to save them. But Carmen was dead. And with her, hope. Leaving now condemned all those people to hell.

The frozen man stepped forward. Ellen shivered. "Trust me. When someone gives you an out like this, you take it."

Ellen looked up into his yellow eyes and saw the pain there. She nodded at his words, turning the choice over in her head. Finally, she whispered, "No." Then, louder, "No. I'm staying. You may not care, but I do."

"The choice has been made," the woman said, turning her back on Ellen and striding back to the center of the stones. Her reflection glanced back at Ellen only once, and maybe there was a tiny shred of pity in her ocean blue eyes.

"Torres! Give me your weapon and collect spare clips," the yellow-eyed man said.

Torres was one of the large men, craggy and weathered. He went from man to man, getting a clip from each, before jogging over and handing the submachine gun to the man in white. Torres looked from the frozen man to Ellen. "That's the safety," he said, "and this is how you reload." He demonstrated how to use the gun, and Ellen nodded.

"Thanks," she said.

"Thank him," Torres said, pulling a pistol and returning to his former position.

She turned to the man in the white suit. He said, "It's all right. I didn't take the out either. Good luck."

"You too," she said.

Ellen went back up the hill, stopping only once at Carmen's body, collecting the axe and the badge. She clipped the tin star to her shirt and set off toward Stillwater.

Appendix

THE TWINS

Magus
- The Twins, Faith and Hope, Mistresses of Diablerie, Stewards of Pemhakamik

Apprentices
- Ash Wednesday, Heir to the Twins, Diabolist
- Rose Cross, Spymaster, Theurgist
- The Machinist, Enchantress, trained by the Artisan, retro-futurist
- Grandmother Coyote, Physurgist, deceased (murdered, killer still unknown)

Familiars
- Ghostwalker, the huntsman
- Blackthorn, dryad, cheerful killer
- Shahmeran, wyrm, fashionista enforcer

THE TWINS cont'd

Servitors
- Gnomes, ghoulish workers
- Orrerites, small living solar systems
    The Keeper of the Menagerie
- Thraxians, demonic warriors
    Hirrust, security for the Seattle safehouse
    Zeryss, part of Rose Cross's security detail
- Vree-ka-vree, urban hunters
- Sadhvi Deva, Ash Wednesday's right hand

Soldiers
- Michael Barnes, head of security for Rose Cross

Mortals
- Cecelia Ho, seneschal of the Seattle safehouse
- Dr. Henry Jeremiah, caretaker of the San Pablo Sanitarium

Locations
- Northwind, extra-dimensional manor house
- The Menagerie, collection of wondrous creatures
- Darius Island, meeting place for emissaries of the Twins and the Lion
- Chevalier Tower, lair of Ash Wednesday

THE PRIESTESS

Magus
- The Priestess

Apprentices
- Kisin, Physurgist, haunted enforcer

Familiars
- Huracan, telekinetic assassin
- Teotl, human battery

THE SERPENT

Magus
- The Serpent

Servitors
- Mimics, humanoid shapeshifters

THE LION

Magus
- The Lion, Master of Physurgy, Steward of Khem

Apprentices
- Zara Iblisa, Heir to the Lion, Physurgist
- Anansi, Necromancer, dark diplomat

Familiars
- Edunara, master of lightning

Soldiers
- Daoud, head of security for Anansi

THE ARTISAN

Magus
- The Artisan, Master of Enchantment, Steward of Ki

Familiars
- Jihaz, the Artisan's finest weapon of war

Servitors
- Rajol Hadidi, the Clockwork Men

Soldiers
- Faisal al-Jarallah, covert agent

THE WOLF

Magus
- The Wolf

THE BUTTERFLY

Magus
- The Butterfly

Acknowledgments

This book could not have been produced without the incredible generosity of my Kickstarter backers who probably have a grossly inflated expectation of its quality. Five people contributed a truly ridiculous amount to the project, and I wanted to thank them personally—Hilary Brizendine, Cynthia Housel, Mana Taylor-Hall, Leila Vandiver, and whyshiroma—all of you have my sincere and undying gratitude.

My wife, Lauri, also deserves the kind of thanks usually reserved for people who rescue kittens from tsunamis. She is the reason *Coldheart* looks like an actual book and not a ransom note. She did the kinds of things you don't even think go into producing a book and did them tirelessly. She put the Kickstarter together, got the rewards done, and was generally the most supportive wife and partner I could have asked for. I mean, she hasn't even murdered me yet.

Lastly, I want to thank my readers. Without you guys, I'm just a crazy person making up lies to entertain himself.

About the Author

Much like film noir, Justin Robinson was born and raised in Los Angeles. He splits his time between editing comic books, writing prose, and wondering what that disgusting smell is. Degrees in Anthropology and History prepared him for unemployment, but an obsession with horror fiction and a laundry list of phobias provided a more attractive option.

Other Books by Justin Robinson

The Dollmaker
Mr Blank
Nerve Zero
Undead on Arrival

COMING SOON
City of Devils
Everyman